Praise for the Novels of
DEBBIE MACOMBER

Window on the Bay

"This heartwarming story sweetly balances friend-ship and mother-child bonding with romantic love."
—*KIRKUS REVIEWS*

"Where *Window on the Bay* really shines is in its portrayal of women who are done raising their children, but are far from done with life."
—*BOOKLIST*

Cottage by the Sea

"A novel that warms like the summer sun."
—*PEOPLE*

"Macomber's story of tragedy and triumph is emotionally engaging from the outset and ends with a satisfying conclusion. Readers will be most taken by the characters, particularly Annie, a heartwarming lead who bolsters the novel."
—*PUBLISHERS WEEKLY*

"Romantic, warm, and a breeze to read—one of Macomber's best."
—*KIRKUS REVIEWS*

"Macomber's patented recipe of idyllic small-town life with a touch of romance is sure to result in a summer best-seller."
—*BOOKLIST*

Sweet Tomorrows

"Macomber fans will leave the Rose Harbor Inn with warm memories of healing, hope, and enduring love."
—*KIRKUS REVIEWS*

"Macomber manages to infuse her trademark humor in a more somber story that focuses on love, loss and faith. . . . This one will appeal to those looking for more mature heroines and a good, clean romance."
—RT BOOK REVIEWS

"There's a reason why Debbie Macomber is a #1 *New York Times* bestselling author and with *Sweet Tomorrows*, we get another dose of women's fiction perfection. . . . In the nooks and crannies of small-town life, we'll find significance, beauty, and love."
—HEROES AND HEARTBREAKERS

Blossom Street Brides

"*Blossom Street Brides* gives Macomber fans sympathetic characters who strive to make the right choices as they cope with issues that face many of today's women. Readers will thoroughly enjoy spending time on Blossom Street once again and watching as Lydia, Bethanne and Lauren struggle to solve their problems, deal with family crises, fall in love and reach their own happy endings."
—BOOKPAGE

"A master at writing stories that embrace both romance and friendship, [Debbie] Macomber can always be counted on for an enjoyable page-turner, and this Blossom Street installment is no exception."
—RT BOOK REVIEWS

"A wonderful, love-affirming novel . . . an engaging, emotionally fulfilling story that clearly shows why she is a peerless storyteller."
—EXAMINER

"Fans will happily return to the warm, welcoming sanctuary of Macomber's Blossom Street, catching up with old friends from past Blossom Street books and meeting new ones being welcomed into the fold."
—KIRKUS REVIEWS

By Debbie Macomber

The Angels Series

A SEASON OF ANGELS
THE TROUBLE WITH ANGELS
TOUCHED BY ANGELS
ANGELS EVERYWHERE

Deliverance Company

SOMEDAY SOON
SOONER OR LATER
THE SOONER THE BETTER
(formerly MOON OVER WATER)

FAMILY AFFAIR
ONE NIGHT
MORNING COMES SOFTLY

The Miracle Series

MRS. MIRACLE
CALL ME MRS. MIRACLE
MR. MIRACLE

Someday Soon

DEBBIE MACOMBER

AVONBOOKS

An Imprint of HarperCollinsPublishers

SOMEDAY SOON. Copyright © 1995 by Debbie Macomber. All rights reserved. Printed in the United States of America. No part of this book may be used or reproduced in any manner whatsoever without written permission except in the case of brief quotations embodied in critical articles and reviews. For information, address HarperCollins Publishers, 195 Broadway, New York, NY 10007.

First Avon Books mass market printing: July 2008
First Harper mass market printing: June 1995

Print Edition ISBN: 978-0-06-307370-8
Digital Edition ISBN: 978-0-06-176360-1

Cover design by Amy Halperin
Cover illustration by Shane Rebenschied
Cover images © Pakhnyushchy/Shutterstock (sky); Iakov Kalinin/Shutterstock (field); canadastock/Shutterstock (scenic hills); Lenar Musin/Shutterstock (walkway/fence); Julia Kuznetsova/Shutterstock (trees); FooTToo/Shutterstock (mountains); Artazum/Shutterstock (house)

Avon, Avon & logo, and Avon Books & logo are registered trademarks of HarperCollins Publishers in the United States of America and other countries.

HarperCollins is a registered trademark of HarperCollins Publishers in the United States of America and other countries.

21 22 23 24 25   CPI   10 9 8 7 6 5 4 3 2 1

To Jane McMahon
A friend for all seasons
Knowing you has blessed my life

PROLOGUE

*T*he screaming had stopped. The shouts, the shots, the terror, were over. Now all Deliverance Company had to do was escape, and every detail of their route had been carefully planned.

Cain McClellan had never been comfortable with this mission, although it was similar to ten others he and his men had handled over the years. It wasn't anything he could put his finger on, other than a feeling. One that caused the hair on the back of his neck to stand straight on end. They'd been lucky, damn lucky. In twelve years he'd never lost a man.

Deliverance Company was good. His men were some of the best trained commandos in the world. That was why they were paid so handsomely.

Only something wasn't right, and Cain knew it. He was a man who lived and died by his instincts, but Tim Mallory and his other men had proved him wrong. Thus far.

The rescue, their specialty, had gone off like clockwork. Deliverance Company was in and out of the jungle compound in seconds, leaving the Nicaraguan government troops stunned and confused. That was exactly the way they'd planned it. By the time the Sandinistas figured out what had happened, Cain and his men would be long gone.

The man they'd saved, a CEO for a big-time manufacturing company, had been in the wrong place at the wrong time and fallen into hostile hands. Very hostile hands. The United States government's options were limited, trapped as they were in political red tape. Cain had been contacted early on by the conglomerate. Such missions were his specialty.

The helicopter was due any minute. According to their plan, the men of Deliverance Company had split and were scheduled to rendezvous in a designated area at fifteen hundred hours.

The eerie feeling returned, the sensation that said something was about to go terribly wrong. Cain's instincts had saved his life more than once, and he didn't take this feeling lightly. He stopped abruptly and looked around.

"Come on," Mallory urged, rushing past him. "We don't have time to waste."

The sudden impact of the explosion knocked Cain to the ground. He landed hard, on his face, and his mouth filled with the slick taste of blood. Shock and pain welled inside him as he staggered to his feet. His breath rasped painfully in his lungs.

Only when he was upright did Cain understand what had happened. Mallory had stepped on a land mine, the force of which had ripped through his right leg and hip. Jagged flesh and bone were exposed where once a healthy, whole man had stood. The acrid stench of explosives hung in the air, mingled with that of blood and sweat. The smell of death hung over them like a winter fog before the smoke cleared.

The ominous sounds of gunfire crackled in the background.

"Leave me," Mallory ground out from between gritted teeth. He gripped his leg with both hands and looked over his shoulder. Cain didn't need him to say anything to know the Sandinistas were quickly gaining on them.

"I'm not going anywhere without you." Cain moved toward the fallen man, surprised by how hard it was to remain upright. His steps wove one way and then the other.

"You haven't got time to waste." It went without saying that either they reached the rendezvous point on time or the chopper left without them.

"It's too late for me," Mallory mumbled, fighting to stay conscious.

Cain reached him, and one glance told him the injuries were massive. He didn't take time to investigate further. He reached for Mallory, preparing to lift him onto his shoulders.

"I've lost too much blood. I'll never make it." Mallory's voice faded as he drifted toward unconsciousness. "Don't risk . . ."

A bullet whizzed past Cain's head as he heaved Mallory's two-hundred-plus pounds onto his shoulders. Blood drenched his shirt and ran down both his arms like a waterfall. Staggering under the weight, Cain strained and raced with his burden toward the meeting point.

"Let me die," Mallory pleaded, sucking in deep breaths in an effort to remain conscious. "The leg's gone, man, and so am I."

"Not yet you aren't," Cain shouted. "You're going to make it."

"I'd rather die."

"Not while I'm around, you won't."

A bullet caught Cain in the arm, a flesh wound, the pain as searing as if someone had branded him with a white-hot poker.

The copter was in sight, its massive blades whirling, stirring up dust and excitement. The sound was deafening, but Cain swore he'd never heard anything more beautiful in his life.

1

Her first mistake was agreeing to attend this Christmas party. Her second was downing a glass of champagne and then, for courage, another.

Her third error in judgment was remembering Michael.

The only reason Linette Collins had agreed to come was that it was easier to give in to Nancy and Rob than argue.

It was well past time for her to socialize again, they claimed. Long past time for her to grieve. Only no one had told her how she was supposed to grow another heart. No one had told her all the time she'd been granted to mourn her husband was two short years.

Her heart had been rubbed raw in the time it had taken leukemia to claim her young husband's life. Since Michael's death the days had blended together, one twenty-four-hour period dragging into the next until the weeks and months had blurred together in a thick fog of disenchantment.

Linette had gotten on with her life, the way everyone

said she should. She went to work every day. She ate. Slept. She managed to do all that was required of her and nothing more, simply because she hadn't the energy. Or the inclination.

Then, out of the blue, when she was least expecting it, she'd found peace. A shaky sort of acceptance that teetered, then, gradually, with time, righted itself.

This serenity happened as if by magic. She woke one morning and realized the pain she'd constantly carried with her didn't seem quite as heavy. The doubts, the fears, the never-ending litany of questions, faded. Unsure of how it had happened, Linette had graciously accepted this small slice of peace, this unexpected reprieve, and clung to it tenaciously.

Each day the feeling had grown stronger, and for the first time in months she felt whole. Almost whole, she amended.

But when she'd stepped into this Christmas party she hadn't been prepared for the festivities to hit her quite this way. The fun, the singing, the laughter, reminded her forcefully that it had been almost two years to the day since Michael's death.

"I'm so pleased you came," Nancy said as she squeezed past Linette. Her sister-in-law smelled of cinnamon and bayberry and looked incredibly lovely in her sleeveless winter green velvet gown. Linette's own white wool dress didn't fit as well as it should. She'd done what she could to disguise how loose it was with a narrow gold belt.

"I'm pleased I came, too," Linette lied, but it was only a small white one and unfortunately necessary. She sipped champagne and forced herself to smile.

"Did you sample the hors d'oeuvres?" Nancy asked. "You must! I spent hours and hours assembling those little devils. Try the teriyaki chicken bits first. They're wonderful." She pressed her fingertips to her lips and kissed them noisily.

"I'll give them a taste," Linette promised.

Without warning, Nancy's arms shot out and hugged Linette long and hard. When she drew back, Linette noticed tears shimmering in her sister-in-law's eyes. Nancy's lower lip quivered as she struggled to hold in the emotion. "I miss him so much," she said, choking out the words. "I still think about him. It doesn't seem like it's been two years."

"I know." Instead it felt as if several lifetimes had passed.

Linette squeezed Nancy's hand. It often happened like this, her comforting others. How ironic.

"Oh, damn. I didn't mean for that to happen," Nancy murmured, pressing her index fingers beneath each eye while she blinked furiously in an effort to keep the tears from spilling down her cheeks.

"It's only natural you should miss Michael," Linette offered, briefly wrapping her arm around Nancy's waist.

"It just hit me all at once that he was gone. I'm sorry, Linette, the last thing you need is for me to remind you of Michael, especially tonight. This is a party, we're supposed to be having fun." Nancy reached for the champagne bottle and Linette's glass, then laughed lightly. "He'd want us to celebrate."

That was true. Michael had always been generous and loving.

"Oh, my," Nancy said a tad breathlessly, turning

around abruptly. Her startled eyes flew to Linette's. "Tell me, how do I look?" she asked, nervously brushing her hands down her skirt.

Linette blinked, surprised by Nancy's lack of confidence. "Great."

"You're sure?"

"I'm positive. Why?"

"Rob's boss and his wife just arrived."

"You don't have a thing to worry about," Linette assured her.

"My makeup's okay?" She dabbed at her cheeks.

"A beauty queen would envy you that face."

Nancy laughed. "Rob's up for promotion, you know."

Linette didn't, but the news wasn't a surprise. She'd often admired her brother-in-law for his intelligence and ambition.

With a toothpaste-ad smile on her lips, Nancy left, and Linette glanced at her watch once more. Ten more minutes, she decided, and then she'd make an excuse and leave. Silently she'd slip back to life without Michael.

THE minute Cain arrived at the Christmas party, he'd noticed her. Like him, she was alone. Uncomfortable. Eager to escape. She was a lovely thing. Petite and fragile. He found himself studying her almost against his will. It wasn't that she was strikingly beautiful. "Winsome" came to mind, although it was an old-fashioned word and not often used these days. But then, she seemed to be a quaint kind of woman.

It was almost as if she'd stepped out of another time and place. Perhaps it was the sense of being lost that he felt. A sense of being alone and slightly afraid, uncomfortably aware of being out of place.

Not afraid, he decided. The more he studied her, the more he realized this woman had walked through a deep, dark valley. He wasn't sure how he knew this, but he'd come to trust his intuition. She sipped from the champagne glass and briefly gnawed on the corner of her lip. Watching her made Cain wonder if she'd made her way completely across that valley. Maybe he should find out. No. He decided to leave well enough alone.

Carrying his drink with him, he slowly made his way through the crowd to find a secluded corner. Andy Williams crooned a Christmas ditty from a nearby speaker.

Cain hadn't been keen on attending this get-together. This was what he got for giving in to curiosity and looking up Rob Lewis. They'd been good friends in high school, and he was interested to see what had become of his buddy since they'd both left the thriving metropolis of Valentine, Nebraska.

Years before, Cain and Rob had been the local football heroes. Cain was the quarterback and Rob his favorite wide receiver. Frankly, he'd enjoyed his brief stint as a celebrity.

Following graduation Cain had gone into the military and Rob to college. They'd talked a couple of times in the years since, a card at Christmas with a few lines, but that was the extent of it.

Since Cain was in San Francisco getting Mallory set up on a rehabilitation program for his hip and knee, it only made sense to catch up with his longtime buddy. In a moment of goodwill and—all right—weakness, Cain had agreed to drop in on this Christmas party.

He was uncomfortable in crowds. He'd never been one to exhibit many of the more refined social graces.

He felt out of place here. Sipping his Jack Daniel's, he returned his gaze to the woman who'd garnered his attention earlier.

Why not, he decided as he stepped around the sofa. It was Christmas, and it'd been a good long while since he'd felt this strongly attracted to a woman. He wove his way between two couples who were attempting to sing a favorite Christmas carol in German and failing miserably. They seemed to be enjoying themselves, and Cain found them amusing.

"A half hour," Cain said, slipping next to her. She stood close to the fireplace, holding the fluted champagne glass in both hands.

"A half hour?" she repeated, gazing at him with wide brown eyes. Doe eyes, big, trusting, sincere.

"That's how long you'd decided to wait before you quietly left."

Her gaze widened. "How'd you know?"

The whiskey burned the back of his throat. "Because that was how long I'd decided to wait before I left."

She smiled then, and he was amazed at the transformation the simple action brought to her delicate features. It was as if the sun had peeked from behind a thick, dark cloud, spilling sunshine. Her eyes brightened and her lips quivered softly.

"I'm Cain McClellan," he said, holding out his hand to her.

"Linette Collins."

"Hello, Linette." The name sounded vaguely familiar, and he frowned in an effort to remember where he'd heard it. Possibly from Rob, who'd attempted to match him up for the evening.

"You don't work with Rob, do you?" Her attention

drifted to his hair, and he realized the high and tight military cut told her he probably wasn't a stockbroker.

"Rob and I are longtime friends," he answered without elaborating. "What about you?"

"Nancy and Rob are my brother- and sister-in-law."

"You're married?" His gaze shot to her left hand. Her ring finger was bare, but the indentation of a wedding band was clearly visible. It was then that Cain remembered where he'd heard her name. Rob had mentioned Nancy's brother had passed away a couple of years earlier and suggested Cain meet the widow. He'd declined.

"My husband died," she explained unnecessarily.

Cain felt a sudden need for another drink. He clinked his ice against the side of the glass and stared at the melting cubes. "Can I get you anything?" he asked, gesturing toward the bar.

Linette set aside her empty champagne glass. "Nothing, thanks."

Cain left her and headed across the room. He wanted to kick himself for being so inept. It was apparent she was ill at ease; perhaps she wanted to talk about her late husband and had been looking for a willing ear.

It didn't matter, because the moment she'd announced she was a widow, he'd grown so uncomfortable that he'd made an excuse to leave her. The thing was he hadn't known what to say. That he was sorry? That sounded phony. He'd never even met the man.

Circumstances such as these made him regret not leaving for Montana at the first opportunity. Instead he'd lollygagged around San Francisco, looking up old friends and making a fool of himself.

When Cain had a fresh drink, he turned and discovered Linette hadn't left the party. He was pleased she'd stayed.

He hadn't wanted their conversation to end abruptly, but he wasn't sure what more he had to say, either.

He studied the bright red stockings hanging from the fireplace mantel and casually walked back to her side. Her gentle smile reached out to greet him.

"Something amuses you?"

"Nancy," she responded, which was no answer whatsoever.

He looked around for Rob's wife, not finding her.

"She mentioned you," Linette elaborated. "I just realized you were the one she'd wanted me to meet."

"Rob tried to line me up with you as well."

"Nancy did this whole song and dance about it being two years since Michael . . . and that there was this old school buddy of Rob's who was in town."

Cain grinned, thinking it had been a good long while since he'd had reason to smile about anything. "I guess we showed them."

"I guess we did." Linette laughed softly and waved her hand in front of her face. "Is it hot in here, or is it just me?"

Standing in front of the softly flickering fire might have had something to do with why she was uncomfortably warm, but Cain didn't mention that. Instead he took her by the elbow and guided her outside to a small balcony that overlooked San Francisco Bay. The lights on the Golden Gate Bridge outlined the well-known landmark, illuminating the skyline in a postcard-perfect silhouette.

A cool breeze drifted off the water, and the sky was crowded with stars that seemed determined to dazzle them with their brilliance.

Linette gripped hold of the balcony railing with both

hands, closed her eyes, and tilted her head upward. When she exhaled, her shoulders sagged appreciatively.

"Nancy said something about you being out of the country a lot of the time. That must be hard."

"It's my job," he said.

"You don't miss home?"

In the last year, he hadn't thought about the ranch enough to miss it. Nor had he hurried to Montana when the opportunity arose. He was a man without ties, without roots. That was the way it had to be.

"I'm too busy to think about it," he answered after a moment, and looked to her, wanting to divert the subject away from himself. "Do you work?"

She nodded. "I own a yarn store called Wild and Wooly, on Pier Thirty-nine."

A knitting shop. It fit. He could easily picture Linette snuggled up on a rocking chair next to a fireplace, her long needles clicking softly as she expertly wove yarn. He found the image inviting, as if she'd asked him to cozy up next to her.

Cain wished he could pinpoint what it was about Linette that conjured up fantasies of domestic bliss. Homespun women didn't generally appeal to him.

It was the season, he decided, when goodwill toward men flourished and a man's thoughts turned to hearth and home. Christmastime seemed to bring out the best in people, himself included, he reasoned, willing to accept the explanation.

"Would you care to dance?" Linette asked him.

"Dance? Me?" Her invitation flustered him. He flattened his hand against his chest as the excuses worked their way up his throat. "I'm not much good at that sort of thing," he managed after an awkward moment.

"Me either. But we don't need to worry about making fools of ourselves, out here." She held up her arms, and before a second protest could form, she was in his embrace.

He tensed, but she didn't seem to notice. Tucking her head under his chin, she hummed along with the music, and gradually he relaxed.

Their feet made short, awkward shuffling movements until Cain realized that there was actually some kind of rhythm to their motions.

The tension slowly eased from his limbs, and he pressed his chin against her temple. She smelled of wildflowers and sunshine. He'd never held anyone more incredibly soft. So soft, she frightened him. He absorbed her gentleness the way a thirsty sponge did water. With her in his arms, he could close his eyes and not see the mangled bodies of men who'd died at his hand. With her he heard the soft strains of joyous music instead of the screams of dying, bitter men as they cursed him on their way to hell.

His grip tightened, and she trembled. Pulling her flush against him, he felt her breath moisten the column of his neck. Cain closed his eyes and savored the feel of a woman in his arms. Linette clung to him, too. He realized, gratefully, that her hold on him was as tight as his on her.

He knew what was happening. He could spend a few hours with this woman who was lovely and pure and forget who and what he was. He could relish her softness and ignore the bitterness of the truth and the hard life he'd chosen.

All this wasn't one-sided. Linette could hold him and

forget the man she'd loved and lost. He was her haven just as she had become his.

As much as he'd like to deny it, Cain needed this woman's touch. He was desperate for her gentleness. His heart, perhaps even his soul, needed this time with this woman.

The music ceased, but he kept moving. It felt good to have her in his arms. Linette broke away from him, and for an instant he resisted, tightening his grip until he realized what he was doing.

Irritated with himself, he dropped his arms and stepped back. Linette Collins made him weak, and that was something he couldn't allow.

"Thank you," she said softly. She didn't need to say it had been a long time since anyone had held her. He knew. This wasn't the kind of woman who bed-hopped. She'd deeply grieved the loss of her husband. Cain also knew she'd grieved alone, without seeking the solace of a lover.

In one way, Cain envied her husband. There would be no one to mourn his passing. No one to stand over his cemetery plot and weep. That was the life he had chosen. The way it had to be. There was no room for gentleness. Not now, not ever. Not if he planned to survive. And he did.

For what?

The question came at him like the pinpoint beam of a laser slicing through his mind. All at once he hadn't a clue why he found it so important to stay alive. He had no immediate family. No heirs.

As far as money went, he could retire now and it would take two lifetimes to spend what he'd accumulated in the last several years with Deliverance Company.

By tacit agreement, he and Linette wandered back to the party, which seemed to be in full swing. Without a word, they went their separate ways. Which was for the best, Cain reasoned. Linette was a sweet thing and deserved happiness. It wasn't likely she'd find that with him. By nipping this attraction in the bud, he was doing her a kindness.

Cain caught sight of Nancy and Rob dancing on the other side of the room. Small clusters of groups were involved in chitchat, something at which he felt completely inept. With little more than a backward glance, he retrieved his coat and left. Later, he'd send Rob and Nancy a Christmas card and thank them for the party. He was half tempted to mention meeting Linette, then decided against it.

In the hallway outside, waiting for the elevator, he sensed someone's approach. It shouldn't have surprised him to find Linette rounding the corner, but it did. She seemed startled as well, and her round eyes widened.

"So we meet again," he said.

When the elevator arrived, they stepped aboard together. He pushed the button for the lobby. Stepping back, he studied the woman who stood beside him. Within a matter of seconds, they would each go back to their separate lives.

Cain experienced a sense of desperation that was foreign to him. Even worse, he felt like a world-class fool. If Mallory knew what he was thinking, or Murphy, Bailey, or Jack, either, they'd lock him up until this bout of insanity had passed. Men like Cain simply did not become involved with women like Linette Collins.

On the ground floor, Cain watched Linette hurry across the street and climb inside her car. He stood rooted, unwilling and unable to move as her Toyota turned the corner and disappeared from sight.

After a moment he drew in a deep breath, then headed toward the rental car he'd picked up at the airport three days earlier.

His name was Cain, and right then he felt aptly christened. His namesake had been the son of Adam and Eve. The first child born outside the gates of paradise.

2 ❧

*L*inette was busy at her shop early Saturday morning when the phone rang. Although she wasn't due to open for another half hour, she reached for the receiver and tucked it between her ear and her shoulder as she unloaded skeins of brightly colored cashmere wool.

"Wild and Wooly," she said automatically.

"I wish you hadn't left the party so early," Nancy mumbled on the tail end of a yawn. It was apparent she had recently rolled out of bed.

"I had to be to the shop this morning," Linette explained. She hadn't slept well, but only because she couldn't stop thinking about Cain McClellan and the short time they'd been together. She toyed hesitantly with the idea of asking her sister-in-law what she could tell her about Cain. So much as a hint of curiosity about the other man might prove to be potentially embarrassing. Nancy was sure to make something out of Linette's inquisitiveness.

If Linette were a little more sophisticated, a little more at ease with the opposite sex, she might have found a subtle way of quizzing Cain. She hadn't because he hadn't seemed keen on talking about himself. What questions she had asked had received answers that were evasive and vague. She'd noticed how he'd quickly turned the conversation to subjects away from anything personal.

She knew he was in the military. Nancy had told her that much when she'd first mentioned him. Linette speculated that his work was involved with intelligence. Probably top-secret stuff that prevented him from discussing details. Funny she could spend so short a time with him and feel as if she understood him.

Like her, he was alone. Like her, he needed someone to hold.

In the entire two-year period without Michael, Linette had never felt more alone than she did now. At first she'd assumed it was because the anniversary of his death was approaching, but gradually she realized it was the Christmas season itself.

"Did you enjoy the party?" Nancy asked, cutting into her thoughts.

"Very much." Thanks to Cain. Forcing her attention back to Nancy, she asked, "How did everything go with Rob's boss and his wife?"

"Great. They're nice people," Nancy said, and then, turning to the apparent reason for her call, she added, "Didn't I see you talking with Rob's friend?"

"Yes, we found each other despite your and Rob's best efforts to keep us apart," Linette said with a small smile.

"I saw the two of you one minute and the next thing I knew you'd both disappeared." Linette pictured Nancy jiggling her eyebrows suggestively.

"We left. Cain's not much of a party person either."

"So you snuck off together," Nancy said, her voice dipping with implication. "That's great."

Before Linette could correct her sister-in-law's impression, Nancy spoke again. "How about the two of us getting together for lunch this afternoon? That way you can tell me all about you and Cain, and I'll let you in on my own little secret."

"There's nothing to tell," Linette protested. "Besides, I don't know if I can get away. The shop's been terribly busy, and I don't feel like I can leave Bonnie alone, especially on a Saturday." It sounded as if she were hedging, but what she said was true. Since this was the last weekend before Christmas, it could possibly be the busiest day of the year for her shop. Lunch would consist of a bite or two of a sandwich between customers.

"I'll pick up something and bring it to you, then," Nancy argued. "I'm dying to hear what happened between you and Cain McClellan."

"But, Nancy—"

"Don't argue. I must say, he's a hunk."

"But—" Before Linette could explain it might be a wasted trip, Nancy had hung up.

Replacing the telephone receiver, Linette sank onto the chair by the cash register. She loved Nancy and deeply appreciated the support and love Michael's sister had given her, but she didn't want to discuss Cain McClellan.

He'd come into her life briefly, and it was unlikely they'd meet again. Ships passing in the night and that sort of thing. He was a man without an anchor, and she was a dock. A concrete dock. Stable, permanent, lasting. Even if they had struck up a relationship, it would be a long-distance one. He'd told her himself he was only in town for a few days.

Linette's prediction about this being the busiest sales day of the year proved to be accurate. From the moment she unlocked the door, she was inundated with customers. Many of the handcrafted items she'd knitted over the autumn months had already sold, but the limited number of wool scarves and baby blankets left were gone by ten that morning.

"Has it been like this every Christmas?" Bonnie asked, sinking onto the chair and removing her left shoe. She rubbed her toes and mumbled something about getting what she deserved for wearing new shoes.

"I don't remember," Linette said.

"Linette," Bonnie said, and exhaled sharply. "I'm sorry. I forgot. It was Christmastime when your husband died, wasn't it?"

"Don't worry about it," Linette said quickly, not wanting to discuss Michael. She liked Bonnie, who was in her mid-fifties and grandmotherly with short gray hair and a thick waist. Her face was round and warmly hospitable. It helped that Linette's lone employee had been knitting for years herself and was knowledgeable about the craft. Linette felt lucky to have her.

The bell above the door jingled, and Bonnie automatically replaced her shoe. "I'll get it," Linette said, pressing her hand against her employee's forearm. "Pour yourself a cup of coffee," she said. "You deserve it." They'd been so busy, neither of them had taken time for a coffee break.

"You're sure?" Bonnie asked, glancing longingly toward the back room.

"I'll be fine."

Linette realized she'd spoken too soon. This latest customer was Nancy. "You're not the least bit busy," her sister-in-law admonished.

"You should have been here ten minutes ago," Linette countered. She straightened a row of white wool, replacing it inside a brightly painted wood bin stacked beneath a large picture window overlooking Fisherman's Wharf. Linette loved the view the window afforded her. With its colorful fishing fleet, the wharf reminded her of a quaint Mediterranean seaport. There'd been plenty of times when she'd gazed out this very window, transported to a world outside her grief.

"I brought goodies," Nancy said, holding up a grease-stained brown paper sack. "The deli packed us sandwiches and enormous dill pickles."

"I didn't think you liked dill pickles."

"I don't," Nancy said casually, "unless I'm pregnant."

It took Linette far longer than it should have to make the connection. "You and Rob are having a baby?"

Nancy's eyes brightened with tears, and she nodded enthusiastically. "I didn't want to say anything until after Christmas, but I can't keep it a secret any longer. We'd almost given up trying. Christopher's eight, and we were beginning to think we couldn't have more children when, whammo." She tossed her arm into the air, grinning broadly. "Another rabbit bit the dust."

The two women hugged, and to her surprise Linette felt tears filling her own eyes. She knew Nancy and Rob wanted another child, but neither one had mentioned a baby in so long that she wasn't sure what they'd decided.

A baby.

She and Michael had yearned for children, but early

in their marriage they'd decided to wait a couple of years. Every aspect of their lives together had been carefully planned. All too soon, however, Michael had been diagnosed with leukemia. Afterward everything had changed. The days came and went, the seasons ebbed and flowed and every sunrise had become a sunset as Michael's life became consumed with dying.

"Be happy for me," Nancy said, hugging her close.

"Of course I'm happy," Linette said, wondering at Nancy's apprehensions.

"It's just that . . . well, I know how badly you and Michael wanted a child, and I guess I was afraid you might feel like you'd been cheated."

"How could I possibly feel cheated, having loved Michael? I'm sorry we didn't have children, but I'd never begrudge you and Rob your happiness. I'm thrilled for you both."

"Thank you," Nancy said, rubbing the moisture from her face. Her shoulders shook, and it took a moment for Linette to realize Nancy was laughing, not weeping.

"I cry so easily lately. Rob doesn't know what to make of me."

Knowing how Rob idolized his wife, Linette strongly suspected he'd think he'd married the most perfect woman in the world no matter what she said or did. Especially now.

Bonnie wandered out from the back room, bringing a freshly brewed cup of coffee with her.

"Bonnie, do you think I can steal Linette away for a few minutes?" Nancy asked, and looped her arm through Linette's.

"Might as well," Bonnie said with an agreeable smile.

"We seem to be experiencing something of a lull, but I don't expect it to last long."

Linette led the way into the back room, which was stacked with empty boxes, most of the skeins of yarn having been sold even before the boxes had had a chance to be emptied.

A badly scarred wooden table stood against the concrete block wall with two equally dilapidated chairs. Linette couldn't remember where they'd found the set, but it had been a welcome addition to their small space.

Nancy claimed the ladder-back chair while Linette scrounged up paper plates and two clean coffee mugs.

Nancy drew out thick sandwiches from the brown paper sack. They were subways covered in wax paper and held together with large toothpicks, with gaily decorated tops.

"Did I mention my appetite's improved?" Nancy said, smiling gleefully at Linette. "Pickles aren't the only thing I find appealing. I swear if this continues, I'll resemble the Goodyear blimp by July."

Linette inspected her half of the sandwich and discovered three different kinds of meat and an equal number of cheeses, plus the usual lettuce, thick slices of tomato, and a variety of other goodies, including sliced green olives.

"All right, tell me about you and Cain," Nancy instructed now that she was settled.

"I already explained there isn't much to tell," Linette said. Juice ran down her forearm when she took her first bite of the dill pickle.

"I saw the two of you together, remember?" Nancy insisted. "And then you were gone. Where did you take off to?"

"Nowhere. We rode down in the elevator together and went our separate ways."

"That's all?" Nancy sounded terribly disappointed.

"What do you know about him?" Linette asked, her curiosity overriding her hesitation. She would have preferred to keep any inquisitiveness low key and any questions indirect. Linette feared Nancy would leap on Linette's interest in Cain and make something out of it that it wasn't.

"Rob and Cain attended high school together."

That much Linette knew.

"Cain went into the military after graduation. From what Rob said, he's only talked to Cain twice in the last twenty years. The first time was about a year or so after Rob was out of college. Cain phoned him and they chatted. Apparently he was a member of the Special Forces and had spent a good deal of time in Asia."

"Asia?" Linette repeated slowly.

"That's what Rob said. When I quizzed him, he couldn't recall much more of their conversation, which is understandable seeing that it was several years back. Apparently some of their friends have asked about Cain over the years, but no one's heard from him. When it came time for their class reunion, no one had an address for him. Apparently Rob's the only one he's kept in contact with from his high school days.

"When Cain phoned last week, Rob was thrilled. The two met for lunch, but Rob said Cain skillfully managed to steer the conversation away from himself."

"He did that with me, too."

"From what little Rob was able to glean, Cain's involved in some kind of undercover activity that consists of rescuing political hostages."

A chill raced up Linette's back.

"You'd think he'd be ready to retire soon. He's got in twenty years or more by now."

He wasn't ready. Linette hadn't a clue how she knew that, but she did. Cain was a man who enjoyed living on the edge, who felt a rush of excitement when he could look danger in the face and not blink.

"He didn't ask to see you again?" Nancy spoke as if she suspected Linette were holding back vital information.

"No." Cain McClellan had come into her life like the softest of whispers and disappeared before she'd had the opportunity to decipher his message.

CAIN knew Francine Holden was the perfect physical therapist for Tim Mallory the moment he laid eyes on her. He also knew Mallory wouldn't agree with him. The highly recommended therapist was a no-nonsense professional who wouldn't put up with any of his friend's usual guff. If Francine Holden was only half as good as Dr. Benton claimed, his colleague had a chance of regaining the use of his right leg. Something that had seemed impossible eighteen months earlier.

It wouldn't be easy, but then nothing in his business ever was. Thank God Mallory was a fighter. If not, he would have died in a Nicaraguan jungle. Francine wasn't a shy, retiring soul whom Mallory would easily intimidate with his temper tantrums and wildly swinging moods.

"Dr. Benton recommended you highly for the job," he said to the woman who sat across from him. Sitting didn't disguise her height. Cain guessed she was close to six feet, with a build that resembled that of a weight lifter. She'd need strength if she was going to be lifting Mallory around. Francine wore her long blond hair in a French braid that stretched halfway down the middle of her back. Her eyes were blue and wide, by far her most striking feature, set deep in a face that was remarkably plain.

"May I see your friend's latest X rays?" she asked, ignoring his compliment. When Cain handed them to her, she held the first set up to the light. "How'd this happen?" she asked.

Cain weighed how much he should tell her and decided he'd be doing them both a disservice with anything less than the truth. "The damage to the knee and hip are the result of a booby trap."

"Booby trap? You mean as in a land mine?"

"Something like that." Cain shifted back on his chair and crossed his legs. "We were in Central America at the time, on a mission."

Slowly her intensely blue eyes left the X rays to connect with his. "What agency were you with?"

"None. We're mercenaries."

"Doing what?"

He shrugged, unwilling to give her any more information than necessary. "What we were paid to do."

"I see."

Cain watched her reaction, surprised that she revealed none, at least none he could read.

"How many reconstructive surgeries has your friend been through?" It was back to business, and Cain was impressed with the casual way in which she responded to the information.

"Ten surgeries in the last eighteen months."

She motioned to the X ray. "When were these taken?"

"Two weeks ago."

"What's your friend's mental state?" she asked before handing him back the film.

"About what you'd expect," he said evasively. Mallory had already gone through a handful of therapists. The latest hadn't lasted more than two days.

"In other words he's depressed, angry, and has done his best to shut out the world."

Cain felt his lips quiver involuntarily with a smile. "Something like that."

"I'm not a miracle worker, Mr. McClellan."

"All I'm asking is that you give it a shot. I'm willing to pay you top dollar." More if need be. Mallory was a good friend. Perhaps the best Cain had ever had. He hadn't left him in the jungle to die, and he wouldn't desert him now, either.

"It isn't a question of money," Francine returned smoothly. "It has to do with grit and spirit. I've been a therapist several years, and I've seen a number of cases similar to your friend's here. At this point he doesn't care if he lives or dies. What happened to his body can't compare with the damage done to his soul."

Cain was amazed by how accurately she'd analyzed Mallory's emotional state. "Can you help him?"

"Maybe. Maybe not. It's up to him," she said thoughtfully. "I can make a more accurate assessment once I meet him."

"Great." Cain eagerly sprang to his feet. "Let's take care of that right now."

A brief smile brightened her plain features. "Have you told him I'm coming?"

Cain hesitated. "No."

"Good."

"It's probably better he doesn't know you're a therapist," Cain suggested, preferring to delay another of Mallory tantrums. The minute his cohort learned that he'd hired another therapist, there was sure to be trouble.

"We won't be able to keep it from him long," Francine said evenly. "He'll figure it out soon enough."

She was right. One look at this titan of a woman and Mallory would know exactly why he'd brought her to meet him.

From the glint in her deep blue eyes, Cain guessed this was a woman who thrived on challenge. All the better, because Mallory was going to demand every ounce of fortitude she possessed.

He led her through the house he'd rented on Russian Hill. Taken with the panoramic view of the Bay, Cain had also liked the countrylike lanes and terraced houses. Perhaps he was thinking the atmosphere would help Mallory, but if that was the case, the high rent area had been an expensive mistake. Mallory had made a prison out of the back bedroom.

Greg, Mallory's attendant, was leaving the room as they approached. He looked from Cain to Francine and then back at Cain.

"He's having a bad day," Greg announced. His expression suggested they'd be better off returning at a later date.

"As long as he's in the shape he's in now," Francine said without waiting for Cain to respond, "every day's a bad day."

Greg smiled and nodded. "Good luck," he said as he stepped away from the door.

Cain knocked once and walked inside without waiting for a response. The room was dark, and it took a moment for his eyes to adjust to the lack of light. Mallory was sitting in the corner farthest from the door, with a blanket over his legs. The once robust man had lost seventy pounds in the last year and a half. His eyes had shrunk back into his head, and his hair was long enough to brush his shoulders. At a glance, he looked like hell. Cain wanted to shout at him, tell him to snap out of this, but he wasn't the one with a shattered hipbone and a knee that had been blown apart.

Cain could walk out of this house. Mallory couldn't stand up, let alone walk. It was easy to make judgments from this side of a wheelchair. Feeling helpless, Cain did what he could, but it seemed like damn little.

"I'm not in the mood for company," Mallory muttered.

"I brought someone for you to meet," Cain said. It would take more than a sour mood to get rid of him.

"Another time, perhaps." Mallory's voice was strained, the frustration and anger leaking through the words.

Francine moved away from Cain and reached for the light switch, flipping it on. The room was instantly bathed in a warm glow.

Automatically Mallory's hands went to shade his eyes, and he cursed under his breath. Cain watched as his friend's angry glare connected with the therapist's gaze.

"Hello, Mr. Mallory," Francine said brightly, "I'm Francine Holden."

Mallory glared disdainfully at Cain as if he'd stabbed him in the back. "Get rid of her."

"Now, Mallory—"

"I said get rid of her."

"I could get offended, but I won't," Francine said,

chuckling. Cain swore he heard a tinge of glee in her laugh and loved it. This was going to work out far better than he'd hoped.

"We're going to become friends, Mallory," Francine said. "Real good friends. For the next two months, I'm going to stick to you like glue, and when I'm through with you," she said, firmly planting her hand on her hip, "I guarantee you won't be sitting in a dark room with a blanket over your head to close out the world."

Mallory ignored her. "All I want is peace and quiet. Is that so much to ask?" he demanded. Cain could almost feel the anger emanate off Mallory in waves. "It's the season, you know."

"Your muscles can't wait while you sit around feeling sorry for yourself." Francine lowered her gaze to his mangled left leg, peeking out from beneath the blanket. Mallory covered it quickly. "Every day without therapy, you risk never regaining the use of that leg. You want to walk again, don't you?"

For the first time Mallory focused the full force of his attention on her. "I don't need you."

"That's where you're wrong. You've never needed anyone more in your life."

Mallory responded with a low snicker.

"We'll get started first thing this afternoon," Francine announced, speaking to Cain. She pushed up the sleeves of her thin sweater as if she could hardly wait to get going.

"Cain?" Mallory pleaded silently for assistance, but Cain purposely looked away. A minute passed before a string of abusive threats colored the air.

"I'm pleased to see you have such an extensive vocabulary," Francine said. "I imagine you'll be using it over the next couple of months. Judging by those X rays, this isn't going to be easy. I promise you one thing, you'll never work harder in your life. But by the time I'm finished with you, you'll be walking. Now," she said, her words bright and cheerful, "are you man enough to accept this challenge, or do you want someone who'll tuck you in at night and read you bedtime stories for the rest of your life?"

"Cain, I'm warning you," Mallory said between clenched teeth. His eyes were as dark and menacing as Cain had ever seen. "Get rid of this Amazon."

"I won't do that," Cain said mildly. "She may be your last chance."

"I don't want this," Mallory muttered, and rubbed a hand over his face. "And I don't want her." He gestured toward Francine. "If you think I need a woman, fine, send me a woman, not Attila the Hun."

Cain glanced at Francine, wondering if Mallory had offended her. Apparently not. Her face remained expressionless.

"Don't worry," she said, "we just need to get to know each other better. Before long we're going to be real good friends."

"Don't count on it," Tim Mallory muttered.

"Oh, but I am," she countered, grinning broadly as she walked out the door.

Cain followed, waited until there wasn't any chance Mallory could hear him and asked, "What are his chances?"

"Good," Francine said without hesitating. "Very good. He's got plenty of spunk. Trust me, he'll need every ounce of that tenacity. We'll start right away."

Cain paused. "I apologize for the things Mallory said."

"Don't worry about it," was her automatic response, but a look flashed in her eyes that told Cain his friend's words had hit their mark. "I know I'm no raving beauty, but that's not why you're hiring me."

Perhaps not, but if she could bring Mallory out of this depression and help him walk again, Cain would believe she was the most beautiful woman in the world.

3 🎐

Cain needed to do some Christmas shopping. That was why he'd come to Fisherman's Wharf. At least that was the excuse he'd used when he found himself wandering aimlessly along the waterfront.

The harder he worked to convince himself his being there had nothing to do with Linette Collins, the more obvious the truth became. He could have arranged for near anything he wanted over the Internet with little more than a credit card and a catalog number.

The only reason he was on the wharf was the ridiculous hope he'd catch a glimpse of Linette. Just one. Without her knowing. Why he found it so necessary to spy on her, he didn't know. Didn't want to know.

As it happened, he located her yarn shop tucked in a corner along Pier 39, the window display as charming and inviting as the woman herself. He stood outside several moments, his hands buried in his lambskin-lined jacket.

Uncomfortable emotions came at him like poisoned darts, infecting him with all the might-have-beens in his life. He'd chosen this lifestyle, thrived on the challenge. No drug could produce the physical or emotional high of a successfully completed mission. No drug and no woman.

Then why was he standing in the cold like a lovelorn teenager, hoping for a glimpse of a widow he'd met briefly one night at a Christmas party? Clearly there were a few screws loose. The military had a word for this: battle fatigue. What he needed was a few uninterrupted days by himself to put his life back in the proper perspective.

Montana. Christmas was the perfect excuse to escape for a few days. It was long past time that he visited his ranch. He heard from the foreman he'd hired every now and again, but it had been well over a year since Cain had last visited the five-thousand-acre spread.

His strides filled with purpose, he walked along the pier until he saw a sign for World Wide Travel. After stepping inside the agency, he moved to the counter and waited his turn. A smartly dressed professional greeted him with a smile and arranged for his airline ticket to Helena, Montana. The only seats available were in first class, but Cain could well afford the extravagance. It was a small price to pay to escape San Francisco and the beautiful widow who'd captured his mind.

Experiencing a small sense of satisfaction, Cain tucked the airline ticket into the inside pocket of his jacket and continued on his way, moving down the waterfront and farther away from Linette. Farther away from temptation.

He was just beginning to think he had this minor curiosity licked when out of the blue, he saw her. For a moment it felt as if someone had inadvertently hit him against the back of the head. He went stock-still.

From the way her shoulders hunched forward he could see that she was tired. She stood in line at a fish and chips place, working to open the clasp of her shoulder bag. The wind whipped her hair about her face, and she lifted a finger to wrap a thick strand of dark hair around her ear.

The smart thing to do was to turn around, without delay, and walk away as fast as his feet would carry him. He'd gotten what he wanted. One last look at her, without her knowing. His curiosity should be satisfied.

Even as his mind formulated the thought, Cain knew just seeing Linette again wasn't nearly enough. He wanted to talk to her and get to know her. He wanted to sit down across a table from her and discover what it was about her that made a man who'd built his life around pride and discipline risk making a world-class fool of himself.

LINETTE was exhausted. She couldn't remember a day when she'd done a more brisk business. Instead of celebrating over the highest gross income achieved in a single workday, she felt like falling into bed and sleeping for a week. She wanted to ignore Christmas, the hustle and bustle, the joy and goodwill.

It was Nancy's news, too, Linette realized. It wasn't that she begrudged Rob and Nancy every happiness. She was thrilled for them. Yet it was all so painful. She ached for the child she'd never have with Michael and all the dreams they'd once shared.

Christmas, coupled with the anniversary of Michael's death and the news of the baby, weighed down her heart as surely as if it had been tied with concrete blocks and carelessly flung into the Bay.

As she advanced toward the take-out window, Linette realized she wasn't hungry. What appetite she'd had vanished. Stepping out of line, she secured the clasp of her purse and turned to head up the wharf.

It was then that she saw Cain. Linette's heart gave a short, rapid-fire reaction. As much as she didn't want to admit it, he'd been in her thoughts most of the day.

His eyes locked with hers as if the distance, the shoppers, the crowded sidewalk and endless traffic, in no way separated them. As if all she had to do was reach out and, like magic, he'd be standing there, directly in front of her.

At precisely the same moment they started walking toward each other, their gazes continuing to hold them as effectively as an embrace.

"Hello." Cain spoke first.

"Hi." She smiled, or at least attempted one. "Fancy meeting you here."

"I had to come down to pick up my airline tickets."

"You're leaving?" It shouldn't have come as any surprise. Cain had never hid the fact that he was in town for only a few days. San Francisco wasn't his home.

"I'll be back shortly after the first of the year."

The news sufficiently lifted her spirits, although there wasn't a single reason to believe she'd be seeing him then. Or ever again, for that matter.

"You changed your mind?" he asked, inclining his head toward the fish and chips stand.

"Yeah. I was looking for something quick and easy. But by the time I arrive home, the fish will be cold and soggy." That wasn't the whole story, but it was close enough to the truth to satisfy him.

By tacit agreement they started walking. The aroma

of fresh fish and thick-cut French fries floated toward them as they strolled along the pier.

"The fish and chips wouldn't be soggy if you ate them right away," Cain said. His hands were buried in his coat pockets, and he condensed his steps in order to keep pace with her much shorter stride. "I was headed that way myself. Would you care to join me?"

Linette hadn't been expecting a dinner invitation, and his offer took her by surprise. "Thank you, I'd enjoy that." She'd enjoy anything that helped her through the loneliness, helped her through this night. Rushing back to her apartment, which stood empty and dark, held no appeal.

His hand cupped her elbow as he led her, not to the fish and chips stand as she expected, but to the restaurant, a well-known and expensive seafood place that catered to a heavy tourist trade.

Because of the hour, they were put on a waiting list and told it might be as long as forty-five minutes before they could be seated. Cain didn't seem to object and Linette didn't, either.

He suggested they wait in the bar, and she agreed, although she wasn't much of a drinker. The lounge was as crowded as the restaurant, but they managed to find a table. An attractive waitress took their order. Cain asked for a Jack Daniel's, and Linette opted for a glass of white wine.

"Busy day?" Cain asked once they were settled.

"Frantic was more like it. There was a lull every now and again where Bonnie—she works with me—and I could take a breather, but those were few and far between. How about you?"

He hesitated as if he weren't sure how to answer her. "I attended to business matters."

She noticed how he turned the conversation away from himself and quizzed her once more about the yarn shop. She answered his questions, but she was deeply disappointed. It was more than obvious that he had no intention of lowering the steel facade he wore like plate armor, to share any part of himself. He was a good listener, but after thirty minutes she ran out of things to say.

As time passed it became more and more difficult to carry on a conversation. Linette finished her wine and set the glass on the small round table.

"Would you care for another?" Cain asked.

"No thanks." She made a show of looking at her watch. "Actually, I think it might be a good idea if I headed home. It's later than I realized, and . . ." She let the rest fade. Making excuses, even plausible ones, wasn't her forte. "Perhaps we could have dinner another time."

Cain's gaze narrowed with confusion as she stood. "Sure," he said. He took out his wallet and left a generous tip for the waitress. He hurriedly spoke to the reception-ist on his way out the door.

Linette hadn't intended for him to follow her outside. "It was good to see you again, Cain," she said, eager to be on her way. She turned, her steps as fast paced as she could make them. His eyes seemed to bore into her back, and it was all she could do not to whirl around and confront him.

Weaving her way in and out of the pockets of pedes-trians, Linette made good time. She'd gone four or five blocks and was just outside the BART station when she heard Cain call her name.

Briefly closing her eyes, dreading a confrontation, she hesitated and then turned around. He trotted across the street. "One question," he said. "Was that a brush-off?"

"It's me," she said, more than willing to accept the blame. "I've had a rough day. Nancy stopped in to tell me she's pregnant and it's almost Christmas." She was speaking so fast, the words nearly collided with one another on the way out of her mouth. "Forgive me if I offended you, but I didn't have the energy to sit through dinner and listen to myself all evening." By the frown he wore, she realized her explanation served only to baffle him further.

"Listen to yourself?" he asked.

"It's apparent you're not interested in sharing any part of yourself with me. Don't misunderstand me, if you don't want to talk, fine, that's your prerogative. It's just that I'm tired and hungry and depressed and not fit company. Not tonight." She clung to her purse strap as if it were a lifeline, eager to be on her way.

A car, not unlike any other, raced past them. Linette saw a youth toss something out the window. His action was followed by several loud bursts of noise. Before who or what had fully registered in her mind, Cain lunged for her, gripping her hard about the waist. Twisting so that he would receive the brunt of the impact, he pushed her toward the sidewalk, which came racing up to meet them. She landed with a thud atop him, bouncing slightly with the force of the fall.

Her breath jammed in her lungs as shock and panic shot through her.

"Are you all right?" Cain asked, brushing the hair from her face as if that would tell him what he needed to know. His touch was gentle and light, although she noticed his hand trembled.

She couldn't answer him, couldn't force the words past the sheer terror that had gripped her throat. Instead she wrapped her arms around him and clung. With her heart thundering in her ear, she sank into the safety of his arms, the warm haven of security.

"I'm sorry," he whispered repeatedly, his hands stroking the back of her head. "I thought it was something else. Apparently it was only firecrackers."

She nodded, her pulse hammering against his chest. Her breath came in rapid bursts as she struggled to regain her composure.

"I didn't mean to frighten you."

Gradually she gained control and eased herself away from him. "I'm fine." She wasn't, but she would be in short order.

He stood and helped her to her feet. A crowd had gathered around them, firing questions. Cain ignored them as if they were alone, ignored the questions and offers of assistance. Linette heard whispers about crazy kids, tossing fireworks into the street like that.

Cain wrapped his arm around Linette's waist and gently led her away.

"I'll drive you home," he said. In no way were the words in the form of a question. She saw the strain on his face.

"I'm fine," she reiterated. Perhaps she was now, but she wasn't so sure of Cain. The self-directed anger radiated from him like the heat from a sunburn.

He helped her inside his car, and when he climbed in

the driver's seat, she rattled off her address. She noticed the hard set of his jaw and the way his hands tightened around the steering wheel.

He didn't say a word on the ten-minute drive to her apartment building.

"I think we can both do with a cup of strong coffee," she said.

His eyes hardened as if he weren't sure he should accept her invitation. "I've done enough damage for one night, don't you think?"

She raised her hand to her face, to brush away a strand of hair, and realized she didn't want to walk into the cold, dark apartment, surrounded by silence, surrounded by memories. Not tonight. Not alone. Like the night of the Christmas party, they needed each other.

"Come up with me." The words were barely audible, and she wondered if he heard her. His hands tightened until his knuckles went white before he reached for the key and without another word turned off the ignition.

Linette led the way into the elevator and down the long, silent hall to her third-floor apartment. She unlocked the door and turned on the light. Inside, she removed her coat and hung it in the hall closet with her purse. Cain removed his jacket and draped it over the end of the leather sofa, as if to say he wouldn't be staying long. He scanned the room and zeroed in on the framed photograph of Michael she'd placed on the fireplace mantel.

Linette moved into the compact kitchen, but Cain gently but firmly sat her down at the octagon-shaped glass table in the dining room. "I'll make the coffee," he announced. He assembled the pot within minutes and started rummaging through her refrigerator. "When was the last time you bought groceries?" he asked, taking a carton of eggs from the top shelf.

She assumed the question was rhetorical, but she answered him anyway. "Last week . . . sometime."

Before she could ask what he was doing, Cain had scrambled eggs and buttered toast. He set the plate in front of her, poured them each a cup of coffee, adding sugar to hers. Then he pulled out a chair, twisted it around, and straddled it. "I'm sorry about what happened earlier. I don't have any excuse, other than to say I acted out of instinct."

Linette had already discerned as much.

"I've been in this line of business for too many years not to react to the sound of gunfire, or in this case a string of ladyfingers."

Linette cradled the coffee mug between her hands and let its warmth revive her. "I know. Nancy told me you were part of Special Forces."

He studied her for a few moments. "What did you mean when you said Nancy's pregnant and it's Christmas?"

Linette's shoulders sagged with defeat. "You're doing it again," she said with an exaggerated sigh.

"Doing what?"

"Turning the conversation away from yourself."

"I am?" He seemed surprised. "All right, fair is fair. Answer my questions and I'll answer yours."

Linette told him about Nancy's visit earlier that afternoon. "My husband and I badly wanted children. I don't expect you to understand. I'm not entirely sure I do myself, but it's like this big hole inside me started bleeding again. I thought it had healed."

Cain sipped his coffee. "Your husband's the man in the photo on the mantel?"

"That's Michael. He died of leukemia two years ago on December twenty-third."

"Ah, so that's what you meant about it being Christmas."

"Yes. It's my fault he lingered as long as he did."

"Your fault?"

She nodded. "He'd been in a coma for a month before he died, and there was no hope. You see, I refused to let him die. I'm convinced the sheer force of my will is what kept him alive. I sat by his bedside for weeks, refusing to leave for more than a few minutes. I feared that without me there, he'd slip away. I couldn't allow that, I couldn't let him die on me, not when I so desperately wanted him to live. And so I clung to him, clung to the hope of a miracle."

She lowered her gaze, reliving those terrible weeks in her mind. "With faith the size of an avocado pit, I expected God to heal Michael. He did, of course, but not the way I anticipated. Michael's free of illness now. It took me a long time to understand that.

"It wasn't until it was almost Christmas that I realized what I was doing to my husband. Michael was ready to go, had been ready nearly the entire month he'd been in the coma. He was waiting for me to release him. When I did, death came quickly. It may sound odd, but it came as a friend and not the bitter enemy I'd imagined."

Cain stood and, taking his coffee with him, started to pace her kitchen.

"Since the anniversary of his death falls so close to Christmas, it's all the more difficult. You see, everyone seems to want to make the holidays better for me. I feel like I'm being suffocated with attention. Everyone tries so hard to pretend Michael isn't really gone. It's like they're playacting that he's away on a business trip or something like that. His parents have had a hard time accepting his death.

"For the past two years, they've insisted I join them for Christmas. I love Jake and Janet, but they're still grieving themselves, and as much as we care for each other, it's all so uncomfortable."

"What about your family?"

"They're on the East Coast, and my parents are as bad as Michael's. At least with Jake and Janet, I'm only trapped a day."

Cain sat down once more. "All right, ask me anything you'd like."

"Anything?"

He nodded.

Now that she had free rein, Linette wasn't sure where to start. "How old are you?"

He laughed. "Thirty-six, and you?"

"Twenty-nine."

"What brings you to San Francisco?"

He heaved a heavy sigh. "One of my men was badly injured eighteen months ago. He's required several extensive surgeries since, and the best hospital and surgeons were here."

"How's he doing now?"

A frown of deep concern creased Cain's brow. "Physically, about as well as can be expected, but mentally he's having a hard time of it. I hired a new physical therapist for him this afternoon, and hopefully she'll last longer than the others. I have a feeling Francine's just what Mallory needs."

A smile courted the corners of his mouth when he mentioned the other woman's name, causing Linette to wonder about the physical therapist. Francine was a feminine name and conjured up the imagine of a sleek, attractive woman who'd managed to capture Cain's attention. If Linette hadn't known better, she would have thought she was jealous of a woman she'd never met, over a man she barely knew.

"Where are you stationed?" she asked abruptly, wanting to change subjects, sorry now she'd asked.

This too gave him pause, and frankly she wondered why. It wasn't as if a military base should be any secret. "I'm out of Miami."

It certainly wasn't any place close, she noted. "You're a long way from home, aren't you?"

"A very long way," he agreed, his voice low and strained.

Linette had the feeling he wasn't speaking about the distance between San Francisco and Miami, either. He was out of his element with her, too. He wasn't accustomed to consoling grieving widows or answering questions about himself. He was a man who issued orders and expected complete and immediate obedience.

"Anything else?" he asked when she wasn't immediately forthcoming with another question.

She shook her head.

He downed the last of his coffee and set the mug in her sink. "I'll leave you, then. You're sure you're all right?"

"I'm fine." She was now.

Cain reached for his jacket and started toward the door. Linette followed him. "Thank you for bringing me home."

"No problem."

"And thanks for listening." She normally didn't spill out her heart like that or burden another with her grief. She'd needed him, and in some strange way she realized he needed her just as badly.

The desire to touch him was suddenly so strong that she gave in to it. She lifted her hand and pressed it against his cheek. His hand joined hers, and he moved his head slightly so that he could kiss the inside of her palm.

"You're going to be fine."

"I know." And she did. But every now and again, mostly when she wasn't prepared, something unexpected would find its mark, reminding her of all that she'd lost. This very day was a good example.

Cain's eyes studied hers carefully. "I'd like to kiss you."

"I wish you would," she confessed.

He smiled and so did she.

Before another second passed, she was in his arms and his mouth covered hers. As if this were where she belonged, had always belonged, Linette melted against him, savoring the feel of his strength. His mouth was hungry and hard, his kisses heady and deep. Before long she was clinging to him. The pleasure was so keen, it frightened her.

Expertly he moved his mouth over hers, molding her lips with his own. When she sighed, he deepened the kiss. She felt empty and aching. She hadn't thought these sensations were possible with another man. She hadn't expected this, hadn't anticipated it.

By the time they broke apart, Linette was convinced desire and need were written all over her face.

Cain stared down on her as if he too had been taken by surprise, as if he were as shocked as she by their bodies' responses to each other.

"Good night, Linette," he said finally.

"Good night, Cain," she whispered, praying the dazed, hungry look had vanished from her eyes.

Slowly, as if it demanded all of his strength to leave her, he opened the door. He stepped into the hallway. "How about dinner tomorrow?" he asked abruptly as if the invitation came as a surprise to him.

"All right."

"I'll come by here at six."

"Perfect."

He left, and she closed the door and leaned against the hard wood. Her knees were shaking, but it wasn't any lingering effect of her adventure that evening. It was the aftermath of Cain's kiss that left her trembling.

At the fireplace, Linette picked up the photo of Michael and stared at the lovingly familiar face for several moments.

"I like him," she told her dead husband, and then, because she believed it was important, she added, "I believe you would have, too."

Sagging onto the sofa, Linette pressed the photo against her chest and closed her eyes. For the last three years she'd felt as if she were living out her life in the eye of a storm. The winds had died down in the last few months, the hailstorm of fears pummeling against her had tapered. And the thunderstorm she'd suffered at Michael's death had eased to a light drizzle.

She smiled to herself, amazed at how fanciful her thinking had become of late. After replacing the photograph, Linette returned to the kitchen. She hadn't eaten the eggs Cain had scrambled for her. Now she reheated them in the microwave, sat down at the table and enjoyed the meal. It was the first time a man had cooked for her in a very long while.

4

Cain tossed his car keys in the air and caught them in his left hand. From the way he was acting, one would assume he was a love-starved teen. That was the way he felt. He paused then, struck by the realization of what he was letting happen. Wanted to happen.

Linette Collins was dangerous.

Not only to his sanity, but to his very life. Cain had seen it happen often enough to other men to know the danger signs. Yet here he was making the same choice, the same mistake.

He was close to losing his own fool head. And all over a woman. Only Linette wasn't an ordinary woman. She possessed special powers. She must in order to tie him up in knots a sailor couldn't undo.

Cain was good at what he did. From the time he was in Special Forces, he'd heard that he was a natural. What that meant, he'd decided years later, was that he didn't give a damn whether he lived or died. It all boiled down to one thing: He had nothing to lose.

It was this that had given him an edge, the steadiest

hand, the clearest head. Now that he'd met Linette, he understood what this advantage had cost him. Over the years, the price had been exacting and demanding.

Roughly, he didn't give a tinker's damn about anyone or anything other than Deliverance Company and the all-encompassing, all-important mission.

He'd held Linette and kissed her, thinking . . . he didn't know what he'd been thinking. Clearly he hadn't been, otherwise he would have known better, would have taken one look at her and run as fast as his legs would carry him in the opposite direction.

A woman like Linette would muddle his mind, would mire his reflexes. A woman like this would be the death of him. Then he'd leave this world as lonely and as miserable as when he'd entered it. It wasn't much of a legacy.

What frightened Cain most was how desperately he needed her. Linette Collins, the gentle widow, had the power to cure his heart. She had the power to cure him of a lifetime of not giving a damn.

Cain sat in his car and thumped his fist against the steering column. He had an idea. A crazy one in light of what he'd been thinking, but one that had presented itself and wouldn't let go.

Before he could change his mind, he climbed out of the car and hurried back into Linette's apartment building. Instead of waiting for the elevator, which he considered too slow, he raced up the three flights of stairs, taking the steps two and three at a time.

He was panting by the time he arrived outside her apartment. Drawing in several deep breaths, he waited until his heart had calmed before he rang her doorbell.

Although he didn't see it happen, he was certain

Linette checked the peephole before unlatching the deadbolt lock.

"Cain?"

"Listen," he said, struggling to sound nonchalant and relaxed, "I just had an idea. Why don't you spend Christmas with me in Montana?"

"Spend Christmas with you in Montana?" Linette repeated slowly.

Cain was beginning to think this might not be such a brilliant idea after all. "You were telling me how difficult the holiday is for you. I'm offering you a solution."

"But . . ."

Apparently she didn't know what to think of his suggestion, because she blinked several times and stared at him with a dumbstruck expression.

"I've got a ranch house there with plenty of bedrooms, so you don't need to worry about sleeping arrangements. I'm not expecting anything more than your company for a few days." He couldn't believe he was doing this. Couldn't believe he was tossing his heart out on a slab for her to either accept or reject.

Perhaps he was trying to make up for all the Christmases he'd missed as a kid, with a father who guzzled every dime he'd ever earned. Somewhere in a hidden corner of Cain's heart, a little boy was waiting for the Christmas tree and the home-cooked turkey with all the trimmings. He'd believed that child had long since matured to manhood, but apparently all it took was the warmth and gentleness of a beautiful widow to reawaken the long forgotten childhood fantasy.

"Listen," he said, feeling more foolish by the minute, "think about it, and when we meet tomorrow evening, you can let me know. It's just an idea, and if you'd rather not come, then it isn't a big deal."

Without waiting for a reply, Cain turned away, wishing now he'd taken more time to consider what he was doing before traipsing upstairs and taking the bull by the horns.

"Cain."

He whirled back around.

Linette had stepped into the hallway. She looked vulnerable and uncertain. "I'll be happy to go."

He shouldn't be this pleased, but he was. Ecstatic. Already he'd determined that Linette was dangerous. Yet here he was inviting her to his home, opening his heart and his life to her softness. He might as well pull the pin out of a hand grenade and drop it at his own feet. All he had to do now was wait for the explosion.

"How soon can you leave?" he asked, burying his hands in his pockets in an effort to resist the urge to kiss her again.

She gestured weakly as if she weren't sure how to answer him. "Tomorrow, but I'll need to make the arrangements with Bonnie, and I need to be back before the twenty-eighth."

"No problem."

She grinned then, and Cain swore he'd never seen anyone with a more beautiful smile.

"You'll call me in the morning?"

He nodded, and took two giant steps backward.

"Good night, Cain."

"Night." It wasn't until he was in his car that he realized he was whistling. He stopped abruptly, wondering what madness had overtaken him. It didn't matter if this craziness had a name, Cain decided. He couldn't remember a time when he'd been this happy.

$\mathcal{F}$RANCINE dressed carefully for her second encounter with Tim Mallory. Not that she had a vast wardrobe to choose from. Her closet contained mostly white uniforms of tops and slacks that afforded her freedom of movement. For the occasional interview and business meeting, she kept a couple of tailored suits on hand, but nothing spectacular.

She wore her hair the way she always did, pulled tightly away from her face in a long French braid that stretched halfway down the middle of her back. She didn't bother with makeup. Never had, even as a teenager. Nature hadn't given her an attractive face, and with nothing to enhance, she figured why go to all the bother.

She parked her car in the driveway and hopped out, taking her gym bag with her. She was eager to get started on this case. She'd always thrived on challenge, and something told her she was going to enjoy working with this particular patient.

Generally she would have preferred starting Monday morning, but the longer they waited before beginning the exercises, the greater the chance Tim Mallory's muscles would atrophy. She'd know soon enough how much his leg muscles had already degenerated.

Tim Mallory might think he was some he-man soldier, but she'd demand every ounce of grit the mercenary ever believed he possessed.

When she arrived at the house, Greg, his personal assistant, opened the door for her. "It's Sunday," he said, looking surprised to see her.

"I know. How's the patient?"

The beefy young man shrugged. "About the same. Cantankerous, angry, and in a generally bad mood."

"Be prepared, then," she said, casting the assistant a sympathetic glance. "Because it's about to get worse. Much worse."

"You're kidding, I hope."

"I wish I was. Come and get me in an hour, and bring ice bags and two aspirin."

"For Mr. Mallory?"

"No," she said with a chuckle. "For me. Mallory and I've only met once, but I can tell this guy's going to give me a migraine."

Greg laughed.

Francine didn't wait for him to show her the way, she already knew the mercenary was holed up in the back bedroom. Probably with the lights off, buried under blankets because the lack of circulation in the lower half of his body left him chilled inside and out.

She found him just where she'd suspected she would.

"Hello again," she said brightly, flipping on the light switch and moving into the bedroom with the determination of a Mack truck.

"What the hell are you doing here?" Tim demanded. He sat up in the bed and grabbed the clock off the bedstand. "It's barely nine."

"I prefer to start early. Beginning Monday morning, I'll be here at six. We'll have your first workout before breakfast."

"Wanna bet, sweetheart?" His dark gaze hardened, daring her to defy him. She noted his eyes were dull with pain and rimmed with fatigue. Her best guess was that he wasn't sleeping much and had the appetite of a bird. That too was about to change.

Francine flattened her hand against her hip. She didn't like being referred to as "sweetheart," especially in that tone of voice, but mentioning it was certain to guarantee he would continue.

"Do I wanna bet? Sure, I'd be willing to place a wager on that."

Mallory's eyes flared, as though he'd welcome the opportunity to send her packing. "Any time, any place."

"Great," she said gleefully. "We'll make it easy. You get out of that bed and walk me to the door, and I'm out of here. Until that happens, big boy, I'm going to be your shadow. I promise you, you'll never work harder than in the next several months."

His blunt features flushed with anger. "I can't walk," he said between gritted teeth. "And you damn well know it."

"Not now you can't, but you will in time."

"Can you guarantee that?"

"No," she returned evenly, unwilling to pull any punches. "But you're going to have to give it your best shot, and I'm here to help you." Rolling up her sleeves, she smiled at him. "Let's get started."

"I don't feel like it." The anger in his eyes intensified as he glared at her.

"I don't suppose you do. No one does, and I'm not going to lie to you, Mr. Mallory. There's going to be pain, plenty of it. For a time, you'll hate me." She rolled the empty wheelchair away from his bedside.

"I already do."

She grinned and promised, "But not nearly as much as you will."

By the end of the first hour of gently working the stiff muscles of Mallory's legs, rubbing them down to encourage the circulation, Francine was invigorated. As she worked, she explained what she was doing and why. She wanted to reassure him there was a payoff for the pain she inflicted on him. From Mallory's tense silence it was unlikely her patient had received the message.

Francine had enough experience to know this procedure wasn't painless, but after the first few protests, Tim lay on his back, his eyes closed, his expression cast in stone.

"How much longer?" he asked after the first hour. His face glistened with sweat, and his chest heaved as he struggled against revealing his discomfort.

"I'm almost finished," she said, working the calf of his injured leg. She elevated it slightly, and as he rolled his head to one side, she saw that he'd gritted his teeth. There was no joy in witnessing pain. It was never easy to see another suffer, no matter how cantankerous the patient. More often than not, her lectures on the benefits of the exercise were for her own ears. She needed to be reminded of the eventual outcome for all this agony.

By the end of the session, what little energy Tim Mallory possessed had vanished. Greg arrived, and Francine asked that he help Mallory out of his clothes and into his swimming suit.

Her patient lifted his head off the sweat-drenched pillow. "I thought you said we were through."

"We are. But now that I've got the circulation going in that leg, I want to put it to use."

"I'm tired."

"I know." She'd wager he was a lot more than tired, but she couldn't allow her sympathy to show.

"Not today."

"Greg," she said, "have him to the swimming pool in fifteen minutes."

The young man grinned and nodded. "I'll see that he's there."

"Good." With that she reached for her gym bag and left the room. She heard Tim protest the minute she was out of the room, but he didn't stand a chance of winning this argument, and he knew it. The mercenary might not willingly own up to it, but he had few options. Eventually acceptance would come, but from what she knew of Mallory's personality, he'd hold out as long as he could.

One thing was certain, he didn't have much energy left to put up much of a fight. At least for now.

𝓛INETTE's first impression of the ranch house was that it looked like something out of a television western. *Bonanza* revisited. The two-story log structure, nestled against the backdrop of the Rocky Mountains, looked as inviting as a port in a storm. An apt description in light of the fat snowflakes lazily drifting down from a thunder blue sky.

"It's beautiful," she told Cain.

"I called ahead and had the kitchen stocked, so there'll be plenty of chow. John Stamp's my foreman, and his wife, Patty, promised to check everything over and have the house ready when we arrived." Cain glanced her way. "Are you tired?"

"Not in the least." They'd spent the majority of the day hopping from one airport to another, and when they'd finally landed, they'd had to drive nearly three hours.

Cain had phoned Linette bright and early that morning and asked if she could make a ten o'clock flight. After a moment of panic, she'd assured him in a calm voice that it wouldn't be a problem, and thanks to Bonnie, it hadn't been.

"I'm more hungry than anything," Cain said.

Gourmet cooking was one of Linette's favorite things. She hadn't been doing much of that lately, not when she was cooking for one. Now she looked forward to impressing Cain with the smooth way she handled herself around a kitchen.

Cain pulled the Bronco into the detached garage and helped her out of the passenger's side before hauling their luggage out of the back end.

The lights from inside the house glowed brightly like beacons of welcome. Linette reached for her cosmetic bag and followed Cain through a thin layer of freshly fallen snow to the house. Several inches had already been shoveled off the pathway.

The door was unlocked, and Linette sighed inwardly at the rush of warm air that greeted her. When Cain had mentioned the ranch house, she hadn't a clue it would be this beautiful or this inviting. From the entryway, she saw a fire flickering gently in the massive stone fireplace. A stairway rounded up one side to a hallway, leading, she suspected, to a series of bedrooms.

Cain removed his coat and hung it in the closet before helping her out of hers.

"If you take care of the luggage, I'll see what I can do about rustling us up some dinner." Eager to explore his beautiful house, she didn't wait for his response.

While Cain carried their suitcases up the stairs, Linette wandered into the kitchen. She stood, awestruck, just inside the door. This wasn't an ordinary kitchen, but a chef's dream. Sparkling copper kettles hung from above a large gourmet island. The appliances looked new, and a quick investigation revealed a walk-in cooler and a six-burner gas stove.

It didn't take Linette long to realize nothing was required of her. Dinner was already prepared and waiting for their arrival. Apparently Patty Stamp had seen to that along with everything else.

Cain soon joined her. "Dinner's ready," she announced.

"That was quick," he teased.

They ate at the dining room table, which was set with linen napkins and a centerpiece made of freshly clipped holly and cinnamon candles. Neither felt obligated to carry the conversation. Linette suspected it was because they didn't feel the necessity to fill the silence with idle chatter. Perhaps, like her, Cain didn't know what to say.

Cain helped her with the dishes, and afterward they drank coffee in front of the fireplace in matching wing-back leather chairs. As he sipped from the ceramic mug, Cain read over some business papers John Stamp had left for him to review.

The fire mesmerized Linette; the flames licked noisily at the logs, and every now and again they'd spit and sizzle as if undergoing some great debate.

Intermittently her gaze drifted to Cain, and she thought about what her parents had said, the warnings they'd issued when they'd learned she was spending the holiday with a man she barely knew. Yet she felt none of their concern.

Cain must have felt her scrutiny because he raised his eyes to her. His gaze softened as it met hers. His look was gentle, almost loving. Neither spoke. For her part, Linette wasn't sure she could. All she knew was there was no place else she would rather be than right here with Cain McClellan sitting at her side.

"I'm not being good company, am I?"

"On the contrary," she hurried to say. "I'm perfectly content."

Her in-laws hadn't known what to say when she'd announced she wouldn't be joining them for Christmas after all. Linette knew she'd stunned them by telling them she was traveling with Cain to Montana. Michael's mother had swiftly phoned Linette's, and within fifteen minutes Linette had received a call from her concerned parents. Once she'd explained how she'd met Cain and what she intended to do over Christmas, her mother had been left speechless. Unfortunately Betty Lawson's silence hadn't lasted long, and Linette had been forced to listen to a tense lecture about the wisdom of her actions.

Apparently both Michael's parents and her own felt she was making a foolish mistake. She couldn't trust her own judgment, they feared. She wasn't herself. Grief had clouded her thinking.

Perhaps they were right.

Linette had certainly never done anything like this before, but then she'd never met a man like Cain McClellan.

She yawned and decided to rest her eyes a moment. She must have been more tired than she realized and drifted off to sleep, because the next thing she knew Cain was whispering close to her ear. Her eyes fluttered open, and she found him standing next to her chair.

"I'm sorry to wake you, but you'll be far more comfortable upstairs."

She smiled sleepily and yawned. "I suppose you're right."

"I'll go up with you," he said, offering her his hand.

He guided her up the stairs and escorted her to the bedroom he'd had readied for her arrival. He pointed out his own room, which was at the far end of the hallway. Linette didn't know whether to be relieved or disheartened that his bedroom was so far removed from her own.

"Can I get you anything?" he asked, poised in her doorway.

"No, I'm fine."

He nodded, and it seemed to her that he wanted to say something more. The look in his eyes intensified, and he hesitated before adding, "Good night, then."

"I'll see you in the morning."

"Speaking of the morning," he said, leaping on the excuse to linger.

"Yes?"

"I thought we'd cut down a Christmas tree and decorate it."

Linette's heart gladdened at the prospect. "That sounds like fun."

The strong sexual attraction between them spit and sizzled much like the logs had earlier. Nor could Linette deny what was happening to her body. A tingling awareness spread through her, leaving in its wake a desire she'd shared only with one other man.

Linette realized that Cain was a full partner in these feelings, but like her, he was bewildered and unsure.

"Good night," she said with a sigh.

He swallowed tightly, nodded, and turned away.

CAIN wandered back down the stairs. Settling back onto the chair he'd recently vacated, he rubbed a hand down his face.

Linette deserved more than he could offer. Already she'd made it clear that she wouldn't be satisfied with the bare bones details of his life. She wanted to know it all.

He couldn't tell her about Deliverance Company.

It was necessary to shield her from the reality of who and what he was. Not knowing would protect her from the worry. Protect her from the harshness of what he did for a living.

After watching Michael die, Linette was a woman who cherished life, and he was a man who often foolishly risked his own. He could think of no way to explain what he did. There wasn't a chance in hell of making her understand, so he hadn't tried. And wouldn't, because every moment with her was too painfully precious to destroy.

The snow fell relentlessly through the night. Cain woke to look out at a thick blanket of the powdery substance. He was in the kitchen drinking his first cup of coffee when Linette joined him the following morning.

She was dressed in jeans and a thick cable-knit sweater. He'd never known a woman could look this naturally beautiful without makeup. Afraid she'd notice how he couldn't keep his eyes off her, he poured her a cup of coffee. She smiled her appreciation when he handed it to her.

"Did you sleep well?" he asked, hoping she had. For his own part, he'd tossed and turned most of the night, tormented by the knowledge that she was only four doors away.

"Like a log."

"Good." Toast popped up from the toaster, and he reached for it, then buttered the twin slices. "John will be by first thing this morning to go over some business matters with me."

"I'd like to meet Patty," she said.

"From what John said, she's just as anxious to meet you."

No sooner had he spoken than there was a polite knock against the back door. John let himself inside, followed by his wife of ten years. Cain watched as Patty's curious gaze moved past him to dwell on Linette. He might have been wrong, but it seemed Patty took one look at Linette and her eyes gleamed with approval.

Cain introduced the couple.

"Did you get a chance to read over those papers?" John asked. He was tall and rangy and wore his cowboy hat low on his head. Patty was short and slightly stocky, with shoulder-length blond hair and blue eyes. The two expertly managed his spread. When Cain had first purchased the place, he'd urged the Stamps to move into the main house. They'd declined, choosing instead to live in the smaller house reserved for the foreman. Cain maintained a small herd, but John had been urging him to build it up, claiming beef prices were better than they had been in a number of years. Cain was taking the advice under consideration.

As he became involved in a lengthy conversation with John, he noted Linette and Patty talking as if they were longtime friends. Every now and again he caught a word or two of their conversation. From what he gathered, Linette was asking Patty about Christmas dinner. Apparently she planned on cooking it herself.

Hard as he tried, Cain couldn't keep his eyes away from Linette. Soon John, who was eager to prove his point, realized it was useless.

"This is the first time you've ever brought a woman to visit," he commented dryly. "Are you and Linette serious?"

Startled, Cain snapped his attention away from his guest. "No," he said abruptly, perhaps too abruptly, because the women stopped talking and looked at him expectantly.

"We're going out to cut down a Christmas tree this morning," Cain said, breaking the strained silence.

"Then we won't hold you up. Come on, John," Patty urged. "These people have more important things to do than talk about purchasing a few more head of cattle."

Cain walked the couple to the door and thanked Patty for having thoughtfully seen to their dinner the night before. He casually mentioned how good the roast had tasted.

"Linette already thanked me," she said, blushing with pleasure at his compliment. "I shouldn't have traipsed down here first thing this morning," Patty went on to say apologetically, "but I couldn't help being curious about your lady friend." Her gaze narrowed as she studied him. "She's a good woman, Cain. I hope you're considering settling down. It's time for you to start thinking about a family." With that she turned and walked away.

It was time all right. Time to have his head examined, Cain decided. That he was foolish enough to live out a schoolboy's dream was one matter, but having his foreman's wife advise him to marry and start a family was enough to turn his blood cold.

"You ready to go find a tree?" he asked gruffly after the couple had left.

"Any time," she assured him.

By the time Cain located a hand saw and found a sled

and rope, the sky had turned an angry shade of gray. "It looks like it's going to start snowing again," he said, wondering at the wisdom of their gallivanting through the woods.

He did this sort of thing routinely, but he didn't know how well Linette would hold up to the physical demands of hiking in the snow. He was about to suggest that perhaps this wasn't such a great idea after all when he saw the disappointment flicker in her eyes.

"It'll be fine," she insisted. "We'll cut down a tree and be back before you know it."

"All right," Cain relented, mainly because he didn't have the heart to disappoint her. Whatever common sense he possessed had taken a flying leap toward insanity the minute he'd met this woman. Why stop now?

Fortunately a copse of trees grew close by. Any one of those would serve nicely. They could walk there and back without much difficulty, he decided.

"This one will do," he said, coming upon the first tree the appropriate size. He reached for the hand saw when Linette stopped him.

"It's too short," she insisted. "And one side isn't as full as it should be."

"Too short? Not full enough?"

"Yes! Besides that, you'll be able to see that you cut down a tree from the house. It'll spoil your view."

It would be a cold day in hell before one blasted fir tree would ruin his view. He wasn't likely to notice the loss of a single six-footer when he owned a forest full.

"All right," he said with limitless patience, "you choose."

Apparently this was what she'd been waiting for him to suggest, because she dragged him halfway up a mountain and down another before she discovered the ideal Christmas tree. Frankly, Cain didn't know there could be so much wrong with so many trees. He would have been perfectly happy with any one of a thousand she'd singularly dismissed for one ridiculous flaw or another.

To think he'd been worried about her physical endurance. By the time she'd made her choice, he was both hungry and tired.

"You're sure about this one?" he asked. One thing was clear. If he ever spent another Christmas with Linette Collins, he was buying a tree in town. And he was purchasing it without taking her with him.

"Positive," she said, and her cheeks glowed pink and healthy.

He hunkered down and sawed away at the trunk, grumbling under his breath. This was his reward. All his life he'd dreamed about cutting down his own Christmas tree. He'd never realized it would be this difficult.

He stood when he'd finished and discovered Linette had vanished. "Linette," he called, his heart pounding hard and fast. It would be just like the fool woman to wander off and get lost.

"Linette," he called a second time. Concerned, he scanned the area as the sense of dread filled him. He left the fallen tree and glanced toward the sky, sure they were about to encounter a blizzard.

When he didn't get an answer, he shouted louder, this time cupping his mouth in order for his voice to carry farther.

"Cain."

Relieved, he whirled around. The snowball's impact caught him square in the chest. For one moment he stood frozen in surprise. It didn't take him long to recover. Before another second had passed, he'd scooped a ball of his own.

"That wasn't wise," he said. She didn't appear to believe him because he was bombarded with three other snowballs in quick succession. He was amazed by the accuracy of her throws.

"Anyone who stands around and waits to be hit deserves what they get," she called out. "Some soldier you turned out to be."

Cain was quick enough to duck behind a tree this time. The snowball slammed against the bark, spraying his face with snow. Cain laughed outright. This was what he got for trusting that little she-devil.

It didn't take him more than a few minutes to work his way through the woods and sneak up behind her. He watched her for several moments, peeking out from the tree, attempting to locate him. It never occurred to her that he could be less than ten feet behind her.

"Linette." He spoke her name softly and let the breeze carry it as though it had been whispered by the angels themselves.

Linette stiffened, her attention keen.

He said her name a second time.

She swung around and blinked incredibly large eyes at him. "Cain? How'd you get there?" She made it sound as if they'd somehow become separated during a Sunday school picnic.

He bounced a snowball from one gloved hand to the other. "You certainly had me fooled," he said, smiling gleefully. "And all along I thought you a sweet and gentle soul."

"But I am." Once more she fluttered her long lashes at him.

"Who would have guessed a woman so beautiful would possess such a wide streak of malice?"

"You shouldn't have complained."

"Complained?" He lightly pitched the compacted snowball in the air, catching it with one hand.

"About the Christmas tree," she said. He noticed the way she was edging away from the tree and guessed she was planning to make a run for it.

"I never said a word," he countered.

"Maybe not out loud, but you were mumbling a number of times, and what you didn't mumble you were thinking."

He laughed, because she'd read him so accurately.

She pitched one last snowball at him, then turned and ran like a jackrabbit, ricocheting from one tree to the next and yelling at the top of her lungs.

The snowball missed him completely. He dropped the one he was holding and took out in a dead run after her. Her agility and speed amazed him, but she was no match for him. He reached her within seconds and grabbed her about the waist.

Laughing, they both went down in the snow. She lay sprawled atop him, but he quickly reversed their positions, pinning her beneath him. Her eyes had never been more clear. They sparkled with laughter and life. Her chest heaved as she smiled up at him.

"You deserve to have your face washed with snow," he told her, holding her hands above her head. "And I'm just the man to do it."

"I'm so sorry," she said in a totally unconvincing lie. "I don't know what came over me. You were cutting down the tree and muttering when all at once this voice inside me said you needed to be brought down a peg or two."

With his free hand, Cain lifted a paw full of snow and held it above her face. "If you're planning to talk me out of washing your face, you'd better come up with something more convincing than that."

Laughing, she squirmed beneath him in a useless effort to escape. "It'll never happen again," she promised, then made the mistake of snickering.

"Until next time, you mean," he told her sarcastically.

"Cain," she pleaded.

"You owe me," he said, his eyes holding hers.

Linette went still, her chest heaving, her eyes laughing. All at once the amusement drained out of her, and she gazed up at him and asked, "Wouldn't a kiss do just as well?"

5 🙝

$\mathcal{L}$ouis St. Cyr wasn't going home for Christmas. A visit on New Year's didn't appeal to him, either. Why should he rush to the loving arms of his family? In Bayamon, the small Caribbean island his father ruled, he was known as "Sonny" or "Junior." He was tired of fitting into the background of his father's ambitions. Tired of living his life to suit his family.

In France he was his own man, and he didn't need his mother's pampering or his father's tedious advice. He didn't need the hassles that went along with being the son of a wealthy landowner turned politician.

His mother had pleaded with him to reconsider, and his father, the great and mighty leader, had threatened to cut off his hefty allowance. But Daddy wouldn't, and Louis knew it.

After all, it was his father who'd insisted he attend the University of Paris at the Sorbonne, his own alma mater. And to think that in the beginning, Louis had balked. He'd wanted to attend Harvard University in the United States, but that was a battle in a long list of battles he'd lost. But no more.

Moving away from his family was the best thing that had ever happened to Louis. He wasn't giving his mother an excuse to drive him home just because she wanted him available for a silly Christmas party.

One small taste of freedom and Louis discovered the elixir to be habit forming. Daddy could push all the buttons he wanted, but Louie boy wasn't responding.

Besides, he was in love. What red-blooded nineteen-year-old would turn down an invitation to spend two glorious weeks with a gorgeous blonde named Brigette? Not Louis.

The nymph had planted herself in his life and in his bed, and he had no intention of allowing her out of either. He might even marry Brigette, he decided. That would make his father sit up and take notice, especially since they'd long since chosen his bride for him.

Angelica was beautiful and the daughter of a long-time family friend, but Louis and Angelica had grown up together. Louis's tastes were far more adventuresome these days.

Louis lay on his back and studied the ceiling tiles. A slow, satisfied smile came to his lips. Brigette was asleep at his side, her blond hair spilled over the thick feather pillow. One shapely leg was sprawled atop a thin sheet, and she breathed softly, her breath gently teasing his ear.

All his life Louis had done what his family requested. All his life he'd accepted that they knew what was best for him. Never again. He was his own man. How much of a man was something Brigette had taken great delight in proving to him.

A sound from the room below distracted him. Louis paused, wondering if the alley cat Brigette fed had somehow gotten into the house. He was about to investigate when his lover wrapped her long, slender leg around his and edged closer to his side when the door flew open.

Sound exploded through the peaceful silence.

Louis's heart nearly burst as two men dressed entirely in black burst into the room. Their faces were covered with camouflage paint. Twin submachine guns were aimed at him and Brigette.

Terror froze Louis's throat muscles as he struggled upright. Brigette grabbed a sheet and held it against her bare breasts and screamed. Her cry was silenced by a popping sound. Blood soaked through the sheet as the woman he loved toppled forward. Louis choked back a strangled cry of grief and horror.

Before he could react, or reach out to the beautiful French woman, he was dragged naked from the bed. Fighting as best he could, he kicked and shoved. Pain exploded against the side of his jaw as he was hit with the butt of the machine gun. Blood filled his mouth, and he gagged and spat out a broken tooth. The two men worked silently, binding his hands behind his back.

"What do you want?" he pleaded, first in French and then in English and German.

They didn't answer.

"Please," he begged as they dragged him down the stairs. Each man had hold of one elbow, and the top of his feet slapped noisily against the stairs. "My father will pay you anything you ask."

The taller of the two men smiled. His teeth gleamed white, and his eyes filled with hate. Sick laughter broke the eerie silence. "Yes, we know."

𝒯HE infamous Christmas tree was decorated. Cain stood back to examine their efforts, then shook his head. It was the sorriest-looking tree he'd ever seen.

"What?" Linette asked defensively. They'd spent the better part of the afternoon stringing popcorn and cranberries. Patty and John's two children, Mark and Philip, had constructed long paper chains out of strips of colored paper, chattering excitedly and generally eating him out of house and home.

The two boys had returned to their place, and Cain and Linette were left alone once more. But Cain couldn't stop studying the Christmas tree. No matter which way he looked at it, it was by far the ugliest thing he'd ever seen.

"The star's crooked," he announced, dragging a dining room chair across the living room carpet. Standing on the cushioned seat, he adjusted the aluminum star he'd cut from cardboard and covered with foil.

"There?" he asked, attempting to judge if he'd done any good. He glanced down at Linette. "Is it straight now?"

"It's exactly right." Linette sagged onto the chair and stretched out her legs. Her arms dangled over the sides. "It's the most gorgeous tree I've ever seen," she said with a sigh of appreciation.

Briefly Cain wondered if she was looking at the same tree he was.

"It would have been better if I'd remembered to buy ornaments." Frankly, it hadn't occurred to him how he intended to decorate a Christmas tree. Never having put up one before, he hadn't given the matter a second thought.

Vaguely, in the back of his mind, he recalled a Christmas when his mother had been alive. Cain couldn't have been any more than three or four. He didn't remember Santa Claus or opening gifts, or any of the traditional things usually associated with the holiday. What he did recall was the sound of his mother singing to him and the lights of the Christmas tree. Like a miser, he'd clung to that memory, one of a few that he had of her.

"I like the tree just the way it is," Linette insisted.

A loud knock sounded against the door, and a moment later Patty stuck her head in from the kitchen. "I'm not interrupting anything, am I?"

"No," Cain assured her, and leaped down from the chair.

"Wow." A grin brightened Patty's pretty blue eyes. "That's some tree." Doing her best to disguise a smile, she held out a plate of decorated gingerbread men. "I figured you two deserved this for keeping my boys occupied."

Cain helped himself to a cookie. Frankly, he'd enjoyed himself with those two hooligans. The boys had been a little in awe of him and eager to please. Cain had met the two Stamp children only once, a year or so earlier, and they'd stayed close to their mother's skirts. He'd never thought much about kids. He wasn't sure he knew how to act around them.

Linette hadn't seemed to have a problem, so he'd followed her example. He talked to them as he would anyone, no matter what their age. Before he quite knew how it happened, he was sitting on the rug with them, stringing cranberries with a fat sewing needle.

"You've got a fine pair of boys," Cain said.

"Thank you." Patty smiled.

"How about some coffee?" Linette offered.

Patty nodded. "That sounds great."

Linette poured coffee and carried the mugs into the living room on a tray. Cain took it from her and set it on the table.

"Actually . . ." Patty began, rubbing her palms together slowly, and Cain noticed the way her eyes refused to meet his. "I've come to ask a favor."

"Sure," Linette said automatically.

Cain knew better than to agree to anything without knowing what it was.

All three sat around the dining room table. Patty's small hands cupped the coffee mug. "Every year on Christmas Eve, John dresses up in a Santa costume and delivers presents to the boys."

Cain could tell what was coming.

"But Mark's in first grade this year, and he told me he doesn't believe in Santa anymore. He's just a little boy, and he wants to believe. The thing is, he'll recognize John. I don't want to carry this Santa thing too far, but I hate to disappoint Philip. He's only five, and he believes Santa's coming Christmas Eve to bring him a train set and cowboy boots."

"You want Cain to dress up like Santa?" Linette asked.

Patty turned wide, hope-filled eyes to Cain and nodded.

Cain raised both hands and shook his head. "I'm really sorry, Patty, but I'm no good at that sort of thing."

"Sure you are," Linette countered swiftly. "You were great with the boys earlier."

Cain ignored her. "I wouldn't know what to say."

Once more it was Linette who protested. "All you need is a few ho-ho-ho's every now and again. Anyone can do that."

Cain cast her a look he hoped would silence her. After the death-defying search for the perfect Christmas tree, he should have known better.

"The costume probably won't fit," he suggested next. Heaven knew he was taller and bigger than John.

"It's one size fits all," Patty said a little sheepishly. "It was a little big on John, so I imagine you'll fit into it just fine."

"I'm sure you're right," Linette said confidently, as if this were a done deal.

Both women turned to him with a look that said if he were any kind of a man, he'd leap at the opportunity to do this one small thing. Cain wasn't about to let a couple of women gang up on him. He refused to give in to the pressure. He had a well-established conscience, and he wasn't going to apologize for not making a complete ass of himself dressed in a red suit.

"I'm sorry, Patty," he said firmly, "but I'm not your man."

LINETTE stepped back to examine Cain in the bright red suit and fake beard. "You're so cute."

Cain cursed under his breath and caught part of Santa's whiskers between his lips. He spat out the fake hair. "No pictures."

"I promised, didn't I?" She'd batted her pretty eyes at him, and he was lost. Apparently there was no end to the ways he was willing to be made a fool for her. Even now he wasn't quite sure how it'd happened.

One minute he'd declared there was no possible way he'd agree to dress up as Santa. The next thing he knew, he was standing in front of a mirror with a pillow strapped to his belly.

What truly frightened him was the easy way in which Linette had gotten him from an out-of-the-question no and into this ridiculous-looking suit. What Tim Mallory and the others would say if they saw him didn't bear thinking about.

Linette adjusted the wide black belt about his middle. "Your cheeks could use a little color."

Cain knew better than to grumble, otherwise he was likely to get another mouthful of beard. He yanked the thing from his face. "You aren't putting any of that stuff women stick on their faces on me."

She gave him an indignant look. "I wasn't going to suggest any such thing."

"Good." He released the beard, and the elastic snapped it back into place.

"You're being a good sport about all this."

Linette didn't know the half of it. He glanced at his reflection in the mirror, and once he got over the shock of seeing himself, he figured he made a halfway decent-looking Santa.

Planting his hands on his belly, he practiced laughing jovially. Not bad, he decided. He tried again, laughing deeper this time.

"How's that sound?" he asked Linette.

"Santa couldn't do any better himself."

Cain studied his reflection once more. Linette was right about the lack of color in his cheeks. He remembered hearing something about Santa's face being bright. He pinched his cheeks hard enough to cause his eyes to water, but the red drained away as quickly as it came.

"I suppose we should go downstairs and wait for the signal," Linette suggested.

Patty was supposed to turn on the porch light when they were ready for Cain's appearance.

"All right," he agreed.

Downstairs, Cain stopped to look at himself in the mirror once more. "Linette," he said seriously, "could you come here a moment?"

"Sure."

He sat on the sofa and when she approached gripped her around the waist and brought her into his lap. She gave a small, startled cry, then laughed.

"And what is it you'd like for Christmas, little girl?" he asked, and for good measure added a couple of ho-ho-ho's.

"It feels so good to laugh again, to celebrate life and not death. I can't think of a thing I need more than what I already have." Her eyes filled with such warmth and happiness that Cain was forced to look away.

He felt as if his well-ordered life were slowly beginning to come undone, not unlike the Christmas presents he'd soon be delivering. Soon it would be too late. It almost was now. He knew what it felt like to hold Linette, to taste her. To feel her silky-smooth skin beneath his fingertips. She was like a madness that had taken hold of his senses.

Neither spoke, and emotion thickened the air until it demanded all Cain's effort to continue breathing. He marveled at the beauty of the woman in his lap. Her laughter was like music.

He'd kissed her twice now but had avoided anything more, promising himself he wouldn't, couldn't get physically involved with her.

Cain's breath burned in his chest. Slowly he removed

the stocking cap and fake beard and set them aside. He wove his fingers into Linette's dark hair and directed her mouth down to his. His kiss was gentle, mainly because he feared what would happen if he kissed her the way he wanted.

All Cain knew was that if he didn't touch her soon, he'd die. His good intentions swooshed down the drain. All the silent vows he'd made about not laying a hand on her vanished.

When he dared to look at her, he discovered her eyes were filled with longings that, he feared, mirrored his own. He raised his hands to her blouse and fumbled with the buttons, his fingers trembling so badly that he could barely unfasten the tiny openings. Linette kissed his jaw, then brushed his hands aside.

"Someone's coming," Cain said.

"What are you doing here?" John demanded. "The porch light's been on for a good ten minutes."

"Sorry," Cain managed, hoping that if John guessed what had delayed him, he'd be kind enough not to mention it. "I got distracted."

"Say, you look great." John slapped him companionably across the back. "How'd you manage to get your cheeks so red? Man, you're good at this sort of thing, aren't you?"

Cain glanced over his shoulder as he walked out of the house to find Linette peeking out from behind the bathroom door. She beamed him a wide smile and blew him a kiss.

There was a limit to what he was willing to do to please this woman. He should tell her, just so she'd know.

A half hour later he learned exactly how much he was willing to do for Linette.

"Church," Cain repeated, nearly choking on a hot buttered rum. He sat with Linette in John and Patty Stamp's living room. His stint as ol' St. Nick had gone amazingly well.

Mark and Philip were busy with their new toys, and Cain was about to suggest he and Linette return to the main house. If the truth be known, he was far more interested in picking up where they'd left off before John's untimely arrival.

"What a wonderful idea!" Linette leaped on Patty's suggestion as if the woman were handing out gold coins. "I didn't dare hope there would be church services anywhere close by."

"It's an old country church. You probably saw the white steeple when you drove in."

"We didn't," Cain inserted, hoping Linette would pick up on his decided lack of enthusiasm for this latest adventure.

She didn't.

"Well, it's there," Patty said, casting him a snide look. She turned her attention back to Linette. "Every Christmas Eve John gets the old sleigh ready and we ride to church in it. I look forward to the sleigh ride every year."

Linette scooted to the edge of her seat, her enthusiasm bubbling over.

"I'm sure there wouldn't be enough room for the two of us," Cain said confidently. He'd seen that old sleigh stored in the barn a hundred times. There was barely room for the Stamps, let alone two others.

"We'll make room," John insisted. "It's the least we can do to thank you, if you get my drift." To emphasize his point, he nodded toward the two boys.

Cain got John's drift all right, but this wasn't the reward he was looking to collect.

"Could we?" Linette's eyes were liquid with a tender kind of wanting. It simply wasn't in Cain to disappoint her. Hell and damnation. This evening wasn't going anything like he wanted.

All right, all right, he revised mentally, perhaps a trip to church was for the best. If he returned to the house with Linette and touched her again, he wouldn't be able to stop with a few deep kisses, and he knew it.

Before either of them had an opportunity to think through what they were doing, he'd be making love to her. Once wouldn't be near enough to satisfy him, either. It would mushroom from there into something completely out of his control.

Cain couldn't allow that to happen.

In the beginning he'd needed Linette's softness as an absolution of who he was and the things he'd done. In a matter of days it had gone far beyond that. His entire body ached for her. This was the kind of ache that a cold shower wasn't likely to help.

"Sure, we can attend church services," Cain said, offering John and Patty a weak smile. He remembered the last time his figure had darkened a church door. He must have been around fifteen, he guessed, and in love with the Baptist preacher's daughter.

An hour later, just before nine, they all climbed into the horse-drawn sleigh. Fat, glistening snowflakes drifted down from a dark, moonless sky. Linette settled next to him, and he wrapped his arm around her shoulder. Because there was no place else for him to sit, five-year-old Philip was nestled in Cain's lap.

Patty and Mark sat across from them, and John sat on the narrow seat up front, guiding the horses.

Philip's head was bobbing. The five-year-old was exhausted, but too proud to admit it. The lad pressed his head against Cain's chest and promptly fell asleep. For a moment Cain suspected something might be physically wrong with his heart. It actually ached. He hurt for the child he was never allowed to be, for the son he never planned to sire. For a simple life in the country that would never be his.

Just then, softly at first, the sound barely above a whisper, Linette started to sing "Silent Night." Her soprano voice was hauntingly beautiful. Soon Patty's voice blended in two-part harmony with Linette's. In all his life, Cain had never heard the old carol sung more beautifully.

By the time they arrived at the church, the parking lot was crowded. A number of other ranchers had arrived in sleighs as well.

He handed Philip, who was fast asleep, to Linette, climbed down, and then helped Patty and Mark down, while John dealt with the horses. When he looked up to assist Linette, he hesitated. Seeing her with a sleeping child in her arms produced that funny ache in his heart once again. Only this time it hit him harder, stronger.

Heaven almighty, what was he doing? The question was there, but not the answer. He didn't belong in church any more than he belonged with this woman. The uncomfortable feeling refused to leave. Talk about a fish out of water. He was a killer. He had no business walking inside a church with these good people.

The thundering music from a pipe organ swelled

through the old church. They sang a number of favorite Christmas carols. Cain hadn't sung in years. At first he mouthed along, not wanting Linette to think he couldn't sing. Gradually, as the music infected his spirit, his voice blended with the others.

Before he realized what had happened, Cain relaxed. The preacher, a silver-haired man around sixty, with a voice a sports announcer would envy, gave a short message about love and peace and goodwill toward all mankind. Heady stuff, if you dared to believe such matters were possible in this day and age of hate and war. But then there'd been hate and war nearly two thousand years earlier, Cain realized.

At the end of the service, tapered candles were passed out to everyone in the congregation. The lights were turned out, and darkness settled over them. Then the first candle was lit. Its warm glow spread like a beacon through the bleak night. Then the pastor lit the candle of the first person in each row, and they in turn passed the flame from one to the other until the entire church glowed with light.

The service closed with the singing of "Silent Night." Cain couldn't participate for the hard knot that gripped his throat. He didn't want to ruin this moment, standing in this country church with Linette at his side.

For the first time in years he felt almost whole. Almost good. Almost clean.

Unfortunately, it didn't last. Within an hour of returning home, Cain was reminded of exactly who and what he was.

ONE moment Linette was sound asleep and the next she was awake. It took her a couple of seconds to remember where she was, then another moment to realize Cain was with her. His face was only a few inches from her own.

"Cain?" she whispered.

The moonlight reflecting off the freshly fallen snow revealed his taut features. The look in his eyes was wild, almost primitive. She could feel every breath he drew and see his pulse throb at the base of his throat.

"Is something wrong?" she asked in a whisper, and knew without his answering that there was.

He shook his head, denying everything. "I need to kiss you."

It never occurred to her to ask what he was doing in her bedroom in the middle of the night. It never occurred to her to refuse his request. She raised her arms and linked them around his neck, and smiled up at him.

"Did anyone ever tell you you're too trusting?" he said as he lowered his mouth to hers.

Linette experienced the familiar, hot excitement as his lips settled over hers. It was as it had been in the beginning for them. A coming home, a renewal of life. One touch and the desperate loneliness she'd lived with since Michael's death eased.

They were staring at each other in the golden glow of moonlight, when Linette realized something was different about Cain. Gone was the man who'd dressed up as Santa in order to surprise two small boys. Gone was the man who'd sat next to her in a sleigh, holding a sleeping child in his arms.

She didn't recognize this Cain. Then again, perhaps she did. This was the man she'd met at Nancy and Rob's Christmas party, the one who took her out to dinner and asked her about her life while freezing her out of his.

Confused and a bit dazed, she attempted to gather her scattered senses. Cain would never hurt her, never take what she wasn't willing to give.

She lovingly stroked the side of his neck and kissed the underside of his jaw. He released his breath slowly, in a barely audible rush.

"Can you tell me what's—"

"No." He answered her question before she had a chance to fully ask it. He kissed her again with a hunger that left them both gasping for breath. When he lifted his head from hers, she could read the desire in his eyes.

Then he was kissing her again, deeply, hungrily. All at once he stopped and broke away from her, rolling onto his back. His chest heaved, and he groaned from between clenched teeth.

Linette was undergoing some heavy breathing of her own.

"Cain?"

It took another moment or two for him to compose himself. He sat up and gently kissed her forehead. "I'm sorry." He rubbed a hand down his face. "I shouldn't be here. It would have been better if I'd left you a note."

"A note?"

"I have to go."

She didn't understand. "Go?"

"I got a call, for a mission."

"Mission? But it's Christmas."

"I know. I've already talked to John. He'll drive you to the airport in the morning. I've arranged for your flight back to San Francisco."

By the time Linette could sit up, he'd made it across the room and was walking out the door. "Cain?"

He paused but didn't turn around.

"When will I see you again?"

His shoulders tensed. "You won't." With that he closed the door.

Linette fell back against the pillow, fighting a hundred conflicting emotions. She had one thing to say for Cain McClellan. He had a hell of a way of saying good-bye.

6 ❧

_F_rancine Holden loved her family. Loved spending the Christmas holidays with them. Loved smothering all ten of her nieces and nephews with a heart full of love and a bounty of attention.

But it wasn't the holiday season or the gifts collected under the brightly decorated Christmas tree that occupied Francine's thoughts this year.

It was her patient, Tim Mallory.

"I swear life gets better every year." Her grizzly bear of a father wrapped his massive arms around his wife of thirty-seven years and planted a noisy kiss on the side of Martha Holden's neck.

"I never understood why a woman as talented and beautiful as your mother married a man like me," Chuck Holden told his daughter.

Francine smiled and pulled down the spices from the oak rack and took them to her mother. Martha's hands were buried in a thick ceramic bowl filled with moistened bread cubes.

"It's times like this that I ask myself the same question," Francine's mother said with a teasing smile. "In case you hadn't noticed, I'm about to stuff this turkey."

"All right, all right," her father said, and laughed. "A man knows when he's not wanted."

Her father walked out of the large family kitchen, leaving the door to swing in his wake. Francine found herself alone with her mother for the first time that day.

"How are things going with your new patient?" Martha asked conversationally as Francine added an extra dash of rubbed sage to the dressing.

Francine hadn't been able to stop thinking about Tim Mallory, especially now, knowing he was spending Christmas Day alone. Rarely had she met a man more bullheaded and irritating. Rarely had she met a man who haunted her thoughts more.

His leg was responding well to the exercises and physical therapy, but mentally, despite her best efforts, she hadn't been able to reach him. It was as if he'd erected a concrete wall between the two of them.

Francine felt as if all she'd done in the last week was continually butt her head against the full force of his stubborn male pride.

"Things aren't going so well."

Francine felt her mother studying her. "Why not?"

"I've only been working with him a few days."

"But . . ."

Francine shouldn't be surprised by how well her mother knew her. "But I don't expect it to get much better. Not unless something happens.

"He doesn't trust me, doesn't want anything to do with me. He'd rather I left him alone." She'd spent several sleepless nights mulling over the problem with Tim Mallory and had found no solutions.

"Tell me about him," her mother prompted.

"His name's Tim Mallory." She gathered her thoughts together, making a mental assessment. Tim was a large, burly man, not unlike her own father, but the resemblance and just about everything else stopped there.

His anger spilled over like a spitting, bubbling cauldron, the heat of it driving nearly everyone away.

"How old is he?" her mother asked next.

"Thirty-five, I believe."

"Car accident?"

Francine shook her head. "He stepped on a land mine." The injury would have killed almost anyone else, she suspected. She had a few other suspicions as well, mainly that Tim Mallory wished he had died that day.

"A land mine?"

"He's a mercenary."

"A mercenary." This bit of information gave her mother pause.

"He's not like what you'd expect." It surprised Francine how quickly she came to Tim's defense. "He's acting like a wounded animal now because he's in pain."

"And you're the one inflicting it."

"Yes." But Tim's agony was far more than physical; the mental anguish outweighed anything else.

"Are his loved ones with him for Christmas?"

Francine shook her head. "He's alone."

"Alone?"

"He's never mentioned any family." Nor had Cain McClellan said anything to indicate Tim had one.

"Why, that's terrible. No one should be alone on Christmas."

Francine didn't have the heart to tell her mother that she suspected Tim Mallory preferred it that way.

Her mother didn't mention Tim again until after the huge dinner had been served. As Francine cleared off the table, she noticed Martha busily working at the kitchen counter.

"What are you doing, Mom?" Francine asked, joining her mother.

"I'm making up a dinner plate for your friend, Mr. Mallory."

"Mom, trust me, he isn't my friend."

Her mother nodded profoundly. "Maybe that's the problem, Francine. It seems to me a man with nc family is in need of a friend. This may be the way to reach him. It's worth a try, isn't it?"

Her mother, with her warm, generous heart, couldn't bear the thought of anyone spending Christmas without being surrounded by loved ones and good friends. Martha didn't understand about men like Tim Mallory. Didn't understand the last thing he'd do was allow Francine into the fog of his pain. From what she knew of Tim, he'd rather starve than eat the dinner she delivered.

"I want you to take this dinner plate to him, and stay and visit until he's finished eating."

Francine knew better than to argue, especially when her mother wore a look that said she wasn't going to listen to reason.

"Take some sugar cookies and fruitcake with you," Martha called to Francine on her way out the door. Her mother added a paper plate full of homemade goodies to Francine's growing stack. "Make sure he understands you're his friend."

"I will," she promised, but doubted that she'd make it much beyond the front door.

By the time she parked her car in Tim's driveway,

Francine was convinced she was making a terrible mistake. She walked up the porch steps with little enthusiasm and rang the doorbell. When no one answered, she got out the key Cain McClellan had given her and let herself into the house.

Stark silence greeted her. Her own family home was filled with the sound of children's laughter and the scent of mincemeat and holly.

"Who's there?" Tim's gruff voice called out from the family room, at the far end of the house.

Francine was grateful to realize he wasn't holed up in the bedroom. "It's me," she called, following the sound of his voice. She found him in the wheelchair in front of the big-screen television set, watching a football game. Probably the same one her father and brothers had been vehemently discussing earlier.

Mallory frowned when she walked into the room. "What are you doing here?" He stared at her with a decided lack of welcome.

She should have given more thought to what she intended to say, Francine mused, too late. Tim Mallory wasn't likely to believe she just happened to be in the neighborhood.

"I thought I'd stop in and see how you were doing." She set both plates on the kitchen counter behind him.

His voice was gruff and unfriendly. "I don't need your pity."

"Good. I'm not offering it."

"Then what are you offering?" He swiveled the wheelchair around and glared at her menacingly.

Francine sat on the ottoman so they'd be at eye level. She studied her palms, debating what she might possibly say to reach him. The man was as obstinate as they came.

"I want to help you," she began slowly, her voice low and uncertain, "but I can't because you won't let me. I was hoping that if we sat down and talked, you might be more comfortable with me."

He looked away from her and back to the television screen. Apparently that was his answer, the same answer he'd been giving her all week. The same answer he'd been shouting at the world since his accident. He was shutting her and everyone else out as effectively as if he slammed a door closed. He didn't want her there, didn't want her anywhere close to him. Physically or mentally.

What her patient didn't understand was that Francine wasn't willing to accept this response. It was going to take a whole lot more than diverting his attention to persuade her to walk out that door.

She walked over to the coffee table, reached for the remote control, and turned off the football game. Then she deliberately set the controller out of Tim's reach.

His eyes followed her movements. His gaze told her it wouldn't take much more for his anger to explode. "We can do this the easy way," she said without emotion, "or we can do this the hard way. The choice is yours."

"Everything in my life has come hard, and it isn't going to change with you, sweetheart." A bitter smile twisted his lips.

She hated the way he said "sweetheart." In no way could it be construed as a term of affection. He made it sound like a four-letter word, as if saying it left an acrid taste in his mouth.

"Oh, that's smart," she muttered sarcastically. "In other words, you go out of your way to make life difficult."

He didn't answer, but then she hadn't expected he would.

"Just go," he ventured after a moment of uncomfortable silence.

"That would be much too easy." She sat back on the overstuffed chair and stretched her long legs onto the ottoman. Crossing her arms, she set her lips in the same stubborn, prim way her mother had so often.

"Just how long do you intend to plant yourself in my house?" he asked gruffly.

"As long as it takes to get you to walk again."

He snickered. "Neither of us is going to live that long."

So that was it. He didn't believe it was possible, couldn't see past the pain and the frustration. The light at the end of the tunnel was an oncoming freight train and not the hope she'd worked so hard to instill in him.

Tim had plunged himself into a cave of despair, crawled through the mire of pessimism, and was waiting for her to give up on him the way everyone else had. With the exception of Cain McClellan. She wouldn't, only he didn't know that. Not yet.

"You're going to walk, Tim Mallory, come hell or high water, and you can count on that because I'm not going to allow you to waste the rest of your life feeling sorry for yourself."

Tim's hands tightened into fists. He clenched his teeth so tight, his jaw went white. Francine guessed that the control on his temper was precarious at best.

"So that's it," he said in a voice best described as a growl. "You want me to walk. You need me to walk. Because if I do, it's a feather in your professional cap. You can't allow me to ruin your perfect record. Can't allow me to smear your lily white reputation."

Francine knew this probably wasn't the moment to laugh, but she couldn't help herself. She giggled.

Tim cursed and wheeled away from her. There wasn't any place he could go that she couldn't follow. He must have figured she was just the type to go after him because he suddenly rotated back around. "Did it ever occur to you that I might not want to walk again?"

"Frankly, no," she returned smoothly. "You want it so damn much you can taste it. You want it so much you're scared spitless. You're more frightened now than you've been at any other time of your life because if you dare to think it's possible, then it won't happen."

"Who the hell do you think you are, Sigmund Freud?"

"Tim," she said, allowing her voice to soften significantly. "I've been a physical therapist for a long time. You aren't so different from the others I've worked with over the years. There's no shame in fear. No disgrace in pain. If anything, it's a common denominator."

The fierce light in his eyes brightened.

"I can help, if you'll let me." She scooted to the edge of the cushioned chair and prayed some of what she'd said made sense in that stubborn head of his. "Listen, Tim—"

"No one calls me Tim," he said.

"No one calls me 'sweetheart,' " she countered without reproach.

He gave a snickering laugh. "I can see why. What did McClellan do, search for the ugliest therapist he could find?"

His verbal attack was so brutal and unexpected that it left Francine reeling. She'd underestimated his ability to find her weakest point and charge full speed ahead.

It shouldn't hurt this much. She should be used to

it by now. Tim Mallory was only saying what others thought, only saying what she knew to be true.

But it did hurt. For several excruciating moments she waited for the pain to fade.

"Oh, so now we're going to get nasty and personal," she said, faking a small laugh. "I have news for you, Tim Mallory. If you think insults are going to send me running, you're wrong. I'm not going to give up on you, even if you've given up on yourself. I'm here for the long haul."

Fire leaped into his eyes. "We'll see about that."

"Yes, we will," she countered, unwilling to budge so much as an inch. But then, neither was he.

ℬOUNCING from one airport to the next wasn't the way Linette had expected to spend Christmas Day. She'd envisioned a turkey roasting in the oven, music on the stereo, and sitting in front of the fireplace with Cain.

Airline food, crying babies, and short-tempered vacationers wasn't her idea of Christmas, but she refused to surrender to self-pity.

Christmas for the last two years had been strained with memories of Michael and her personal struggles with grief. Major on the majors, Michael had once told her. She'd dug her nails into a rock and hung on until the holidays were over.

Her time with Cain, although cut short, had been a reprieve. She couldn't help wondering where he was, what he was doing, couldn't help worrying. Just a little. Even when she knew he wouldn't want her to fret.

The first thing she'd done when she'd arrived at the airport was to buy every newspaper she could get her hands on. She tore through the pages, hoping to find some clue from world events that might prompt the army to call for Cain in the middle of the night.

Political unrest was everywhere, but she could find nothing to indicate the reason Cain had been obligated to leave so suddenly. But then, she realized, whatever had happened wasn't likely to be made public. Yet.

His abrupt departure had come at her from left field. He couldn't possibly have meant what he'd said about not seeing her again. She was convinced of that.

Surely he wouldn't have touched her and kissed her the way he had if that was his intention. It simply wasn't possible, and she refused to believe it.

The plane landed in San Francisco late that afternoon. the sky was dark, the weather gloomy. The gaily decorated Christmas tree in the center of the terminal sagged to one side, and the poinsettias had lost several red leaves. The tree looked the way Linette felt.

As she made her way to the luggage carousel, she noticed a man standing off to one side, scanning the crowd, holding up a piece of cardboard with her name printed on it.

"I'm Linette Collins," she said, not sure what to expect.

"The limousine's waiting outside."

"The limo? I didn't order one."

"You didn't." He looked perplexed and reached inside his black suit jacket, pulling out a sheet of paper. "The job order and payment came in early this morning from Cain McClellan." He looked at her expectantly.

"I see," she murmured, and smiled softly to herself.

She'd hear from Cain again. Linette was willing to stake just about anything on it. Otherwise he would have let her find her own way home.

$\mathcal{F}$RANCINE arrived bright and early the morning following Christmas. She found Greg in the kitchen, nursing a cup of coffee, looking as if he weren't quite awake yet. As a morning person, Francine was the type who woke up with a song in her heart and a smile on her lips. True, she petered out in the early evening and was generally in bed before ten, but that had never bothered her. She wasn't the sort to have much of a night life anyway.

"Good morning," she greeted Greg cheerfully. Francine was especially happy this morning, encouraged by her meeting with her patient the day before. At least each knew where the other stood.

Tim Mallory didn't know the meaning of the word *stubborn* until he'd locked horns with her. Although he hadn't given her any reason to believe she'd reached him, she felt as if their little talk had helped clear the air.

"How was your Christmas?" she asked conversationally, and took a mug out of the cupboard. She poured herself a cup of coffee, savoring the first sip.

"Great. I think the beastmaster had company."

"How's that?" It didn't immediately occur to her that Greg was referring to her as Tim's company.

"There were two dirty plates. It looks like someone brought him dinner. Apparently he enjoyed whatever it was, except for the fruitcake."

"He ate?" Francine couldn't conceal her delight. She'd assumed he'd toss the two plates in the garbage before he'd stoop to accepting her peace offering.

Greg eyed her suspiciously. "It was you?"

"I stopped by, yes." She stirred a teaspoon of sugar into her mug, avoiding eye contact.

"Hey, don't tell me you're falling for this guy." Greg sounded concerned.

"Don't worry," she said, and raised her right hand. "A therapist knows better than to fall in love with her patient. It can cause all kinds of problems."

"Good. You're too nice a person to get hurt."

"Speaking of the great and mighty one, how's Tim this morning?"

"So it's Tim now?" Greg closed his eyes and slowly shook his head.

"All right, how's Mr. Mallory?"

Greg continued to study her with a worried frown. "About the same."

"Great," she said, and set aside the coffee mug. "I'll have him ready for you in an hour."

"I'll be there."

Carrying her bag with her, Francine made her way down the hallway to the back bedroom. She knocked once and let herself into the room. To her surprise, Tim was sitting up, dressed and ready.

"Morning," she said as if nothing were out of the ordinary.

"I don't want you to get any ideas," Tim said gruffly.

"About what?"

"About me being awake and ready this morning. I couldn't sleep, so I figured I might as well wait for you." He reached for the alarm clock. "You're five minutes late."

"Sorry." She managed to swallow a smile, knowing he wouldn't appreciate her finding his behavior humorous. Actually, she was ecstatic, but she dared not let him know.

"See that it doesn't happen again. Knowing McClellan, he's probably paying you top dollar for this."

"He had to," she told him. "You'd already scared off every therapist in a three-state radius." She reached inside her bag for the cream, applied it to her hands, and started working his calf muscles.

"I don't suppose I'd be lucky enough for you to quit voluntarily." Although he said the words, the antagonism and fighting conviction were missing.

She paused in her manipulations to smile up at him. "I'm not leaving, come hell or high water. That's one thing you can lay odds on, Tim Mallory. I've never quit on a patient yet."

"Maybe you should start." He sucked in his breath at a stab of pain. The fact that he was willing to acknowledge the sharp discomfort was another sign her visit had done some good.

"Remember," she told him in gentle tones, "there's no shame in pain."

"And damn little glory," he shot back heatedly.

"That'll come later, when you're standing on your own and walking."

"With a walker." He grimaced, and she wasn't sure if it was caused by her manipulations or the thought of being dependent upon assistance to move about.

"You'll need the walker for a time," she agreed. "But not for long."

"Sure, then I graduate to a cane for the rest of my life."

"A cane beats the hell out of a wheelchair."

He didn't respond with a biting comment, which was another bit of encouragement. Francine felt like singing.

It seemed Tim didn't have anything more to say. He submitted to the exercise with ill grace, which wasn't a whole lot more than what he'd been doing the week previously. She talked to him as she warmed up his muscles for the more strenuous exercises. His silence didn't dissuade her.

She chatted on about Christmas with her family and told him about her nieces and nephews. Not that she thought he was paying attention. She hoped that the sound of her voice would help put him at ease.

"Do you come from a large family?"

His question caught her unprepared. She feared he was being sarcastic and that by answering, she was stepping onto a rifle range where he could fire insults.

"In number or in size?" she returned in an effort to minimize any damage he planned to inflict.

"Number," he returned, seemingly surprised by her question.

"I have three younger brothers. All married."

"And you?" He asked the question from between gritted teeth.

"Am I married? No."

"Divorced?"

"I've never been married."

"Why not?"

"It's none of your damn business."

He laughed as if he found her answer amusing. "Which means no one's ever asked you."

Francine could feel the heat crawling up her neck. She'd walk out of this room before she'd admit to the truth of that. "What about you?" The best defense was a good offense. At least that was what her father had claimed. But now that she thought about it, he might have been referring to football.

"What about me? Am I married? Hardly."

"Which means every woman you ever asked turned you down."

"No," he said in what easily could have been mistaken for a friendly tone, if she didn't know better. "It means

I've never asked. I haven't been so much as tempted. It'll be a cold day in hell before I consider marriage."

"I see," Francine said smugly. "You're the love 'em and leave 'em type."

"You got that right."

Their conversation was followed by a companionable silence.

"You date much?" Tim asked her out of the blue.

"Some." Damn little if the truth be known, but she wasn't about to tell him that. "What makes you ask?"

"No reason."

After the warm-up exercises, Greg arrived and readied Tim for the more strenuous session in the swimming pool. He was crabby and exhausted by the time she finished. She knew he'd eat a good lunch and sleep a portion of the afternoon. But she wasn't through with him for the day. Not by a long shot.

ALL Louis St. Cyr felt was pain. His jaw throbbed where the butt of the gun had been slammed against his face. Part of a tooth was missing, and every time he drew in a deep breath a stab of agony shot through him. He didn't dare move his jaw, and he suspected it was broken.

He hadn't a clue where he was. His kidnappers had taken him for a long drive. The minute they'd arrived, he'd been shoved inside a dark closet. Twice a day one of the two men opened the door and thrust in some food and water. Louis had drunk the water, not caring about the pain in his jaw or his molar. After two days he'd attempted to eat something and found he couldn't.

He lay on the closet floor and tried not to think about what was happening to him. He tried not to think about

Brigette. Instead he closed his eyes and remembered his mother. If he could make himself focus his thoughts on her, the pain wasn't nearly as bad.

He thought about a blue dress she'd worn when he was a young boy. He'd loved the shade against her whiskey-colored skin and the way her skirt had billowed out at her hips when she whirled around.

Louis had asked her to spin for him so he could see the skirts twirl, then he'd laughed and laughed. The sound of his boyhood amusement filled his ears now.

Louis recalled the time he'd been sick with chicken pox and his mother had sat by his bedside and read him to sleep. His younger sister, Anne, had been ill at the same time.

Louis missed Anne.

He didn't want to die. Not like this. Like an animal trapped in a cage.

Tears shimmered in his eyes. He wanted his mother. He wanted his family.

He heard voices on the other side of the locked door. Strange new ones, talking in a language he didn't recognize. They were deciding his fate, and he couldn't understand what they were saying.

A sob swelled in his chest, and he choked off a cry of anguish. He'd be damned if he was going to let those bastards see him cry.

But then he was already damned.

He must have blacked out because the next thing he knew he was being jerked out of the closet. With little care to his injuries, he was slammed against a wall.

An involuntary moan escaped his lips. He bit it off as soon as he could, refusing to give his captors the satisfaction of knowing the pain they'd caused.

The lights blinded him. It demanded every ounce of strength he possessed to remain upright. Someone shouted at him angrily, but he didn't understand what they said. And even if he had, he wouldn't have followed their instructions.

Someone grabbed him by the shoulders and pulled him upright. Louis hadn't realized he'd slid down the wall. He opened one eye long enough to see the submachine gun aimed at him.

So this was how it was to end. He was to be shot like a criminal before a firing squad.

He squared his shoulders, praying death would come quickly and that he could face it with dignity. He wouldn't grovel. Wouldn't plead for mercy.

He was a St. Cyr and would do his family proud. He pictured his father's strong, proud face in his mind and clung to the memory of his mother and young sister. He prayed God would mercifully claim his soul.

A grinding, softly discordant sound followed.

Curious, Louis St. Cyr squinted into the bright lights. Only then did he realize they weren't going to shoot him.

His captors had taken his picture.

7

"You'll come for New Year's, won't you?" Michael's mother pressed Linette. "We haven't seen you in far too long." Then, as if she needed to dole out additional incentive, Janet Collins added, "We missed seeing you on Christmas." The guilt was being tossed Linette's way at breakneck speed.

Sighing inwardly, Linette closed her eyes, wishing she were the kind of person who could refuse graciously and not feel bad afterward. The last thing she wanted was stress between her and Michael's family.

If only she could invent something that sounded believable. Her hand tightened around the telephone receiver. Bonnie was watching her out of the corner of her eye, waiting for Linette to make a decision.

"How was your Christmas?" Janet continued when Linette didn't answer immediately.

"Wonderful." The two days preceding the holiday had been filled with happiness. The vivid memory of trekking through the snow and cutting down the Christmas tree with Cain would stay with her a long time. The

snowy ride in the sleigh with the Stamp family, singing Christmas carols in two-part harmony with Patty,
warmed her heart still. As did the Christmas Eve church
service with Cain standing at her side, her hand clasped
firmly in his.

"I'm pleased you had such a good time with your . . .
friend," Janet continued, and then added with a labored
sigh, "Christmas just didn't seem right without you. I do
hope you'll come for New Year's. You will, won't you?"

"Ah, perhaps I could make it for dinner."

"That would be perfect. I thought we'd eat around
three."

"I'll see you then," Linette said, and after a few parting words of farewell, she replaced the telephone receiver. She didn't dare look at Bonnie, already feeling
her employee's censure.

"So you gave in to the pressure," Bonnie said.

"I couldn't think of any way to say no."

"You might have said you had other plans."

"Yes, but I don't. Not really. Michael's parents are
dear people, and they mean well. It's just that they continue to play this 'let's pretend' game."

"It's easier than having to deal with the loss of a son,
isn't it?"

"I suppose. To hear them speak, it's as if Michael is
away on an extended trip and will return at any moment, so they dare not change a thing until that happens."

"And when you're with them, they want you to play
along," Bonnie added as if she'd met Michael's family
herself.

"Exactly."

Linette walked over to the rack of knitting books and

straightened them, mulling over the conversation with Janet Collins.

"How are Michael's parents going to deal with it when you start dating again?"

"I don't know." Judging from their reaction when she changed her plans for Christmas, Linette didn't think they were going to handle it well. "He was their only son."

"Is this bit of news significant?"

"Not really. It just explains why they've clung to me."

"What they want," Bonnie said in that gentle yet cautious way of hers, "is for you to become a living memorial to their dead son."

"You can't be sure of that," Linette chastised, although she was beginning to suspect her friend was right.

"Perhaps I'm way off base," Bonnie agreed, "but it's an educated guess. Think about what's been happening the last two years with you and your in-laws. If you were to fall in love and remarry, they wouldn't be able to continue pretending Michael's alive. It would mean having to face the bitter truth that the son they loved and cherished is forever gone."

The truth of Bonnie's words tolled in her ears like a church bell on Easter morning. Her friend was right, and Linette knew it.

"The longer you continue to play along," Bonnie added, "the more difficult it will be for you *and them* to move forward in life."

Until Linette had met Cain, the charade the Collinses continued to play hadn't seemed pressing or important. Linette had gone along, hoping the time would come when they'd be ready to face the reality of Michael's passing. Linette realized now that she'd done them both a disservice. Instead of helping each other through the grieving process, they'd hindered one another. What surprised Linette was how blind she'd been to the truth.

"I think it's time to clear the air," Linette said bravely.

"Good girl." Bonnie gave her an affectionate hug.

Linette gave the meeting with her in-laws a good deal of thought over the next few days. On New Year's Day she arrived at their house shortly before three. She carried a wicker basket filled with fresh rolls she'd baked that morning. She was dreading this dinner and the confrontation that was sure to arise.

"Linette." Jake, her kind-hearted father-in-law, answered the door and immediately pulled her into his embrace. His hug was filled with warmth and affection. "We're so pleased you could make it."

Janet walked out of the kitchen, smiling broadly. "My dear, you are lovelier every time I see you." She kissed Linette's cheek and then leaned back as if to get a better look at her. "You're looking a little pale."

"I'm fine."

"Your timing couldn't be better. I've just finished setting the table."

A look at the three place settings told Linette her sister-in-law and family wouldn't be joining them. Now that Linette thought about it, she wasn't sure Nancy had spent Christmas with her parents, either.

When the meal was ready the three of them gathered around the table. "Nancy and I had lunch right before Christmas," Linette said conversationally. "She told me her good news. You must be thrilled."

"Of course we are," Janet said in a way that caused Linette to glance at her mother-in-law.

"They were here for Christmas, weren't they?" Linette asked. She'd made the assumption that Nancy would be joining her parents as she had in years passed.

"No," Jake answered, his eyes revealing his hurt.

"Unfortunately Nancy and I had a bit of a misunderstanding," Janet said, busying herself by buttering a roll. She took inordinate care in doing so, Linette noticed, spreading the butter evenly over the surface of the roll.

"It's nothing serious," her father-in-law said quickly. "Of course we couldn't be more pleased about having another grandchild."

All at once it was as if a thick fog had cleared in Linette's mind. "The misunderstanding was over Michael, wasn't it?" Nancy hadn't said anything to Linette about a disagreement with her mother, nor would she. But her sister-in-law's eagerness to match her up with another man told Linette everything she needed to know.

"Don't you worry your pretty little head about Nancy," Jake said hurriedly. "I swear this is the best ham we've had since last Easter." He directed the comment to his wife in a blatant effort to change the subject.

"How was Christmas?" Linette asked, seeking a way to put the conversation back on an even keel while she digested what she'd learned.

"Lonely," Janet supplied with a beleaguered look. "We missed you. I have to tell you, Linette, both Jake and I were worried sick about you. When we learned that you barely knew this young man . . . why, anything could have become of you."

"I met Cain through Rob and Nancy."

"As I understand it, this man was a high school friend of Rob's, and the two of them haven't seen each other in several years. There's no saying what kind of person he is now."

"You were angry with Nancy because she introduced me to Cain." Knowing she had been the reason for the rift between mother and daughter greatly saddened Linette.

"And when we didn't hear from you right after Christmas, we didn't know what to think."

This was an additional serving of guilt, dished up with a look meant to instill shame.

"I have a thriving business, you know," Linette said in explanation, although that had little or nothing to do with the reasons she hadn't contacted her in-laws.

"We understand how busy you've been." Jake had always been the peacemaker in the family. Linette noticed that he seemed to be growing uncomfortable with the nuances of their dinner conversation.

"I only hope you won't be seeing this young man again," Janet said without emotion as she reached for the molded gelatin salad.

Linette frowned. "Why would you wish for that?"

Janet blinked. "Because of Michael, of course."

"Michael has been dead for over two years."

Her mother-in-law paled slightly. "I realize that, dear, but by the same token, you're vulnerable just yet. Two years is no time whatsoever to grieve over the loss of a husband. Anyone could step in and take advantage of your tender heart. Jacob and I feel strongly that there should be someone to look out for your best interests. Someone who loves you and can guide you during these difficult days."

To hear her mother-in-law speak, it sounded as if Michael had passed on only recently and Linette had been a child bride.

"It's been two years," she said a second time. "I'm perfectly capable of looking out for my own life and my own interests. I appreciate your kindness and your concern, but I prefer to make my own decisions."

Jake nodded, but Janet's gaze clashed with Linette's. "How do you think Michael feels, knowing you took off with a man you barely know?"

"Michael doesn't feel," Linette responded, and her voice trembled.

"But Michael knows. Don't think he doesn't know what you did." Janet's voice elevated with disapproval.

"And what did I do?" Linette asked calmly.

"It's done and over with now," Jake inserted, glancing from one woman to the other. "Let's put it all behind us. Janet tells me she made pecan pie for dessert." This remark was directed to Linette.

"Michael's favorite," Linette whispered. Janet would bake pecan pie for Linette until her dying day and not know her daughter-in-law didn't like pecans.

"We all love pecan pie," Janet said stiffly.

"It isn't one of my favorites."

"Don't be ridiculous," Janet flared, her eyes flashing with resentment. "You love pecan pie."

"If I eat the pie and tell you how good it is, then it's almost like Michael being here, isn't it?" Linette suggested softly.

Janet ignored her and looked across the table at her husband. "All these years and never once does she tell me she doesn't like pecan pie. You'd think she'd have said something before now." Janet slid her knife across the sliced ham with enough force to mark the plate.

"What you're really angry about is that I spent Christmas with Cain McClellan." Her appetite gone, Linette set her napkin beside her plate.

"I'll tell you this much," Janet said in arctic tones, "I would never have believed you were the kind of young woman who'd travel with a man you'd only met once. Heaven only knows what went on between you two."

"Janet, please," her husband warned softly. "Linette is with us now. Let's forget all about Christmas."

"God knows what she did to disgrace Michael's memory."

"Janet," her father-in-law pleaded once more, "drop it, please."

"No," the older woman snapped. "Let's clear the air once and for all." She turned her attention to Linette. "If you're going to remain our daughter-in-law, if you're going to honor the memory of our son, your husband, then we simply can't have you behaving in such an undignified, tasteless manner."

"I see," Linette said. The vehemence of her mother-in-law's words felt like a cold slap. "In other words, you don't want me to see other men."

"Of course we want you to date again," Jake insisted in a hurried effort to smooth the waters.

"But only after the appropriate time for mourning," Janet added, her voice not as impassioned as it had been earlier. "Michael has only been gone two short years."

"I'm ready to date again," she said. It would be a disservice to mislead them, especially now. Scooting back her chair, Linette stood. "I love you both so much," she said, pressing her hands against the side of the table. "It hurts to know that I've disappointed you. I loved

Michael with everything there was in me to love. And he loved me. I know that he wouldn't have wanted me to spend the rest of my life as a living memorial to him."

"All we're asking—"

"All you're asking," Linette said, cutting off her mother-in-law, "is for me to pretend Michael isn't really gone. I can't do that anymore. I won't be involved in this charade any longer."

"I think you've said enough." Janet slapped her linen napkin down beside her plate.

"Maybe it would be better if we discussed this at another time," Jake suggested with a pained expression. "We certainly didn't want for our time together to—"

"Can't you see what Linette's done?" Janet demanded of her husband. "If you look at her, you can see it in her eyes. She's disgraced Michael's memory. She's pushed him out of her life. It makes me wonder if she ever really loved him."

Linette knew she couldn't stand to listen to much more of this. She hurriedly found her jacket and moved toward the front door. Looking back, she found Jake standing behind his wife, who remained sitting at the dining room table.

His hands were on Janet's shoulders as he attempted to comfort her. He glanced up, and Linette saw that his tired eyes had filled with tears. Her own were fast welling with emotion.

"Good-bye," Linette said sadly. Unless matters changed, she doubted that she'd ever be back.

CAIN was beginning to feel the faint stirring of faith that Louis St. Cyr might be alive. His family had recently received a photograph of the youth. He didn't look to be in good shape, but it was proof that he was alive. Or had been within the last week.

The boy's family had wept with joy at the sight of their son, despite his condition. It was the first bit of encouragement they'd been given following the ransom demand. Unfortunately there was no hope of fulfilling the requirements. If the kidnappers had asked for money, they might have been able to work out a deal, but the terrorists weren't interested in cash. The ransom note had been delivered four days earlier, demanding the release of three political prisoners.

What the kidnappers didn't know was that the day of the kidnapping, the three prisoners had been extradited to the United States for a long list of offenses. A senator who was aware of the situation had recommended that Louis St. Cyr Sr. contact Cain. News of the extradition had been kept out of the media. If it were released, Louis junior would be as good as dead.

The problem now was finding out where the terrorists were holding the teenager. The best information Cain had been given had led him to a series of dead ends. Once Deliverance Company knew St. Cyr's whereabouts, the strategy for the rescue mission could be planned. But finding the youth was proving to be highly difficult.

The boy's parents were frantic with worry. From what Cain understood, the mother was on sedatives. Deliverance Company was doing what they could, but it seemed like damn little.

Exhausted, Cain made his way into the back bedroom. He hadn't slept in over twenty hours. He was past sleepy, past tired. He'd reached his limit of endurance and knew it.

As he shrugged off his clothes and turned back the sheets, Cain knew with his resistance this low, he wouldn't be able to keep thoughts of Linette out of his mind. He closed his eyes and waited for her to come.

As his head settled against the thick pillow mattress, she appeared in his mind's eye. It took him a moment to realize she was standing on the porch outside his Montana house.

It was dusk, and she was dressed in moonbeams. Light shimmered around her, drawing his attention, causing his heart to swell with a longing so intense, it was painful.

Silently he called out to her. In slow motion she whirled around, and when she saw it was Cain, she broke into a wide smile. With wings at her heels, her arms open, she raced down the steps and rushed toward him. Her arms were as wide as her heart. As wide as the love she had to offer him.

Just before she reached him, she vanished.

Cain knew this was because he'd vowed he wouldn't be seeing her again. Nor would he allow her to mess up his mind while he was on a mission. Too many lives depended on his having a cool head and a steady hand. The potential to hurt others with a single slip, a single lapse, was all the warning he needed.

So he dreamed of her, and even then certain restrictions applied. She would always remain out of his reach.

Fantasizing about Linette was a compromise Cain had made with himself. He'd banished all thoughts of her from his daytime activities but lowered the mental gates of his resistance at night.

She visited him often. Cain wondered if it were possible for any woman to be as beautiful as Linette was in his sleep-induced memories. He wondered if any woman could be as giving, as loving, or as charming as he remembered Linette. It didn't seem possible.

Caught between the lure of sleep and the cold reality of this world, Cain tried to think about the nineteen-year-old boy he was attempting to find and rescue. The photo image of the youth flashed in and out of his mind, refusing to stay.

It was as if Linette had stepped forward and insisted this was her time with him. If he was going to dwell on business, then he could do it while he was awake. This time was hers, and she'd been waiting impatiently for him to join her.

Rolling onto his side, Cain gave his mind free rein to take him where it would. After a moment he found Linette in her apartment. He scanned the room until he located the cardboard star he'd made for the top of their Christmas tree. She'd placed the aluminum-covered ornament on the fireplace mantel as if it were a valuable piece of artwork.

A peace settled over Cain like a warm blanket in the coldest part of winter. A tranquillity he could give no name.

Linette hadn't forgotten him, either. It was a fantasy, he tried to tell himself, conscious enough to filter out what was real and what wasn't.

He hadn't a clue of what had become of that ridiculous-looking star he'd crafted. Why he should feel the least bit of anything to think Linette had brought it back with her was beyond his comprehension.

Nevertheless, he could feel the pressing worries of the day leave him. His shoulders relaxed, and the tight muscles in his neck slackened. All at once he was free to walk into the waiting arms of slumber.

At the knocking sound, he bolted upright out of a dead sleep. "Come in." He wiped a hand down his face in an effort to clear his thoughts. Once asleep, he was a man who rarely dreamed. Over the course of his life, he recalled only a handful of times he'd remembered his dreams. But this night he remembered. All too well.

"It's Jack." The communications expert for Deliverance Company walked into the bedroom. "You asked me to come for you if there was any news."

"Is there?"

"We think so."

"Give me two minutes to get dressed."

"You got it."

Cain sat on the edge of the mattress and gathered his wits. The dream continued to plague him. Normally he would have shrugged off something like this, but this particular dream involved Linette. The details of it were as vivid as if he'd been living it. She was in a hospital waiting room, pacing and filled with nervous energy. He didn't know whom she was there to see or what the problem was. All he'd felt was the overwhelming urge to take her in his arms and comfort her.

He needed coffee. Needed to tuck the woman who dominated his dreams back into the locked mental compartment. Needed a clear head in order to deal with the problem of rescuing Louis St. Cyr. Before it was too late, if it wasn't already.

"Morning," Murphy said when Cain appeared.

"What have you got?"

"Good news," Murphy said, grinning widely. "We've

located the house outside of Paris where they're keeping the kid."

"And the bad news?" There was always the alternative to go along with anything positive.

"It's going to be a bitch to get him out."

"So what's new?" Rescues rarely came easy, no matter how well planned.

"His captors are a group of fanatics with plenty of sympathizers holed up with them. They're armed to the teeth, and would welcome any excuse to kill the kid."

"Sounds like just the sort of mission we specialize in," Cain said with a grin, and slapped Murphy across the back. "Call Bailey and Stan. We've got work to do. While you're at it, get us the first available flight to Paris."

Already Cain could feel the adrenaline pumping. Deliverance Company was about to do what they did best. If good luck and the fates were with them, there was a chance they could save this poor kid.

8

$\mathcal{F}$rancine knew Tim was well past the point of being tired, and still he pushed himself. He insisted they stay in the pool and go through the series of exercises one last time, driving himself, and her, to the brink of exhaustion.

Francine had been ready to get out of the swimming pool forty minutes earlier.

"Enough," she insisted. "If you work too hard, you'll damage the muscles." For a moment she feared Tim was going to ignore her.

His shoulders heaved with the effort of his exertion. He swam to the far end of the pool, nodded and lowered his head as he caught his breath.

"I'll call for Greg," she said, ready to walk up the steps and out of the pale blue water.

"No." Tim reached for her arms and stopped her. He was sitting on the third step from the top, the water lapping about his shoulders. "Not yet."

"But you're exhausted."

"I know. I won't do any more exercises today. Just

stay with me a couple of minutes until I get my wind back."

"All right." She sat on the step beside him. They'd been working for most of the afternoon. The progress her patient had made in the past two weeks astonished her.

She hadn't thought it possible for a man to make such a complete turnaround in attitude. Francine had the impression Tim still didn't like her, still didn't want her around. He tolerated her company, but most important, he respected her and acknowledged that it was through her efforts he would walk again.

If there was one thing she'd accomplished with Tim Mallory, it had been hope. Somehow she'd managed to get it through that thick skull of his that he would walk again.

When she arrived first thing in the morning, he generally acknowledged her cheerful greeting with a grunt. It didn't trouble her. A grunt was worth a thousand demands that she leave him alone.

Francine knew the workouts in the pool were the ones that drained her patient the most. But his energy level increased daily. His progress was nothing short of phenomenal. The fact that he was taking an active role in his recovery thrilled her and gave her more hope than the physical improvements she witnessed.

"Are you ready yet?" she asked.

"No," he said gruffly. He looked away from her. "Listen, there's something I've been meaning to say." His voice wasn't any less brusque, but Francine could tell that he wasn't angry. If anything, she read a certain hesitancy in him.

"Yes?"

"I'm not much good at this sort of thing." He paused and cleared his throat.

Francine wasn't sure what to make of this. "Not good at this?"

"Apologies," he muttered thickly.

"You don't owe me an apology."

"The hell I don't," he said, and raked a hand through his thick wet hair. "I said some nasty things to you when we first started working together. Things I regret now. I want you to know I didn't mean what I said about you being unattractive."

The room went quiet. Even the water in the pool seemed to go still. A tightness gripped Francine's throat. "It doesn't matter. It's long forgotten." She attempted to stand, but he took hold of her arm.

"There's more." His curt tone was back.

"More?" Francine looked away, not wanting to see his expression or have him read hers. This discussion embarrassed her acutely. Tim hadn't insulted her with anything she didn't already know. Her body wasn't going to be mistaken for that of a model. Nor had she been graced in the looks department. Her features were too blunt for that. Too round. She was large boned, and she'd learned long before that men liked their women small and delicate. The fact that she could bench press more weight than most men wasn't something a fragile male ego could handle.

Tim's hand caught her by the chin, and he turned her face toward his. His deep, dark eyes met hers. "I was wrong about you from the first. You're really quite lovely."

She was about to tell him it was time they left, when

he kissed her. The action stunned her so much that the words were trapped in her throat, forever lost.

The kiss was gentle, a delicate pressing of his mouth over hers. Francine wouldn't have guessed that Tim was capable of such tenderness. She trembled and raised her hands to his bare chest in order to shove him away and tell him how inappropriate it was for them to be doing this.

Not only was it inappropriate, it was wrong. The cardinal rule with a therapist was never to become romantically involved with a patient. But he caught her hands in his and continued, and soon she was fully involved in the kiss herself.

After a moment, he drew back. Francine lowered her gaze, but she could feel him study her. He seemed as surprised by what he'd done as she was.

Neither spoke. Francine didn't know what to say, and she strongly suspected Tim was fast thinking of an excuse. Something that would assure them both that it had been a fluke, not to be repeated or mentioned hereafter.

His eyes lingered on her face, until she was certain her cheeks were red enough to be mistaken for cooked lobster.

"You're an incredible woman." His voice was as rough as moonshine.

Francine knew she had to escape before she found herself believing what he said. She swallowed, and her heart, her silly, romantic heart, seemed to stick in her throat. What she needed now was some witty comment that would lighten the mood and remind them that what they were doing would only lead to problems. Instead her throat felt as if it had been stuffed with a whole apple and her eyes were filled with tears.

He wiped the moisture from her cheek, and before she could object, he kissed her again. This time it was much different. Much better. Much deeper. Much more intense.

She was afraid, almost desperately so, but not because Tim frightened her. Never that. He tempted her, and she couldn't give in to that fascination.

He deepened the contact.

By the time he broke off the kiss, Francine's heart thundered in her ears. Her eyes remained closed and her head fell forward. She'd been kissed, but never quite like this.

"I've been wanting to do that all week," Tim whispered, smoothing the hair from her face.

"I should go."

"No," he said roughly, insistently. "Not now. We've only gotten started."

She lifted her questioning eyes to his. "What do you mean?"

"Mean?" He laughed lightly and kissed her gently. "What else could I mean? I'm dying to make love to you, woman. Don't tell me you haven't noticed."

"What?" It was all Francine could do not to leap out of the water right then. As a matter of fact, she hadn't noticed, hadn't thought of him in those terms. Nor would she.

"Come on, sweetheart, there isn't any reason to play coy with me. It isn't necessary. We're both adults, and I want you, and if the way you kissed me back is any indication, you're just as hot for me."

She stared at him as if he were speaking in a foreign language.

"I've been a long time without a woman, so the first few bouts are going to be hot and fast. Just be patient and I promise to make it up to you later."

Francine was struck dumb. She glared at him and blinked several times before she found the strength to pull herself free of his embrace. Although her knees were weak, she managed to step out of the water.

"Is something wrong?" Tim asked.

She reached for her towel and wiped the moisture from her face. "I don't know what led you to think I'd be willing to share a bed with you, Tim Mallory, but frankly, I'm not interested."

Her refusal must have come as something of a shock, because he looked at her as if he were sure he hadn't heard her right. "The hell you aren't," he said after an awkward moment.

"When I go to bed with a man, it'll be for reasons other than the ones you gave me. You want a body to relieve your physical frustration. Any woman would do. Any body. I just happen to be convenient."

"You're as hot for me as I am for you."

Francine didn't have an answer to that because she feared it was true. "Look at me, Tim," she said, "really look. Do you think that because I'm not svelte and beautiful that I'd be willing to settle for anything less than a man who loves me?"

His gaze narrowed suspiciously, and then he groaned and wiped a hand down his face. "You're a virgin, aren't you?" He muttered several curses as if her lack of experience were some great detriment. Some great deficiency on her part.

Francine pressed her lips together firmly. Hell would freeze over before she gave him the satisfaction of knowing he'd hurt her.

"I'll send for Greg," she said on her way out.

*L*INETTE stepped into the foyer of her apartment building and unlocked her mail slot. She anxiously sorted through the envelopes. She hadn't heard from Cain, and although she repeatedly told herself it didn't matter, it did.

She was beginning to believe he'd meant what he said. That he wouldn't be seeing her again. No matter how hard she tried, she couldn't make herself believe what they'd shared hadn't been something very special. He was special.

Cain had gifted her with the precious promise of the future. Until they'd met, she hadn't been able to look beyond a single day. She had no dreams. Cain had proven that in the two years since she'd lost Michael, she hadn't lost her heart. She could feel again. Could respond to a man's touch.

Apparently she had been nothing more than a passing fancy to him.

Linette let herself into the apartment, tossed the mail onto the kitchen counter, and slipped out of her pumps. She was about to survey her cupboard for dinner ideas when the doorbell chimed. A quick check in the peephole revealed her sister-in-law.

"Nancy," Linette said happily, unlocking the door. "This is a pleasant surprise. Come in." She'd meant to call Nancy all week, but with one thing or another, she hadn't gotten around to it. If the truth be known, she had delayed making the call for fear Nancy would ask her about Cain. And she just wasn't sure what to say.

"How are you feeling?" Linette asked.

Nancy peeled off her coat and collapsed onto the overstuffed sofa. She tucked her feet beneath her and settled in as if she meant to stay a good long while. "Dreadful. I've spent the last week with my head poised above the toilet."

"Flu?"

Nancy shook her head. "Morning sickness."

"Can I get you something? Tea? Water?"

"Nothing, thanks."

Linette sank onto the chair opposite her sister-in-law. "I've been meaning to call all week. I had dinner with your parents on New Year's."

Nancy's gaze shifted away from Linette. "They aren't happy with me just now."

"I know."

"You know?"

"I'm afraid they aren't exactly overjoyed with me, either. As you're probably aware, they didn't think it was a good idea for me to spend Christmas with Cain."

Nancy flattened her hand against her chest. "I was responsible for the two of you meeting, and my parents . . . well, mostly it was Mom, seemed to think I'd dishonored Michael's memory by introducing you to Cain."

"So I heard. I didn't realize what was happening with Mom and Dad," Linette said softly. "I knew that they found dealing with Michael's death difficult, and they were more comfortable ignoring the fact he'd died. But it's gone beyond that now."

"I've been tempted to say something to you for more

than a year now," Nancy murmured, "but it's difficult, and I didn't want to do anything to ruin our relationship, especially when the one with my parents was becoming more and more strained."

"They don't want me to date. I didn't realize that or the reason why until I met Cain. They feel threatened and afraid. I can understand that, but at the same time I can't live my life in order to please them."

Nancy looked worried. "You're seeing Cain, then? You never said anything about him when you returned from Montana, and I didn't want to pry."

Linette clenched her hands together, wanting to disguise her disappointment and not sure if she could. "I haven't heard from him."

Her sister-in-law released a heavy sigh. Her shoulders sagged, and she closed her eyes momentarily. "That might be for the best. You don't know how concerned I've been. I've been so afraid you would fall for him."

Linette didn't understand. It was Nancy who'd worked so hard playing the role of matchmaker, eager to introduce her to Cain. As it happened, they'd met on their own. "You'd rather I didn't see Cain again? But why?"

Linette shifted positions, looking decidedly uncomfortable. "Rob and I were talking last night, and I was saying how disappointed I was that you hadn't called and told me how everything went over Christmas. I made some pithy comment about how nice it would be if the two of you fell in love. Then I said something along the lines that it might be difficult for the two of you, being that Cain's in the military and all. Long-distance relationships can be tricky."

"I think you might be right." Having Cain in the military certainly hadn't helped matters thus far. Linette was left hanging, waiting to hear from him. At the same time she wasn't sure he would contact her.

"I was afraid something like this was going to happen," Nancy said, breaking into her thoughts.

"You don't like Cain?" Linette didn't understand.

"I don't know him well enough to like or dislike him. But after what Rob told me, I regret ever suggesting the two of you meet."

"What Rob told you?"

"Yes, last night out of the blue, my dear husband drops this bombshell. Cain isn't in the military. He's—"

"Of course he is," Linette interrupted. "He was called away on a mission early Christmas morning. He didn't want to leave any more than I wanted to see him go."

Nancy's features tightened. "Rob told me Cain McClellan is a mercenary. Rob assumed I knew, and I told him I didn't and that I didn't think you did, either. He suggested we get together and talk."

Mercenary. The word echoed in Linette's ears like a giant gong, but instead of fading, the sound grew louder and louder, more and more deafening.

"Linette?"

It took an instant for her to realize that Nancy was speaking to her. "In other words, he's a hired killer," she said slowly.

"Yes. I'm sorry, so sorry. I feel like such a fool."

Linette forced herself to give Nancy a reassuring smile. "You didn't know."

"But I should have questioned Rob more thoroughly before I suggested introducing you two. I don't think Cain's a bad person, don't misunderstand me. It's just that . . . well, you've already lost one husband, and you don't need to get involved with a man in a high-risk occupation like his."

"You're right, I don't." Linette's fingernails dug painfully into her palms. If there was one single thing she had learned during Michael's illness, it was how very precious life is. She couldn't bear the thought of anyone wasting a gift of such value.

"What upsets me most is the big stink I made with my parents. They asked me all these questions about Cain, looking for one small thing to discredit him. Mom was furious with me and Rob, and when I learned what he was, Linette, I can't tell you how upset I've been. Thank God she never found out."

"There's nothing to worry about. No harm done."

"You're sure?" she asked with a heavy sigh. "I can't tell you how guilty I've felt over all this."

"Don't," Linette insisted. If she was angry with anyone, it was with Cain. He'd clearly misled her, clearly chosen to let her believe he was in the service. She knew why. Had she known the truth, she would never have agreed to travel to Montana with him. Would never have become involved with him.

"I hope this doesn't mean you're going to be gunshy," Nancy continued, then smiled. "No pun intended. Cain's just one man, and if you were attracted to him, then there are bound to be others, don't you think?"

"Of course." But Linette wasn't interested in anyone else. In time she would be willing to try dating again, but not soon. As it was, she felt like a yo-yo on one of those around-the-world spins. Her emotions had been looped around almost full circle. A feeling of emptiness swamped her.

She knew what Cain had told her before he'd left was true: he wouldn't be contacting her again. He couldn't risk involving his heart any more than she could allow herself to care for a man who'd built his life around death and destruction.

"I'd better go," Nancy said after a moment. "I hate being the bearer of bad news."

"I don't want you to feel guilty over this," Linette said, handing Nancy her coat.

"I can't help it. I'm my mother's daughter. I cut my baby teeth on guilt. Little happens in this world that I can't find a reason to accept some of the blame."

Linette laughed, and the two women hugged. "Don't look so worried," she said, and unlocked her front door.

"But I am. You're going to be all right, aren't you?"

"Of course."

Nancy hesitated, and Linette knew her sister-in-law wished there was something she could do or say to set matters right. Nancy, however, had already paid a hefty price. She'd stood her ground against her parents on Linette's behalf. That hadn't been easy and had helped pave the way for her confrontation with the Collinses later.

After Nancy had gone, Linette sat on the sofa, suddenly cold. She wrapped a hand-knit blanket around her shoulders. In the worst part of Michael's illness she'd sat in exactly this position, with this same autumn-colored afghan tucked about her like a security blanket.

She'd needed it then. She needed it now.

THE force of the explosion knocked Cain onto his belly. His breath gushed from his lungs as the wind was knocked out of him. He lay there in intense pain, too stunned to move.

What the bloody hell had happened? The only thing he could think was that the explosives had gone off too soon. It wasn't supposed to go like this.

The explosion had been planned as a diversion. Unfortunately, the only ones it had distracted were the men of Deliverance Company. Not a single man was in position. The whole mission had literally blown up in their faces.

They weren't ready. This was a hell of a way to announce their arrival. If the terrorists holding Louis St. Cyr had any brains, and they must have, they'd quickly figured out this was a rescue attempt gone awry.

Instinct took over, and Cain leaped to his feet and ran around the side of the building, dodging the rapid fire of a machine gun. Out of the corner of his eyes he saw Jack and Murphy crash through the underbrush to join him. Jack literally hurled himself behind the building, cursing as he slammed onto his stomach. Murphy followed.

"It's too soon," Jack said as though Cain hadn't figured that much out himself.

As far as Cain could see, they had two choices. Ignore the fact that all their careful arrangements had gone up in smoke and go in after the kid.

Or get out alive, while they could.

One thing was certain—if they turned tail now, the kid was a goner. For all Cain knew, the teenager might already be dead. There were no guarantees he'd survived one moment beyond having his photo taken. He'd been held hostage for nearly three weeks as it was. The odds of his surviving the first few minutes following the explosion were slim to none.

"We're going in," Cain decided.

His men followed without hesitation.

He was the first one through the door. The first one to fire his weapon, spitting death at a faceless enemy. The first one to see just how big a disaster they'd walked into.

One man fell and then another. Bullets whistled past Cain, hitting the wall directly behind him. He fell to the ground and rolled, firing as he twisted. If they were going to kill him, he sure as hell wasn't going to make an easy target.

𝒥T had been almost a month now that Francine had been working with Tim, and in all that time she hadn't dreaded a morning more than this one.

She wasn't sure she could look Tim in the eye. Wasn't sure she could pretend he hadn't touched her, hadn't kissed her, hadn't told her he wanted to make love to her. At first she was tempted to call in sick and arrange for a substitute, but that was a coward's way out. Sooner or later she was going to have to face her patient again. The way she figured it, she'd prefer to get this over with as quickly as possible.

After some deliberation, Francine decided she was going to walk into his bedroom the way she always did. She would greet him the same way she did every morning and pray to high heaven he didn't mention what had happened in the pool.

"Good luck with the beastmaster," Greg told her when she let herself into the house. "He's in one bear of a mood."

Francine was afraid of that, but prepared. She walked down the hallway to his bedroom, feeling very much like Marie Antoinette facing the guillotine.

She knocked lightly, and after squaring her shoulders

and gathering her composure, she let herself into the bedroom. "Good morning," she said as if nothing had changed between them. It hadn't, because she wouldn't allow it.

Tim was sitting in his wheelchair, dressed and ready. He raised his head expectantly when she walked inside. He seemed surprised to see her.

"Morning," he murmured. "I didn't know if you'd be here."

"Why not?" Which was a ridiculous question, and one she immediately regretted. "We have work to do," she said, not giving him the opportunity to answer.

"I expect you want me to apologize," he said in the same gruff-affectionate tone he often used with her. "If you do, then you've got a long wait."

"The only thing I expect of you, Tim Mallory, is for you to walk again. It's the reason I was hired, and by all that's holy, that's what I intend to see happen."

"I have a vested interest in walking myself."

"Good," she answered, relieved. "Then we're on the same wavelength."

"What about yesterday?" His gaze held hers.

Her cheeks felt hot, but she ignored the ready way in which her body betrayed her. "What about it?"

"I suppose you want to forget about it."

"I . . . think that would be best."

"Fine," he said, but he didn't sound pleased.

"Good."

"When will I start walking again?" he demanded with thick impatience.

"We need to take this one step at a time, no pun intended. First we've got to get your leg strong enough to support your weight. For the last month I've been working at building up your muscle strength. You're gaining weight and getting stronger every day, but we have a ways to go."

"When can I stand?"

It was true that he'd gained weight, but he remained weak, and she hated to take any chances. Physically he could handle a setback, but emotionally . . . she wasn't so sure. Thus far everything had been going along smoothly.

"You think you're ready now?" she asked.

"I was ready last week." A hint of a smile touched the edges of his mouth.

Francine couldn't keep from smiling herself. "All right, big boy, let's see what you can do."

She started out with the rubdown, the way she did every morning, massaging his muscles, warming them up for the more strenuous work-out that would follow.

He was sprawled across the top of his mattress as she kneaded the thick muscles of his injured leg. She worked hard, preoccupied with the task.

"You aren't talking," Tim muttered.

"Not talking?"

"You're usually a regular chatty Cathy. In the beginning I would have sold my soul to shut you up, but I've grown accustomed to your prattle."

It was true Francine generally made a point of chatting to put him at ease. But all at once she didn't seem to have anything to say. She wasn't entirely sure what she'd been telling him all these weeks.

"It's your turn to entertain me," she suggested.

"Me, talk? I'm not much good at that sort of thing."

"I'm all out of stories."

"Tell me about the time your brother locked you out

of the bathroom and then jumped down the laundry chute so you couldn't get ready for your date."

"I was all of sixteen, and fighting mad."

"And this was the night of your first real date," he said, filling in the details for her. "You had to answer the front door with hot curlers dangling from your forehead, and it was your date, fifteen minutes early."

"So you think that's funny, do you?" She swatted him playfully across the butt.

"Ouch."

"Listen, big boy, you don't know what pain is until I'm finished with you."

Tim chuckled, and to the best of her knowledge it was the first time Francine could remember hearing him laugh. It surprised her to realize how much she liked him. As he was being slowly freed of his disability, she was seeing more and more of the man he'd been before the accident. The more she saw, the better she liked him.

A knock against the door was followed by Greg, letting himself into the bedroom. He was carrying the portable phone.

"It's McClellan," Tim's attendant told her patient.

"Thank God." Tim sighed with relief, and Greg handed him the receiver.

"Do you want me to leave?" Francine asked.

He shook his head.

Although Francine could hear only one side of the conversation, it was clear that Cain had been out on some kind of mission. At first Tim seemed worried, but he became more and more relieved as the conversation continued.

"He wants to talk to you," Tim said when he'd finished. He handed Francine the phone.

"This is Francine Holden," she said, although an introduction wasn't necessary.

"How's the patient?" Cain's voice sounded as if it were coming from the bottom of a deep well. She wasn't sure if it was from a poor connection or the distance.

"Cranky. Stubborn. Impatient. Better."

"I like the last part best. It seems he thinks he's ready to stand."

"We'll see. If matters progress the way they have, it's possible for him to be walking within another month."

Her prediction was met with stark silence. "I don't believe it," Cain said after a tense moment. "I didn't dare believe it would happen."

That had been Tim's mistake as well. He didn't dare to believe it, either. "Wait until you see the changes in him."

"I have to be in San Francisco next week," Cain announced. "I'll be by the house to see this amazing transformation myself. I didn't think it was possible. Thank you, Francine."

"Don't thank me yet." It was much too soon for that. They had a long way to go and almost all of it was uphill.

When she was finished, she handed the telephone back to Greg, who was waiting outside the door. Tim's attendant left, and she returned to his bedside.

"They did it," Tim said, sounding jubilant.

"Did it?"

"Rescued some poor kid who was being held as a political prisoner. Cain said everything that could go wrong did, but they managed to pull it off. The teenager's back with his family, and Deliverance Company is taking an all-expenses-paid trip to the Bahamas, recuperating in the sunshine."

"Was anyone hurt?"

"Only minor injuries." Tim clenched his fist. "Damn, but I wish I'd been there. I'd give my eyeteeth to be in the thick of it again. They could have used me, too."

"It appears to me," Francine said stiffly, "that you've been in the thick of one too many missions as it is."

"Hey, don't go all soft on me. Fighting is what I do best. In case you haven't noticed, I'm damn good at it."

"I can tell," she muttered sarcastically.

Tim was silent for a moment. "If I didn't know better, I might think you actually cared."

"What I care about is seeing you whole and healthy, but I'll tell you right now, I'm not working this hard for you to go off like some white knight to get yourself shot up again."

Tim slapped his hands together. "You do care!"

"I don't," she said in what was a blatant lie. And Tim knew it.

"You know," he said, sounding almost gleeful, "I just might grow on you. I wouldn't be a bad lover, you know. Fact is, I've never had any complaints. We could have some good times, you and me. Some real good times. What do you say, Francine?" He waited for a response, and she answered him with a blistering look. Tim burst out laughing.

"I don't think you're the least bit amusing."

"I wasn't trying to be. I'm dead serious."

"Tim, please, don't."

"Has anyone ever told you how expressive your face is?"

"I think you're ready for the pool."

"I'm ready all right." He jiggled his eyebrows. "And after a few kisses you'd be ready, too."

"Would you stop?" she demanded, sterner this time. She didn't know how to react to his teasing. He seemed bent on making her blush, on seducing her with words.

"You know what I wish?" he said, rolling onto his good side and elevating his head with his elbow. "Just once I'd like for you to wear one of those swimsuits with a zipper up the front."

"That is the most ridiculous thing you've ever said to me, Tim Mallory."

"Just once."

"Exactly why would you care what style of suit I wear?"

"Because, my sexy Amazon, I'd take great delight in opening that zipper."

Her face filled with raging color.

Tim laughed boisterously. "My guess is you've got a pair of the most beautiful breasts I'm ever going to find. Someday you're going to show them to me, and then I'm going to show you how a man satisfies a woman."

He was saying these things just to fluster her, just to disconcert her. "Unless you stop right this minute, I'm walking out and calling for a replacement."

"No, you won't," he said confidently.

Francine seethed inwardly. "What makes you so certain?"

"Because," he said, smiling with a grin that would rival that of the Cheshire cat, "you're crazy about me. Only you don't know it yet."

9

It was one of those winter evenings that Linette referred to as a Sherlock Holmes night, when San Francisco and the Bay Area were shrouded in a thick fog. Linette closed up the shop for the day, tired and lonely. Bonnie had left an hour earlier, leaving her to an endless stack of paperwork. Now she was ready to head home.

The lights along the pier glowed as through a lacy veil as she ambled along, mentally listing chores. The cashmere yarn a customer had ordered had arrived, and she'd forgotten to have Bonnie phone her. She needed to pick up stamps in the morning. Her dry cleaning was ready.

As she came to the end of the pier, Linette hesitated. There, silhouetted against the fog, against the glow of a fading lamp, stood Cain. He was waiting for her, his hands buried deep inside his pockets.

"Hello," he said.

Linette's throat closed up on her. She wasn't prepared for this, hadn't believed it would be necessary to prepare herself. Cain had assured her she wouldn't see him again.

It had taken her far longer than necessary to accept the truth of this. Far longer to accept the reasons why.

"I figured I owed you an explanation."

Still she didn't move, didn't speak.

"Can I buy you dinner?" He glanced down the waterfront to the restaurant they'd gone into when they'd first met.

"I have an appointment," she said when she found her voice.

"A date?" His eyes narrowed with the question.

"No, an appointment."

He looked as if he weren't sure he should believe her.

"I do volunteer work at City Hospital two nights a week, counseling families of cancer patients."

It took him a moment to digest this information. "How long before you need to be at the hospital?"

She checked her watch, hardly able to believe that they were having this civilized discussion. It was all she could do not to scream at him for deceiving her, for the cruel way in which he'd said good-bye.

By all that was right, she should ask him to get out of her life. She'd been perfectly content until he'd come along. All right, not *perfectly content,* but close to it. By all that was right, she should tell him that. Unfortunately, it demanded every ounce of self-control she possessed not to hurl herself into his arms.

"I'm due at the hospital in forty minutes."

"That's time enough." He motioned toward the restaurant. "Will you have a drink with me, Linette?"

"Why didn't you tell me you were a mercenary?" she demanded.

"Would you have come to Montana with me if you'd known?"

"No."

"That's why."

"Was having me with you that important?"

He waited a moment before answering. "Yes."

Linette closed her eyes, fighting the urge to go to him. She didn't know what had brought him back to San Francisco. Didn't want to know, because she was afraid he'd returned for her.

"All right," Cain admitted with a sigh. "It was selfish of me, I'll admit that. If you're looking for an excuse to hate me, then you've got one."

"I don't hate you."

"That's the problem," he said roughly. "Maybe you should."

He held out one arm to her, and without hesitation Linette walked into his embrace.

CAIN's eyes slowly drifted closed. He'd dreamed of this moment for weeks. Of holding her against him, of savoring her softness. He was tired of fighting a battle he couldn't win. Tired of pretending he was strong when he wasn't. Tired of waiting. He rubbed his jaw against the softness of her hair and breathed in the fresh scent of her.

Linette buried herself in his embrace and inadvertently moved against the tender flesh of his injury. Cain swallowed an involuntary moan.

"You're hurt?" Linette abruptly moved away from him, which produced an even greater pain for him. He'd waited too long for this moment to have it cut short.

"A flesh wound," he said, making light of the pain.

He held out his good arm to her once more, but she ignored the unspoken invitation.

"How'd it happen?" she pleaded, and then shook her head. "I don't want to know. Don't tell me. I don't think I could bear it."

Bright tears glistened in her eyes. She struggled to hide the emotion from him as if this weakness embarrassed her. Her tears had a curious effect upon Cain. A curious need reached deep inside him and tightened like a clenched fist.

"It's nothing," he said, longing to reassure her enough to bring her back into his arms. "Come on, let's go have that drink."

She hesitated but didn't protest when he reached for her hand. He cupped her fingers around his elbow, which was an excuse to have her close. It felt right to have her there. Powerfully right.

Instead of going inside the restaurant the way they had previously, Cain stepped up to the fish and chips stand and ordered two beers. When he turned around, he found Linette had taken a seat at one of the brightly colored picnic tables situated next to the stand. Fog swirled around the area, muting the lights.

Cain handed her the Styrofoam cup and sat across the table from her. The simple pleasure of studying her, watching her expression, fed his need.

Keeping her head lowered, she asked in what appeared to be a casual tone, "So what brings you to San Francisco this time?"

He could have lied, could have made up a song-and-dance about some business venture. Mallory was a convenient excuse, and he could have told her about the two-hour meeting with his friend. He hadn't openly lied to her yet, didn't plan on sugar-coating the truth, even at the risk of her anger.

The stark truth was that he hadn't taken the first available flight out of the Bahamas because of Tim Mallory. He'd returned to the Bay Area because he couldn't stay away from Linette another minute.

"I came to see you."

Her eyes drifted closed, and she whispered, "I wish you hadn't."

This woman wasn't good for his ego, Cain could see that.

"We don't have to decide anything right now," he said. "Let me take you to dinner tomorrow night and we can talk this out."

"I can't."

She was making this damned difficult. "Another appointment?"

"No, a date."

Cain felt as if he'd been sucker punched. Years of training enabled him to conceal his reaction.

"I can't believe this," Linette muttered, and her hand fussed nervously with her purse clasp. "You misled me. You eluded the truth, knowing how I'd feel about a man who kills for a living. You said I wouldn't see you again, and then bingo, you pop back into my life just when I've accepted a blind date."

A blind date. Cain felt better. Mildly better. But then she could date a hundred men at one time and it wouldn't be any of his business. He had no claim on her.

He'd been involved with other women over the years. Several of them had had an active social life when he was away. It had never troubled him. Why should it now? He wasn't looking for someone to sit by a window and wait for his return. What came as an emotional blow was how possessive he felt toward Linette.

"Then of course you should go on your date." She'd never know what it cost him to make that suggestion. The thought of another man holding her, another man kissing her, making love to her, was enough to set his teeth on edge. Yet he sat across from her as if he hadn't a care in the world, when in reality he was damn near having a stroke.

The silence was tense. Linette was the one who broke it.

"How were you hurt?" The words came quickly, as if she regretted the need to know.

He could make up something to satisfy her curiosity but didn't. "A rescue effort."

"You were on a mission."

Generally Cain didn't relay the details of his assignments. He would make an exception with Linette, mainly because he felt he owed her that much. "Terrorists kidnapped a nineteen-year-old boy, the son of an important man. We found where they were keeping him."

"The teenager? What happened to him?"

"He's alive. He's recuperating at home with his family."

"Did anyone else get hurt?"

"Yes," Cain said, unwilling to disguise the truth again. "Four men were killed."

She took a moment to digest this information. "Any of your men?"

He shook his head. They'd been fortunate. He'd come away with the worst of it, two cracked ribs and a bullet that had grazed his side. A couple of inches in the other direction and he would have lost a kidney. And would not be sitting across from Linette now.

"How long will you be in town?"

"A few more days."

"Then where will you go next?"

"Florida. I have a compound there for training purposes."

"So you have another mission?"

"Not right away." Clearly she didn't understand that his assignments were never planned in advance. He was often called, as he had been early Christmas morning, without warning. Desperate voices in desperate situations. Lives depended on his quick response. It had been hell leaving her that day, but Linette didn't know that.

She glanced at her watch.

Cain could take a hint. "I'll walk you to your car."

The four-block trek passed with lengthy lapses in their conversation. Neither seemed to know what to say. This meeting had gone badly. She'd already learned what he'd come to tell her.

When they arrived at her car, she turned to him, her keys in her hand. Cain held himself stiffly away from her, knowing she was about to ask him not to contact her again. He didn't blame her.

Taking matters into his own hands, Cain reached for her. She came without resistance. Not even a token one.

They exchanged a slow, sweet kiss. Then, like the gathering turbulent winds of a storm, the kiss changed. If this was the last time she would see him, then Cain was determined she would remember him. If she was going to date someone else, he wanted the imprint of his kisses on her lips.

Linette broke away, her shoulders heaving. "Why did you have to come back?" she asked.

"I couldn't stay away."

She was the one who kissed him, being careful of his injury. She pulled aside his coat and flattened her hand against the bandage. Her touch was gentle and caring.

"You're going to be killed someday," she whispered, and bit into her lower lip.

He tried to make light of her fears. "We all have to die sooner or later."

She shook her head. "I couldn't bear to bury another man I love."

Cain realized he was asking a good deal of this woman. He couldn't be anything less than fair. "If you want me to leave you, I will. I'll never contact you again. All you need do is ask."

Her silence encouraged him. He kissed the underside of her jaw, nibbled at her earlobe, and rubbed his hand down the small of her back. This was crazy, and they both knew it. Forbidden fruit was sweeter by far. No woman had ever been sweeter.

The words to send him out of her life never came.

"I'll pick you up Saturday," he said between deep, lingering kisses, his heart pounding with triumph. For the first time Cain could remember there was music in his soul, and all because a beautiful young widow had agreed to have dinner with him.

TIM Mallory had never been more glad to see anyone than Cain McClellan. Cain had arrived the day before, and the two men had talked nonstop for hours. Then Cain had made some weak excuse Mallory didn't understand and left. Frankly Mallory wondered what was so all-fired important.

If he didn't know better, Mallory would think a woman was responsible. But in all the years he'd known

Cain, he'd never seen his boss lose his head over a woman.

Although Mallory remained self-conscious about having to use the walker, it felt so good to be in an upright position that he didn't care. He gladly accepted the imposition of a metal contraption since it meant he could stand.

Walking was another matter. Thus far all he'd managed to do was shuffle about awkwardly, but Mallory had never been prouder than the moment he'd first placed one foot in front of the other. An Olympic gold medal winner couldn't have been more pleased with himself.

Naturally Mallory griped long and loud about the walker to Francine. But only because he derived a good deal of pleasure in complaining when she was around; also it kept both of them on their toes.

Thinking about his physical therapist produced a smile. In the beginning, Mallory had viewed her as a bully. Even now he couldn't picture Francine as any angel in white.

He enjoyed baiting her, enjoyed watching the color creep into her face. Other than the one time he'd kissed her, there'd been no sexual contact between them, but not because of any lack of effort on his part. The woman had a backbone of iron. He should know, since he'd suffered a head-on collision with that stubborn pride of hers on more than one occasion.

Mallory had never told her how furious he'd been Christmas Day when she'd dropped by uninvited. He had to hand it to her, though, she'd given as good as she'd taken. Not until later that day did he realize how alive he felt. After spending the majority of eighteen months on his backside, to have the blood pumping through his veins again felt damn good.

"I can't believe the progress you've made since I last saw you," Cain said. He'd arrived shortly after Mallory's morning workout in the pool and was staying for lunch. Mallory was grateful to see his friend, but frankly he was going to miss having lunch with his feisty therapist.

"I have to tell you, it feels good to be standing," Mallory said in response to Cain's comment. "I won't be needing the walker much longer."

"You most certainly will be needing that walker," Francine announced, leaning against the doorjamb, her arms folded. "Just because everything's progressing quickly doesn't mean you're going to be walking all on your own by next week."

She'd changed out of her swimsuit and back into the basic uniform she favored. Damp tendrils of hair framed her face. Tim drank in the sight of her, wondering how he could have ever thought of her as unattractive. It was true, she wasn't a classic beauty, but then the Miss America types never had appealed to him.

She was Francine. Stubborn. Demanding. Spunky. And one hundred percent woman.

His therapist might think his ultimate goal was to walk again, but she was wrong. Somehow, some way, he was going to get this sexy Amazon beauty into bed with him. Mallory spent a good portion of each night planning just that.

Greg delivered their lunches. Soup, salad, and a couple of thick sandwiches. Mallory was hungry. An appetite was something novel. Food hadn't appealed to him for months. He wasn't sure when it had happened.

Sometime around Christmas, he guessed. About the time Francine had waltzed into his disgruntled life.

"Didn't I tell you you'd be back with Deliverance Company someday?" Cain said, looking too damn smug to suit Mallory.

"Yeah, but it'll never be the same." There would always be limitations now. He wouldn't be able to do all he had before the accident. One thing was sure, he refused to be a weak link on the team's chain.

"There's plenty you can do."

Mallory frowned. "I want to be in the field."

"Fine, I'll put you in the field."

Francine stepped into the room, her eyes flashing. "What do you mean, you'll put him in the field?"

"Mallory says he wants to be in on a mission, then I say he's in."

"No, he isn't." Francine circled the table like a shark closing in on dinner. Mallory had seen her like this often enough to know when to keep his mouth shut. He knew to bide his time and wait until he had the advantage before tackling her when she was in this frame of mind.

"If you think I've worked this hard with this man just so you can haul his sorry butt out on some crazy soldier-boy escapade and get hurt again, then I suggest you rethink your game plan."

Cain's jaw sagged open. Few dared to cross Cain McClellan. It did Mallory's heart good for his boss to get a taste of the sheer brute stubbornness he'd faced in the last few months.

"You can trust me, Francine," Cain said with admirable restraint. "I'm not going to put Mallory in a position where he'll be hurt."

"If that's the case, then kindly explain how he nearly lost his leg." She folded her arms and shifted her weight to one foot with ill-concealed impatience.

"Perhaps I should clear this up," Mallory suggested.

"Stay out of it," Francine snapped.

"I'll handle this," Cain insisted.

The two glared at each other while Mallory calmly ate his sandwich. If the truth be known, it was all he could do to keep from laughing.

Cain left without explanation early that same evening, and Mallory was disappointed. He'd counted on the two of them talking over old times and sharing a couple of drinks. Being with Cain filled him with eagerness to return to Florida and the good friends he'd left behind.

After he'd first been injured, Mallory had spurned their efforts to help him. He regretted that now. Regretted the things he'd said and his childish behavior.

Thinking Cain was going to be around for the evening, Mallory had given Greg the night off as well. Now, with both Greg and Cain out of his hair, he was left to his own devices for dinner.

He mulled over his options. He could order out and have it delivered. Or he could cook something himself. Not an impossible task. Actually he welcomed the freedom to move about the kitchen. Before the accident he'd cooked the majority of his own meals. The idea of tackling this simple project appealed to him.

After checking out the freezer, he decided upon a thick T-bone steak. Two thick T-bone steaks. Why not? After the afternoon workout with Francine he deserved a reward.

He was fumbling around the kitchen, shocked by how quickly his energy left him, when the doorbell rang. Before he could do anything but wonder who it could be, Francine flew into the room like a small tornado.

"We need to talk," she said, her eyes snapping.

He stared at her for a moment, wondering what burr she had up her butt, when she apparently noticed he was standing in front of the stove with a steak dangling from his hand.

"Exactly what are you doing?" she demanded. Not waiting for him to answer, she whirled around as if looking for something. "Where's Greg?"

"I gave him the night off."

"And your friend, although I'm using that term loosely?"

"Hell if I know where he went. He left about an hour ago."

"He left you?" She made it sound as if Cain McClellan should be strung up from the nearest tree.

"I don't need a baby-sitter, Francine."

"Then kindly explain what you're doing with that steak. And what's that?"

Mallory looked at the cast-iron skillet, surprised by her question. "A frying pan."

"I know that much. What have you got in it?"

"Salt. You sprinkle a teaspoon or so on the bottom, turn it up on high, and sear the steak. That way the meat doesn't stick to the pan."

She shook her head as if this were the most ridiculous thing she'd ever heard. "What were you planning to cook other than that T-bone?"

"I hadn't given it much thought."

"Sit down," she ordered.

Actually Mallory was more than ready to do exactly that. "You're getting bossy in your old age, aren't you?"

"Do you want dinner or not?"

"You cooking?"

"Yup. Any objections?"

He felt like whistling. "None. I like my steak rare."

"How rare?"

He thought about it a minute. "So rare a good vet would have that cow back on its feet."

Francine laughed softly.

Mallory made his way to the table and sank onto the chair. Not until then did he notice the therapist was wearing something other than her uniform. She had on jeans and a cable-knit sweater the color of winter wheat. The sweater did an admirable job of showing off her curves. Other than when they were in the swimming pool, he hadn't paid much attention to her body.

This was one hell of a woman, only she hadn't figured it out yet. He just prayed he was around when she did.

"Do you always wear your hair in a braid?" he asked.

"Yes." She was busy at the stove.

"Why?" Tim watched her remove the pan from the burner and set it aside. Not exactly a promising start if she was cooking his dinner.

"It keeps the hair out of my face."

He should have suspected it was something as utilitarian as that. "I don't mean to question your obvious culinary skill, but exactly what are you doing?"

Francine turned about, a surprised look on her face. "Cooking dinner, what else? I thought you should have something other than protein. There's a couple of potatoes in here I was going to slice up and fry, and while I was at it I'll grill a few onions. I'll fix a salad, too."

She opened the refrigerator and bent forward, searching through the contents of the vegetable bin. This particular view of her soft derriere was something Tim had never seen, and it surprised him by how incredibly sexy he found this woman.

"How about gunslinger's sauce?"

The question came out of left field. "I beg your pardon?"

"You'll like it, I promise. It's flavored with whiskey."

"Yeah, but what do I put it on?"

She straightened and turned around. "Your steak, of course."

"Naturally," he echoed with mild sarcasm. "What else are you cooking up? Boot Hill broccoli?"

She laughed, and the sound of her amusement caused him to smile. Holding a carrot in her hand, she waved it at him. "We're still going to have that talk."

"Anything you say, dahlin', only feed me first."

She blinked at the endearment and quickly reverted to the task of salad making. "I'm not your dahlin', your sweetheart, or anything else."

"Yes, but with a little sweet talk you could be."

She grated the carrot as if she intended to puree the thing. "If you continue in this vein, I'll walk right out that door."

"And leave me here half starved?"

"Yes."

Mallory didn't doubt she would, either. "All right, I'll be good."

She continued slicing tomatoes and tossing those with the lettuce, and Mallory continued studying her. He liked her. Francine was his equal in every way. In all his years, he'd never met a woman like her.

Finished with the salad, she set it in the middle of the table. Recognizing this as an opportune moment, Tim caught her around the waist. "Take your hair out of the braid," he said.

She blinked down at him as if he'd spoken in Greek, then braced her hands over his, although she didn't shove them aside. "Why?"

"Because I want to see you with your hair down." Not waiting for her to refuse, he reached behind her back until he found the end of the French braid and released the clasp. The long, thick strands sprang free, almost bouncing in their eagerness to comply with his wish.

"Tim, please," she whispered. "I don't think this is a good idea."

"Sit," he ordered. He wanted to look at her without getting a crick in his neck. With his good leg he dragged a chair away from the table and gently eased her onto it.

She kept her eyes lowered, refusing to look at him. "I wish you wouldn't," she whispered.

"That's too bad." He splayed his fingers through the soft blond hair, draping the abundance over her shoulders. Leaning back on his chair, he studied the effect. His heart caught in his throat at the beauty he found her to be. How could he have been so blind? Francine Holden literally took his breath away.

"I better slice the potatoes."

Mallory edged his chair closer to hers. "Don't leave," he said, weaving his fingers through her hair and using it to urge her mouth toward his.

"I . . . I thought you were hungry."

"I'm famished," he whispered just before his mouth settled on hers.

Mallory was convinced neither one of them had anticipated the explosion of fire and need that would erupt between them. He'd intended to go slow and easy, introduce her gradually to his touch, coax and soothe her as he would before riding a feisty mare. But the minute she welcomed his kiss, encouraged his touch, Mallory was lost.

His lack of control surprised even him. He kissed her long and hard a number of times. Instead of appeasing his appetite, it increased a need for more of her. Never in all his life had he needed a woman more.

Not any woman, either. He needed Francine. Mallory didn't know much about love. But he knew a hell of a lot about sex. What he felt for her was an off-balance configuration of both, he decided. At the moment the scales tipped toward sexual satisfaction, but not at the expense of hurting her.

Mallory needed Francine.

He wanted her with him. At the end of the day when she walked out the door, he immediately calculated how many hours would pass before he'd be with her again. She dominated his thoughts. The monotony of many a long, torturous night passed while he filled his head with thoughts of her.

"Tim . . ."

All she said was his name, but the way she said it, low and sensual, warm and wanting, caused his body to tighten. He felt lost, and she was the home he'd never had. The love he'd never secured.

He struggled now, breathing hard in an effort to regain some semblance of control. He reminded himself she was innocent. He couldn't allow himself to forget that. Nor could he make love to her for the first time on the kitchen floor. But heaven only knew how long it would take him to drag his way into the bedroom with that cursed walker.

He eased her closer and bent forward and nuzzled his face between her breasts. Francine nearly came off the chair. She moaned and clamped her arms around his head.

"Go to my bedroom," he instructed her, kissing the underside of her jaw.

"Your bedroom," she repeated as if she were a robot.

"Wait for me there."

"But . . ."

"Please, Francine, just this once do as I ask."

"Should I . . . do you want me to undress?"

"Yes."

Reluctantly she moved away from him. Her parting word as she rushed from the room was, "Hurry."

Mallory didn't need any such inducement. He had his shirt off even before he was upright. His hands gripped hold of the walker, and he raised himself out of the chair, using the contraption for leverage. He wasn't looking at any watch, but he suspected he made record time, shuffling his way down the long hallway.

His bedroom door was closed, but it would take a lot more than a little thing like a door to stand between him and Francine.

He walked inside, not surprised that she'd left the light off. Actually he preferred that they made love in the dark. Although Francine was intimately familiar with his body, Mallory found himself self-conscious. This was different.

He closed the door, and the room became pitch black. Slowly, he made his way to the bed.

"Tim, before we make love, don't you think we should talk?"

"Later," he promised gently. He appreciated her fears,

but he wasn't going to destroy this time with a lot of foolish chit-chat. As it was, he felt as if he were about to explode.

Awkwardly he climbed into the bed next to her. Unfortunately there was barely room for the two of them in the hospital bed. Holding Francine close, he kissed her slowly, sensually, and felt a heady rush of desire at her ready response.

She'd done as he asked and removed her clothes. Mallory took several moments to run his hands down the silky-smooth texture of her skin.

The problem Mallory hadn't anticipated was exactly how they were going to accomplish this. He hadn't made love to a woman since his accident.

Rolling onto his good side, he pressed her body flush against his. Her breasts snuggled against his torso. He lifted her leg and eased it over his scarred hip.

"What about . . . you know?" Francine said.

Mallory could hear the self-consciousness creep into her voice. *You know?* He didn't.

"What about what?" he asked, hiding his eagerness as best he could and suspecting he did a damn poor job of it.

"Birth control." Her tone was hesitant and unsure, her words barely audible.

In all his adult life, Mallory had never been so desperate for a woman that he'd forgotten something this important. Worse, he realized he didn't have anything with which to protect her.

"I don't have anything here," he confessed.

"Oh."

As much as he wanted to make love to Francine, he couldn't do this, couldn't love her and then worry that his seed had taken shelter inside her generous body.

"It doesn't matter," she whispered hesitantly.

"Unfortunately, it does," he said between gritted teeth, and reached for the lamp on the stand next to the bed. "The last thing I want is to create another illegitimate child."

10 ❧

*C*ain had never wooed a woman. Frankly, he wasn't sure how to go about it. When he arrived outside Linette's apartment Saturday evening, he hoped he'd covered all the bases. Flowers. Chocolates. Chilled champagne.

To be on the safe side he brought along a fresh bouquet of flowers. Roses, carnations, yellow lilies, and a few other blossoms he couldn't name. It was the biggest bouquet he could find, and it had cost him plenty. But he would have gladly paid ten times that hundred bucks if it would help his cause with Linette.

The box of chocolates was an ultrarich French variety, and the champagne was Dom Pérignon.

With his arms full, Cain had a difficult time ringing the bell. Linette opened the door and smiled when she saw him. Funny what a little thing like a smile could do, Cain mused. One tiny one from her, and he would have gladly trekked up three flights of stairs on his knees. She wore a pretty blue dress and was so strikingly lovely that for an embarrassing moment he couldn't take his eyes off her.

"I came bearing gifts," he said finally, and stepped inside. His first thought was to set everything aside and drag her into his arms. Surely one small kiss wasn't too much to ask. He didn't, however, for fear he'd upset their evening. He dared not risk offending her.

"I'm a little early," he said apologetically.

"I am, too," she said, taking the flowers out of his arms and carrying them into the kitchen. Standing next to her sink, she closed her eyes and buried her nose in their scent. "They're beautiful. Thank you."

Cain set the frilly box of candy and the bottle of champagne on the countertop while Linette reached in the cupboard below and brought out a vase. She filled it with water and carefully arranged the bouquet inside it. When she finished, she set it in the center of the dining room table.

"Our reservations aren't for another hour," he told her. "Would you like me to open the champagne?"

"Please." She retrieved two flutes from the china hutch while Cain manipulated the top off the champagne bottle. The popping sound shattered the silence.

"I've never tasted Dom Pérignon before," she said, smiling up at him. "From what I understand it's very expensive."

"It's not too bad."

Cain filled the two glasses. "Shall we drink to us?"

She bit into her lower lip, then nodded. "To us," she said with a gentle smile. Cain touched the rim of his glass against hers.

They each sampled the champagne.

"So," he said, walking into the living room and taking a seat. He leaned back casually against the thick cushion. "How'd your blind date go?" He hadn't intended to start off their evening with an interrogation of her evening, but a stomach-twisting bout of curiosity got the best of him.

He'd spent the majority of the night before wrestling demons, thinking about Linette dining, laughing, and enjoying the company of another man. It wasn't something he looked forward to repeating any time soon.

Linette laughed softly. "You don't want to know."

"Sure I do." He'd feel a thousand times better if the blind date had turned out to be a horror story. They could laugh together over what one was obligated to do for well-meaning friends. He might even relate a couple of fiascos of his own just so she'd feel better.

"His name is Charles Garner."

She wasn't immediately forthcoming with details, so Cain helped her along a little. "What's he do for a living?" She seemed to be studying the champagne bubbles.

"He's an attorney."

"Divorced?" Already Cain had him pictured as a greedy son of a bitch. To his way of thinking, a fair portion of lawyers were known charlatans. At least the ones he'd been in contact with over the years were.

"No. His wife died of leukemia. The same rare type that killed Michael."

This was beginning to sound less promising. "So the two of you had a lot to talk about," Cain commented with less enthusiasm.

"Yes, only we didn't talk about leukemia. Neither one of us wanted to dredge up the pain of the past."

"I see." If Cain understood her correctly, she was

telling him the two had formed this automatic kinship, born out of their shared experiences.

"Charles is probably one of the nicest men I've ever met. He's gentle and sweet, determined to be a good father to his two children."

"So there are children involved?" This didn't bode well, either. Cain recalled how much Linette wanted a family. This man came complete, a package deal, something Cain could never offer her.

"Charles has two boys. Jesse's seven and has bright red freckles and Steve's five and as cute as a bug's ear."

Already she knew their names. Cain could fast see that the flowers, candy, and champagne weren't going to cut it. At the rate this conversation was going, human sacrifice wouldn't, either.

It was as if Linette had found the perfect match. Mr. Impeccable was everything Cain wasn't and would never be. Her blind date could offer her the security she needed. Something she sure wasn't going to get with him.

"He sounds wonderful," Cain said with a sorry lack of enthusiasm.

"Charles is."

If Cain had a lick of sense, he'd set aside the wine-glass, reach for his coat, and walk out now. Instead he was a glutton for punishment. "When will you be seeing him again?"

It seemed to take an inordinate amount of time for her to answer. "I won't be."

Cain's head snapped up so fast, he heard a bone in his neck pop. "You won't?"

"No." The admission came soft and low.

"Why wouldn't you? This guy sounds ideal for you."

Linette rolled the stem of the glassware between her palms. "It wouldn't be fair to Charles."

"Not fair?"

"To accept another date would mislead him into thinking we could have a relationship."

"You don't want a relationship with Charles?"

"No." She raised her head so that her eyes slammed into his. Her beautiful, expressive gaze snapped with irritation.

"The whole time I was with Charles, all I could think about was you," she said, her lips pinched as if it cost her a good deal to admit this. "He took me to a fabulous, ultraexpensive restaurant, and instead of enjoying myself the way I should have, all I could think about was how much I'd rather be with you. What have you done to me, Cain McClellan?"

Cain had no answers to give her. Although he had several questions of his own.

"I was thoroughly miserable the entire night," she admitted, and then added on a spirited note, "Don't you dare smile, either."

"I'm not smiling."

"You most certainly are. I shouldn't have told you about Charles. I'm sorry now I did."

"I'm very pleased you did." He set aside his champagne glass, reached for her crystal flute, and placed it on the coffee table. Then he lifted her fingers to his mouth and kissed the tip of each one. "I have a few complaints of my own about you, Widow Collins." His lips moved over the inside of her wrist, his tongue making slow circles over her smooth skin. "You've haunted my dreams from the moment we met. It's because of you

I'm here in San Francisco when I promised myself I'd never see you again."

"That's another thing I want to discuss with you."

He noted the irritation had left her voice. Draping one of her arms over his shoulder, he reached for her free hand, then repeated the procedure of kissing her fingers, turning over her hand and exposing her wrist to his mouth. Then he moved his tongue over the inside curve of her elbow and placed her unresisting arm on his shoulder. Her wrists dangled behind his neck.

"I don't think it's a good idea for you to kiss me," she said, her voice reedy and thin. Her resistance would be token at best, Cain guessed.

"Why not?" His heart clamored loudly in his ears, the way it always did when she was this close. His thumb and finger lifted her chin so that she was forced to meet his eyes.

"Because every time you do . . ." The words trembled reluctantly from her lips. She paused.

"Yes," he coaxed.

She shook her head, refusing to say more.

"Because every time we kiss," he repeated, and then finished the statement for her, "you want me to make love to you."

She pulled away from him immediately; her arms slid from his shoulders and fell free. The truth of his words burned in her eyes.

"How do you think I know this?" he asked her gently. "It's because I want the same thing."

"I can't . . . I won't become sexually involved with you."

"I know that, too. It's far better that we don't make love." There was danger in emotional commitment. Danger in allowing himself to become accustomed to her softness. This woman was deadly. He'd known that from the first. Yet he defied the danger again and again by seeking her out.

Cain hadn't a clue where this relationship would lead. Didn't know anything beyond the complicated realization that he couldn't stay away from her.

Francine gladly accepted the shopping date with her mother. She'd been looking for an excuse to casually talk about her relationship with Tim. Martha Holden was both mother and friend to Francine. There were several important questions she needed answered, but she didn't want to be obvious about her reasons for wanting to know.

They met at the Embarcadero at Nordstrom's. Who would have ever believed Francine would have the most important discussion of her life in women's lingerie? Certainly not her.

It all began naturally. "How long did you and Dad date before you were married?" Francine asked. As she recalled, at the time her mother had been an English literature major and her father an apprentice plumber. Both families had been left shaking their heads in wonder at the explosive romance that developed between the two.

Francine's father was a burly giant, reaching nearly six feet six inches. Everything about him was big. His hands were monstrous, his feet so large they had to special order his shoes. Her mother, on the other hand, was a full foot and two inches shorter and a delicate soul who loved poetry, classical music, and English literature.

As fate would have it, Francine had favored her father's side of the family. She reached six feet by the time she was fourteen and was several inches taller than two of her own brothers.

"Your father and I met in September and married in October a year later," her mother answered.

Actually Francine knew this but wanted to ease into the discussion. "What attracted you to Dad?"

Martha Holden smiled softly and held a black lacy bra against her stomach. She looked straight ahead and into warm memories, Francine suspected.

"I was much too young to know about love," Martha Holden began. "He was such a bear of a man, even more so then, but his heart has always been big and gentle. Soon after we met, I saw him bend down and comfort a little boy who'd fallen off his bicycle. There was something so tender and caring in the way he talked to that child. I think it was then that I fell in love with him."

Francine made busy sorting through a rack of satin pajamas, her eyes avoiding her mother's. "Did you and Dad sleep together before the wedding?"

Her mother, who'd been busy checking bra sizes, hesitated. "No," she answered softly. "I realize that isn't what you expected to hear. Not in this day and age, not then, either, for that matter. We met during the sixties, in the age of free love, when AIDS and the like wasn't a consideration."

"I admire your restraint," Francine said, sorry now she'd brought up the subject, which was far more personal than anything she'd asked previously. "It must have been difficult being so much in love."

"Congratulate your father, then. If it had been up to me, we would have lived together two months before the wedding. He was the one who insisted we wait. Trust

me, Francine, I did everything I knew to break his resolve, but your father wanted things right for me."

"Are you glad you waited?"

Martha laughed. "Yes, but not for the reasons you're
thinking. You were born nine months to the day after
the wedding. I don't think either of us anticipated me
being so fertile."

Francine was certain her cheeks had turned crimson.
She'd come very close to testing her own fertility with
Tim. Hoping her mother didn't notice her red cheeks,
she picked out a pair of pajamas, a new bra, and some
bikini underwear and paid the cashier.

"How's the patient coming along these days?" her
mother asked, broaching the very subject Francine had
hoped to avoid.

"Good. He's improving more every day."

Her mother tucked her arm in Francine's. "How long
have you been in love with him?"

Francine felt like bursting into tears. She had hoped
she hadn't been that obvious. The best answer she could
give was a shrug. "He's a mercenary, Mother. Can you
believe I could do something so stupid as to fall for a
soldier of fortune? To complicate matters even more,
he's a patient. Good therapists don't allow this sort of
thing to happen."

"You're only human. Now stop being so hard on
yourself!" She led Francine away from the lingerie department. "Come on, let's take a break and you can tell
me all about what's been happening between you and
Mr. Mallory."

Before long they were sitting across a table from each
other.

"I'm so angry with Tim, I can barely work with him."

"Angry," her mother repeated. "I thought you said you were in love with him."

"I am. On Friday I learned that he's chomping at the bit to get back in the field with his cronies. The man's a crazed fool. He was nearly killed the last time. I didn't work this hard to watch him go off and get himself killed."

"Do you normally care what your patients do after therapy?" her mother asked.

"No," Francine answered softly.

"What did you expect him to do once he started walking again?"

"I don't know. I guess I didn't think about it. But I never believed, not for one moment, that he'd be fool enough to risk his life again."

"Have you—"

"Made love?" Francine finished for her. "No, but it was close. We . . . Tim didn't have a condom, and he refused to risk it. His mother wasn't married when she had him. Apparently he was tossed from one foster home to another."

"In other words, he was the one who put an end to it?"

Francine nodded but avoided meeting her mother's eyes.

"He must feel deeply about you, Francine. If he didn't, he wouldn't have cared about the risk, despite his own background. Why should he when he'll be gone shortly?"

"Afterward I thought about what happened."

"Yes," her mother coaxed.

"And I realized I went to bed with him for all the wrong reasons. I love him, yes, but in my heart that was only a small part of my wanting to make love."

"You thought it would keep him in San Francisco," her mother supplied for her.

Francine's head shot up. "That's exactly what I hoped, but I know now it would never have worked. Every day Tim drives himself harder and harder with one goal in mind. He's eager to get back to Florida. Get back with his friends."

"In other words, he's eager to leave you."

"Yes."

"Let him go, Francine."

"You make it sound so easy. I know what you're going to say—if it's meant to be, he'll come back. I wish it were that simple, but it isn't."

"What can you do to hold him here?"

Francine had already given this matter a good deal of thought. "Nothing."

Her mother patted her hand gently.

"It isn't fair. This is the first time in my life that I've ever been in love. There hasn't been another man I ever loved like this. He may be the only one I ever will."

"Perhaps."

However painful, Francine was grateful her mother didn't try to convince her otherwise. It had taken her nearly thirty-six years to fall in love the first time. She'd be over sixty if she had to wait that long again.

All at once Francine had the incredible urge to laugh. It started out as a soft giggle, then gained in intensity until she was nearly doubled over.

"Francine?" Her mother was looking at her strangely.

"Monday morning when I arrived at the house," she said between breaths, "Tim had a case of condoms delivered."

"I beg your pardon?"

Francine wiped the moisture from her cheeks. Leaning toward her mother, she lowered her voice. "Tim had one hundred and forty-four condoms brought to the house just in case we found ourselves in similar circumstances. I swear he has them planted in every room. There's even an ashtray full of condoms by the pool."

"I think I could grow to like your Mr. Mallory."

"That's the problem, Mom, he isn't mine."

"Don't give up just yet," her mother said softly. "Life has a way of working matters out for the best. If you lose him, then that was the way it was meant to be. My guess is that he knows less about love than most men. He's as perplexed about the whole thing as you are. Give him time."

Francine mulled over her mother's words of wisdom that night. The following morning she arrived at Tim's house at her usual time. Her job was nearly finished now. At the rate her patient was progressing, he'd be able to walk, with the aid of a cane, inside of a month. His progress thus far was nothing short of phenomenal. Nothing short of a miracle.

Tim was sitting up in bed, waiting for her.

"Morning," she greeted him, setting her bag on the chair. His gaze followed her every move, the same way it had for weeks. It was all she could do not to ask him to stop watching her.

"Morning," he returned, sounding downright chipper. "I gave Greg the night off," he said, and waited as if he expected her to respond.

"So?"

"So, I thought I'd invite you over for dinner." He jiggled his eyebrows suggestively.

"Who's cooking?" she was foolish enough to ask.

"We both will be if everything goes the way I'm planning."

"Tim, please."

"That's what you'll be saying all right."

Francine swore his grin stretched from ear to ear. "Is everything one big joke to you?" she demanded.

"No." He reached out and caught her hand, bringing her closer to the edge of the mattress. "Come on, sweetheart, there's no need to be shy about this."

Francine closed her eyes, unable to offer a suitable argument.

"I can understand you not wanting to fool around during work hours. I've tried to respect that the last couple of days, but I have to tell you, honey, it's hard."

"What about Cain?" She couldn't believe she was seriously contemplating doing this.

"No problem. He's been gone every evening as it is. If you want, I'll ask him to stay away."

A strained silence passed.

"This is highly unethical."

"Irresponsible on both our parts," Tim added softly.

"Foolish in the extreme."

"Crazy."

Francine smiled and whispered, "I bought lacy underwear the other day."

Tim groaned. "Don't tell me you have it on now."

"I do."

His eyes slammed closed, and his fingers tightened around hers. "Six o'clock. Salad, steak, and champagne," he said.

"What's for dessert?"

Tim grinned as if he were absolutely delighted she'd asked. "You and me, my love. You and me."

"*H*AVE you got a minute?" Mallory asked Cain early that same afternoon. Cain was reading the morning paper at the kitchen table when his friend joined him.

"Sure." He wasn't scheduled to meet Linette until after six. He'd gotten two tickets to the symphony as a surprise, knowing how much she'd enjoy it. In a thousand lifetimes he never would have believed he'd willingly sit through a bunch of men and women in tuxedos playing musical instruments. He liked songs with words.

"I've been meaning to talk to you, too," Cain said, setting aside the newspaper. He didn't know what was going on between Mallory and the therapist, but apparently it was more than met the eye.

"I need a small favor," Mallory said, looking a bit sheepish.

"You've got it."

"Would you mind staying away for the night?"

"Staying away?"

Tim heaved a deep sigh. "If you must know, I'm going to have company."

"For the night?"

"For the whole night."

Cain studied his friend carefully. "Is this someone I know?"

"Yeah," Tim answered defensively. "It's Francine."

This was what Cain feared. "Do you think that's wise?"

"I didn't ask your opinion, McClellan. I don't care if it's wise or not. She's coming."

"If it's a woman you want, I can arrange—"

"There's only one woman who interests me." His words were packed with irritation.

After meeting Linette, Cain knew the feeling. He'd bumped heads with Mallory's therapist once already, and he'd strongly suspected then a romance was brewing between the two. What he didn't know was his friend's feelings toward Francine.

"All right, you got it," he said. "I'll spend the night in a hotel."

"I appreciate it," Tim said, and then waited before asking, "You wanted to talk to me about something?"

"Yeah." Now, however, he wasn't sure. "It has to do with Francine."

"What about her?" Mallory's whole posture was defensive, and Cain wished he'd chosen his time more carefully.

"I'm not going to give you advice, if that's what you're thinking."

"I appreciate that."

"But . . ."

Mallory grinned. "Somehow I thought there was going to be a 'but' in this."

"I just want to warn you that a woman can really screw up your head." He was one to talk! He'd been following Linette around like a calf after its mother from the moment he'd arrived in town.

"We've both seen it happen," Mallory commented.

"You're coming back to Deliverance Company?"

Mallory's shoulders went back with surprise. "Of course."

"You aren't going to let some woman change your mind?"

"Hell, no."

Cain relaxed and reached for the newspaper once more. "Good. You had me worried there."

𝒯HE calls didn't always come in the middle of the night. No sooner had Cain finished speaking with Mallory than the phone rang. The crazy part was, Cain didn't give a thought to the fact that he was being called back to work. The first thing that went through his head was that he wouldn't be able to take Linette to the symphony after all.

An hour earlier he'd issued unwanted advice to Mallory when he should have been saying it to himself. Linette had him twisted in such tight knots, within a matter of days he'd forgotten who he was.

Cain listened as Murphy outlined the details of the case. This time it was a cultural attaché being held political prisoner. In Central America. Jungle. Heat. Death.

When Cain finished with the call, he immediately dialed the airlines and scheduled his flight to Florida. The mission would be planned from there. Two of his men were flying in from other parts of the country. They'd rendezvous first thing in the morning and leave together from there.

But first, before he did anything more, Cain had to talk to Linette. He dreaded this moment more than anything he could remember in a long while. He dreaded it more than he had leaving her at Christmas.

Linette looked surprised when he arrived at Wild and Wooly, and her eyes brightened with pleasure. But something about him must have told her why he'd come, because he watched the happiness quickly drain away.

"You're leaving?"

He nodded.

She said something to Bonnie and walked into the back room.

Cain followed her. He found her sitting, her back against the wall, her hands clasped in her lap. When she looked up, he noted that her eyes were bright.

Cain's heart constricted as he knelt down in front of her and cupped her hands in both of his.

"Where?" she asked in a whisper.

"Central America."

"What happened?"

"A man. A good man with a wife and family was taken hostage by a faction looking to pressure the government. He's an American."

"Then why don't we send in the army or something?"

What she was really asking, Cain realized, was why he was the one who had to go.

"They can't do that."

"But why?" she pressed, and Cain realized she was trembling. She freed one hand and stroked the side of his face. "Why?" she repeated.

"It's long and involved. The United States government doesn't negotiate with terrorists. I'm not entirely sure I can answer the wheres and whys myself. All I know is that Deliverance Company has been contacted."

She lowered her head. "Do you have to go?"

"Yes, Linette. This is what I do."

"What about your broken ribs?"

"They're healed enough."

"But—"

He stopped her by gently pressing his finger against her lips. "I'm leaving. My flight takes off in less than two hours. I came because I wanted to tell you myself." He kissed her bunched up fingers, wishing with everything inside him that he could calm her fears. "This is who I am. I'm good, baby, real good. Don't worry, all right?"

"When will you be back?"

"I don't know. Someday soon."

"You won't take any unnecessary chances, will you?"

"I'm not going to do anything stupid."

"There isn't any chance you'll be killed, is there?"

Cain closed his eyes and wished he could lie to her. "I can't make that promise."

Her trembling increased. "I know," she said.

11

*P*aul Curnyn was going to die. Not once had he doubted the certainty of his fate. The only question that remained unanswered was how and when.

Bound and gagged, beaten and bloody, he steeled himself against the pain that throbbed through his back and legs. The sound of his own screams echoed in his ears.

He closed his eyes and felt tears burning for release. He silently damned his captors for reducing him to this level of weakness. He couldn't deal with much more of the pain. Couldn't keep from screaming. If they continued to torture him, he wouldn't have the strength to keep from begging them to stop. He prayed his family would never know how much he'd suffered.

His family.

Paul's mind focused on his wife, Delores, and his two children. Jennifer and Sean. He wished now he'd been a better husband and father. Wished now he'd cared less about making a name for himself at the State Department and more about his family. He prayed his children would remember him.

Paul tensed as one of his captors approached him. Out of the corner of his eye, he saw the man remove his revolver from a leather holster and point it at Paul's temple. The steel barrel felt cold and evil against his skin.

A flurry of Spanish erupted between the men. The one who held the gun shouted the loudest. The dialect was one Paul wasn't fluent enough with to fully understand. What words he was able to translate sent chills of terror scooting down his spine.

Paul heard the gun hammer pull back and closed his eyes.

IT would have been easier, Francine decided, if she and Tim hadn't planned their lovemaking. It felt cold and calculating to know in advance what they were about to do. Worse to know why she was doing it. He hadn't declared his love, only his need, but her reasons for coming weren't any more sterling. If she satisfied him in bed, then maybe, just maybe, he wouldn't be so eager to leave her.

Francine swallowed tightly. She felt like an emotional wreck. Over the years she'd heard from her friends and read in a variety of accounts that the first time a woman made love could be painful. She didn't fear the pain as much as she worried about disappointing Tim with her complete lack of expertise. She must be some kind of idiot to think that she could hold a man with her sexual favors when she was a virgin.

By the time she stood outside the house, Francine's stomach was queasy. She breathed deeply several times in an effort to calm her fractured nerves. Then she painted a bright smile on her face, opened the door, and walked inside, carrying her overnight bag with her.

"Anyone home?" she called out cheerfully.

"In here."

Tim was waiting for her in the kitchen. One thing was sure, she was in no mood to eat anything. All she could think about was getting this ordeal over with as quickly as possible.

"Hi," she said, unable to meet his eyes. She'd worn her hair down, the way he liked it, and wished now she hadn't. It kept falling over her shoulder and getting in the way.

"So you decided to come after all." He didn't sound particularly delighted to see her.

"Yeah."

"I hope you're hungry. I sent Greg out for Chinese, and he brought back enough food to feed an army."

"I . . . I don't have much of an appetite yet."

"Me either."

Francine chanced her first look in his direction. Tim was sitting at the table with an atlas spread open. Apparently he'd developed a sudden interest in Central America.

"Greg's gone?" she asking, glancing around.

"I told him to get lost for the night."

Not exactly a delicate way to announce Tim was expecting company.

"That kid's getting to be a real smart-aleck. Seems he felt the need to lecture me about you."

"He knows about us?" The question slipped out before she could censor it.

Tim's laughter lacked any real amusement. "Cain figured it out, too. I haven't exactly had much of a social life lately. You're the only woman who's been around in the last year and a half. Neither man is blind or stupid."

"I suppose it only makes sense they'd know."

"Were you planning on hiding it from them?"

"No." But by the same token she wasn't exactly planning on holding a symposium on their relationship, either. "What did Greg have to say?"

"That you were a fool for getting involved with me."

"He should have told me that, not you." Although to be fair, he had warned her.

Tim muttered something under his breath and then said, "I suspect Greg's half in love with you himself."

"Greg?" Francine didn't believe it for a moment.

"So you're not hungry?"

"No."

"Me either," he confessed. He closed the atlas, but Francine noticed the way his gaze lingered over the volume cover.

They sat in silence, and it seemed neither one of them knew what to say next.

"I suppose we should get at it, then."

"Get at it" certainly didn't leave a lot of room for romance.

"I suppose we should," she answered, stiffening. Tim wasn't teasing her the way he had before, taking delight in making her blush. Nor did he appear to be overly eager to make love when the suggestion had dominated every word and action for weeks.

"Why don't you go in the bedroom and get undressed," he suggested.

Francine expanded her lungs with a giant breath. "I don't think that's a good idea."

"Not a good idea?" His eyes shot to hers. "Why not?"

"This isn't working," she whispered, more to herself than to Tim, amazed that she'd managed to come this far.

Tim leaned back on his chair and studied the ceiling tile. "All right," he said, and released his breath forcefully. "I apologize. My mind's been on other things. Cain's gone."

Francine didn't understand. "It was my understanding that you were going to ask him to leave."

"I mean gone as in he's been called away on a mission," he explained.

"A mission." It made perfect sense to Francine now. Tim longed to be with his friend on some field of death rather than stuck in San Francisco with her. If she'd ever needed a reminder that he would dally with her, use her, and then callously leave her, she had it now.

Tim glanced at his watch. "He'll land in Florida in a couple of hours. Murphy's there, and Jack and Bailey are flying in this evening. My guess is they'll land by tomorrow afternoon."

Francine listened intently, concerned for their safety.

"Timing is everything in these cases. For all we know, that poor bastard could already be dead." Agitated, Tim flexed and unflexed his hands.

Francine scooted back the seat, stood, and reached for her bag.

Tim looked over at her. "Where are you going?"

"Home."

He frowned. "Why? Listen, I know our night hasn't gotten off to a good start, but that doesn't mean we can't have some fun together."

Francine held up her hand while she waited for her thoughts to sort themselves out. "On second thought, I don't think our making love is such a good idea after all."

Tim reached for his walker and pulled himself upright. "What do you mean?" he asked. His eyes were grave and dark. Disappointed.

"I meant exactly what I said. You're looking for a good-time girl. Someone to take your mind off your boredom for the next couple of weeks before you head back to your friends."

Tim's frown darkened to a glower. "What you're really saying is you've changed your mind."

Francine wasn't going to argue the point with him. "Yes."

"Come on, sweetheart, we got off to a bad start, but that doesn't mean we have to call the whole thing off."

He brought up another point she couldn't argue. "The only thing you have to offer me is a few weeks of casual sex. I thought that would be enough, but I see now that it isn't. I'm sorry to disappoint you, but I need more than you're willing to offer."

Briefly, he closed his eyes as if praying for patience. "What's wrong? Do you need me to pretty it up with a few flowery words? Fine. I can do that. You'll get what you need, and I'll get what I need. It isn't such a bad deal."

"I'd be a fool to turn you down."

He smiled for the first time. "Exactly."

"No thanks." She felt considerably foolish. It might have worked if he hadn't been drooling over some atlas. It was a vivid reminder of exactly who and what he was. A vivid reminder of what she was willing to become.

"No thanks," he repeated sarcastically. "Listen, sweetheart, you've apparently got some hang-up about sex all of a sudden. It's a perfectly natural human function. There's no need to mess it up with a bunch of other emotions. I've always called a spade a spade and admired you for doing the same. Don't disappoint me now."

"I don't want you to leave," she said in a rush. "You don't need to be a soldier. You could do anything, be anything at all. You don't have to—"

"So that's it," Tim said, his face tightening with irritation. "You seem to think you can use that body of yours for leverage to wrap me around your little finger. I got news for you. It ain't going to work. Go ahead and walk out that door," he challenged, and pointed the way out to her.

Francine's hand tightened around the handle of the overnight bag before she turned away from him.

"But before you leave, you'd best think about the real reasons you're going."

"I don't need you to tell me why," she snapped.

"That's not the way I see it. You're backing down because you're chicken. You're afraid, so own up to it. Because this bull about me insulting you is a crock of . . ." He let the unspoken word hang between them.

"All right," she said, turning back to face him. "You hit the nail on the head. I'm afraid." And she was. She was scared spitless that she was giving her heart to a man who would love her one night and forget her name the next. Afraid he would forever mark her life and then calmly walk out of it.

"There's no need to be afraid." His words were soft and full of inducement. "Let me love you, Francine. Let me show you what it can be like between us. If you still want to leave afterward, then fine, you can go. Just don't walk out now. We've only just begun, sweetheart."

Francine battled back emotion.

"Come on," he coaxed once more. "Let's sit down and

have dinner. That's all I'm asking. It's a shame for all this food to go to waste." He gestured to the table behind him. "We've come this far. Let's not turn back now."

Francine wavered. Dear sweet heaven, what was the matter with her? Never once in all her life had she thought of herself as weak. Tim made her that way, and she hated it. She'd suffer more than a few regrets if she gave in to him now. On the other hand, she'd be left wondering the rest of her life what it would have been like with him. God help her, she loved him.

Francine walked over to him and stood in front of the walker. She crouched down and set her small suitcase on the floor, then wrapped her arms around Tim's torso. His eyes brightened with anticipation as she kissed him.

His mouth opened to hers, taking advantage of her generosity. With his one free hand, he wove his fingers into her hair and kissed her with a hunger and need that left her clinging and weak in the knees.

"This is more like it," he said, and brought her lips back to his. He kissed her twice more, each kiss more potent than the previous one. They were both left trembling with desire.

"You've got far too many clothes on," he said, his voice little more than a whisper. "Now go to my room, strip, and wait for me. We've got all night for me to appease those fears. But you never know, it might take longer." He released her slowly, as if it demanded every ounce of will he possessed to do so. "I only hope one case of condoms is enough."

Francine stepped back, took a moment to catch her breath, and then pressed her hand to his cheek. "Goodbye, Tim Mallory, and thank you."

His eyes widened as if she'd slapped him. "Good-bye?"

She reached for her bag and literally ran for the door. She feared if he said one word more, she wouldn't have the strength to leave him. And leave him she must, for her own peace of mind.

Two days later Greg phoned Francine at home.

"Hello, Greg," she said, immediately regretting not contacting him herself. She owed Greg more than the brief letter of resignation she'd had delivered to the house.

"How are you?"

"Great." A lie, but the truth would only depress him.

"The beastmaster got your letter."

"I should have stopped in and said good-bye to you. I'm sorry, Greg."

"No problem. Listen, this isn't any of my business, but I want to make sure that Mr. Mallory . . . I want to be sure he didn't hurt you."

Francine braced her forehead against the kitchen wall. "Of course not, what makes you ask that?"

Greg hesitated. "No reason. It's just that . . . well, never mind. It isn't important. He's gone, you know."

"Tim's left San Francisco?" She straightened in shock.

"Yeah, he had me book the first available flight to Miami as soon as he read your letter."

"I see."

"I hope that list of instructions you gave him wasn't important. He crushed it up into a ball and threw it across the room."

"He'll be fine," Francine assured Tim's assistant. She would be, too, in time.

"I CAN'T tell you how much I've enjoyed this last month," Charles Garner told Linette. He'd unexpectedly stopped off at the shop and stayed until closing time.

He was a striking-looking man, Linette thought, kind and good-natured. But he didn't make her heart zing the way Cain did. She didn't spend time with him and then wonder how long it would be before she saw him again. But none of that mattered, she reminded herself.

Linette had made the painful decision not to see Cain again. He'd been in Central America five weeks now. These silent days without him had been some of the most agonizing of her life.

It would have helped if he'd contacted her in some way. She hadn't heard so much as a word from him. Not even a postcard. For all she knew, he could be dead. Each day of not knowing was hell. The fears ate her alive. The interminable waiting. Was he hurt? Dying? Had he forgotten her completely?

Linette tried not to worry about Cain. Tried not to think of him in some foreign jungle, hurting, perhaps dying. Tried not to think of standing over the grave of another man she'd loved and buried.

The first week after he'd left had been the worst. She rarely slept, and when she did, her dreams were filled with horror scenes involving Cain. She lost five pounds in eight days, weight she couldn't afford to shed.

Bonnie was the one who sat her down and talked some sense into her. It seemed crystal clear when her friend said it. Cain was a mercenary. Fighting and killing was his profession. Either accept him as he was or break off the relationship. It was one or the other.

Afterward Linette knew what she had to do. As painful as it was, she realized Cain wasn't going to change. She also realized she couldn't accept living with the risks he took. She wanted to tell him, only there hadn't been any word from him.

He wouldn't catch her off guard this time, she vowed. If he showed up unexpectedly the way he had before, she'd be prepared. What she intended to tell him was all planned out.

She wouldn't allow her heart to take control next time. No matter how glad she was to see him. No matter how light-headed and dizzy the sight of him made her.

"How are the boys?" she asked Charles, determined to keep her mind off Cain.

"Great," the attorney answered. They were standing outside her yarn shop, and he took the key out of her hand and locked up for her. "They loved it that we went roller-skating with them. They like you, Linette."

"I like them, too."

Charles smiled as he handed her back her key chain. "I thought we might get together next weekend. The boys have been hounding me to take them kite flying. No better month than March for that. I thought we'd go down to Golden Gate Park and give it a shot. Are you game?"

"Sure, that sounds like fun."

"Later, I'll arrange for a sitter for the boys and take you out for a night on the town. I thought we'd start with dinner and then take in a play. I understand *The Phantom of the Opera*'s in town. Getting tickets shouldn't be too much of a problem."

"It might be. Why don't I cook something up at your place, and we can rent a couple of videos? The boys can help with dinner. They did a great job cooking the spaghetti last week, remember?" Linette enjoyed her time with Charles's young sons immensely. The two youngsters had helped ease the sting of missing Cain far more than her dates with their father.

Charles hesitated. "You still think about Cain, don't you?"

Linette lowered her eyes and nodded. "I'm sorry, Charles, really I am."

"I take it you haven't heard from him?"

"Not a word." Nor did she have an address where she could write him.

"Once he does contact you, then you can put the relationship to rest. It's over. You know it, but he doesn't."

Linette bit into her lower lip and nodded.

"You're sure this is what you want?" Charles asked, studying her. He was far more understanding about her relationship with Cain than she'd expected him to be. He'd talked to her about it on several occasions, and he'd helped her realize how futile linking her life with Cain's would be.

"This is what I want," she said quickly—perhaps too quickly, because Charles frowned and reached for her hand, clasping it firmly in his own.

"You can't tie your life up in a dead-end relationship. There's no future in loving a mercenary."

"I know all that." She didn't need Charles to tell her what she'd struggled so painfully to acknowledge herself. Loving Cain was like living next to a volcano. He was going to be killed. Sometime. Somewhere. Someday soon. Without notice. Kill or be killed.

"We'll have dinner out, then?" Charles coaxed. "And the play?"

"All right," she agreed, wishing she could dredge up more enthusiasm for the outing.

Charles had a good heart. The problem was that Linette found him dull. She sincerely hoped Cain hadn't ruined her for other men.

He walked her to her car and kissed her cheek. "I'll pick you up around ten Saturday morning."

"I'll be ready."

When she arrived back at her apartment, Linette forced herself to fix dinner. After dining on a frozen entree she'd cooked in her microwave, she took a long hot bath and climbed into bed. She read for a while, then turned off the light. To her surprise, she felt herself drifting off to sleep almost immediately.

The sound of the phone caught her in the middle of a dream. She lifted her head from the pillow and glanced at the clock. Realizing it was the phone and not her alarm, she lifted the receiver and pressed it to her ear. She hadn't a clue who would phone her at two in the morning.

"Hello," she said, still half asleep. Her eyes were closed and her voice sounded drugged.

"Linette."

The connection wasn't good. Static buzzed and hissed over the wires.

"Linette, it's Cain."

Her eyes flew open then, and her heart kicked into double time. "Cain?" she cried, and sitting upright, she grabbed hold of the telephone receiver with both hands. "Where are you?"

"Some hellhole of a town in Central America. You'd think a country this size would know what a pay phone was. Never mind that. How are you?"

His voice faded in and out. "Fine," she said, louder this time. "What about you?"

"I'm fine. Don't sound so worried."

"Did you find . . ." She wanted to ask him about the American he'd told her about, the one who'd been kidnapped, but static erupted on the line.

"We found him. He was dead."

"Oh, no."

"Listen, I don't know how much longer this line will last."

"Cain, please, I need to talk to you." She was shouting, frantic for him to listen to her.

More static, this time so loud and discordant, Linette was forced to hold the phone away from her ear.

"Cain," she cried, afraid the line had been disconnected.

"Can you hear me?" His voice faded again.

"Only a little."

"I'm flying directly from here to San Francisco. I should land—"

"No," she cried. This wasn't how she intended to tell him, but she couldn't have him rush to her, believing she'd be waiting for him with open arms. For the thousandth time she cursed herself for not having the strength to tell him face-to-face before he'd left.

Static again.

"Linette?"

"I didn't know if you were alive or dead," she said, angry now.

"I know, baby, I'm sorry. Dear Lord, I've missed you. I promise to make it up to you."

"Don't come," she shouted. "Stay away from me. Please, just stay away. I don't want to see you again."

"You don't mean that."

"I do. I'm dating Charles now. It's over between you and me, understand?"

"Linette—"

The phone went dead. Linette stared at the phone, not knowing if Cain had hung up on her or if the connection had been cut. It didn't matter. She'd said all she wanted.

Slowly she replaced the receiver. Her hands trembled as she brushed the hair out of her face. Lying back down, she gathered the blankets around her and hugged the spare pillow, burying her face in its softness.

It was over.

"ANOTHER beer?" Mallory asked Cain.

"Sure. You buying?"

"Yeah." Mallory raised his hand to attract the bartender's attention. It was a seedy place in a bad part of town, where the music was slow and the women fast. Frankly, Mallory didn't care about either. As long as the beer was cold he didn't give a damn.

"You haven't had much to say," Mallory commented. He noticed Cain had been withdrawn ever since he'd returned from the last mission.

"You don't seem to be much of a conversationalist yourself."

"I've got an excuse."

"Excuse?"

"I'm walking, aren't I? It takes a lot of concentration to put one foot in front of the other."

Cain smiled, but the amusement didn't reach his eyes.

The bartender set two bottles of beer on the counter.

Mallory paid him, and the old guy drifted down to the other end of the long bar to talk to the cocktail waitress. Mallory glanced at the buxom blonde, and his stomach clenched. With a few minor changes—all right, major changes—in her appearance the woman could have been Francine.

Mallory didn't want to think about the therapist. Instead he turned to his friend. "Tell me about Paul Curnyn."

"There isn't much to say. My guess is that he was killed the first couple of days after he was kidnapped."

"Did they torture him?"

"It looked that way."

"The bastards."

"My sentiments exactly," Cain muttered. He raised the beer bottle to his lips and hesitated when the cocktail waitress came into view.

Mallory watched as the blonde's gaze connected with Cain's. He'd seen the look before.

"You've got an admirer," Mallory whispered. "You interested?"

"Maybe." Cain tipped the beer bottle and took a deep swallow. "If I don't want her, maybe I could talk her into trying her luck with you."

Mallory laughed. "I'll do my own talking."

"You interested?"

Mallory had to think about that. It had been a good long while since he'd had a woman. He should be frothing at the mouth, but he wasn't. It was all he could do to pretend.

"You can have her."

Cain turned and studied him. "Does this have anything to do with Francine Holden?"

"No," Mallory snapped. "It doesn't have a damn thing to do with anything."

Cain's eyebrows arched. "What happened between the two of you, anyway?"

Mallory sighed and rubbed his jaw. "If you must know, not a damn thing."

"But I thought—"

"It didn't happen."

"Why not?"

Mallory slapped his beer bottle onto the surface of the bar with enough force for it to make a loud clanking sound. Both the bartender and the cocktail waitress stared at him.

"She went off on the fact I wasn't offering her a gold ring and a house with a white picket fence." He paused and frowned. "I'm telling you right now, this is the last time I have anything to do with a virgin."

"So you won't be seeing her again?"

Mallory downed half his beer. "Hell will freeze over first."

Cain was silent for several moments. "Women are nothing but trouble."

"Ain't that the truth." Cain wasn't going to get an argument out of him.

Mallory studied his friend closely. Something was troubling McClellan, and had been ever since he'd returned. Whatever it was, Cain had kept it to himself.

"Are you sure you don't want the waitress?" Tim asked. She wasn't half bad looking, and with his eyes closed he could pretend she was Francine.

"I'm sure," Cain answered after what seemed a long time.

"Maybe we're being hasty here. We're both healthy,

strong American men with time on our hands and a
pocket full of coins going to waste. She looks like the
type who wouldn't mind letting us both sample her
wares."

Cain laughed softly. "Sorry, I'm not interested."

As a matter of fact, neither was Mallory.

12 🙐

I don't know what your problem is, Mallory, but whatever it is, fix it. I'm not taking any more of your bull." With that Jack Keller slammed out of the office.

Cain stood up and walked over to the door. Mallory sat at a desk in the room across the hallway from Cain's. He crumpled up the sheet of paper and tossed it toward the wastepaper basket. His aim was off, and the paper fell to the floor. Apparently Mallory had lost his touch, because several bunched-up papers circled the garbage container.

For two months Cain had stood by silently and watched what was happening to his old friend. He felt useless to help. Mallory was bored and restless, cranky and uncommunicative. Each man in Deliverance Company had wrangled with him over one point or another in the last few weeks.

Cain made it a policy not to become involved in squabbles between his men, unless they interfered with their work. Thus far, all Mallory had accomplished was to make himself the least popular team member. It was almost as if he wanted to give Cain an excuse to fire him.

Until now, Cain had been patient, perhaps more than he should have been. He knew the source of the mercenary's trouble was a certain physical therapist. Cain had given his friend extra slack, but unfortunately Mallory had used it to fashion a noose around his own throat. Something had to be said, and unfortunately he was the one who'd have to say it.

He'd bide his time, Cain decided, closing his office door and returning to his desk, wait until Mallory's temper had cooled, and then they'd sit down and clear the air, man to man.

Problem was, he admitted as he took his seat, he could appreciate Mallory's problem since he suffered a similar fate himself.

It had been three months since he'd last seen Linette. He'd spent countless hours convincing himself to stay out of her life. The problem was he was a selfish bastard. He derived little satisfaction from being noble. little consolation for stepping aside so she could date Mr. Perfect Attorney and smother a couple of motherless boys with a heart full of attention.

As it was, he wasted far too much time thinking about Linette. He wasn't a man who knew much about love. For most of his life he thought himself incapable of the emotion. Now he wasn't so sure.

Linette didn't want to see him again. She'd begged him to leave her alone. Cain had no option but to comply. He couldn't love her and bring worry and pain into her life. She'd suffered enough.

In reviewing his time with her, however brief, he

sought some way to thank her, some way of letting her know that in his own way he cared deeply for her. If the emotion had a name, it was probably love, although he found it difficult to admit that even to himself.

The answer came to him one afternoon as he looked through the papers in his safety deposit box. Soon afterward he contacted his attorney and had his will changed.

When he died, Linette Collins would become a wealthy woman. Cain had invested his money wisely. Other than the Montana cattle ranch, he owned several apartment buildings, plus a house in the Caribbean. With the aid of a financial adviser, he'd accumulated a fortune in stocks and bonds.

Money meant little or nothing to him. As a young man it had been everything. No longer. If he believed Linette would accept it, Cain would give everything to her now. He didn't need anything. Except her, and she was lost to him.

A knock sounded. Mallory opened the door and stuck in his head. "Have you got a minute?"

"Sure." Cain gestured toward a vacant chair.

Mallory came into the office, closed the door, and ambled toward him. He limped, but it was barely noticeable.

A team of surgeons had told Cain that Mallory's chances of walking again were less than fifty-fifty. If the injured man did manage to walk, he'd require the assistance of either a walker or a cane.

Mallory, with Francine Holden's help, required neither.

He sank onto the chair across from Cain. Although Mallory's health had vastly improved in the last six months, he was discontented. His color was good and he'd regained his strength, but he was as listless and un-happy as he'd been when confined to a wheelchair.

"You have something on your mind?" Cain asked.

Mallory snickered. "You might say that. It seems I've been something of a bastard lately."

"Seems that way." Cain wasn't going to lie. "Do you want to talk about it?"

Mallory leaned back on the chair and rubbed his eyes. "I'm not sure it'll do any good."

"Give it a shot," Cain advised.

Mallory straightened, leaned forward, and pressed his elbows to his knees. "I've lost it."

"Lost what?"

"Whatever it was that made me a good soldier. I thought once I returned to the compound with you and the others it would all come back. At first I assumed it was because I was gunshy, but it's more than that.

"When it comes right down to it, I don't want to do this anymore. My heart's just not in it."

Cain's first instinct was to argue. Mallory hadn't given himself near enough time. He'd been back to the compound for less than two months, not nearly enough time to make this kind of drastic decision.

Cain would have put up an argument if Mallory hadn't used the word *heart*. *My heart's just not in it.* Mallory's heart, Cain strongly suspected, was back in San Francisco with a feisty physical therapist.

"What are you going to do with yourself?" Cain asked, and restrained himself from reminding Mallory that he had yet to participate in a mission. One good rescue could change everything. Then again, involving Mallory in a mission, with his current attitude, might jeopardize them all.

"I don't know what I'll do. At least I haven't made a firm decision."

"But you've been thinking about it."

"Some," Mallory admitted hesitantly. "Several years back I bought a ten-acre spread on Vashon Island in Washington State. It's a beautiful piece of property on a hill overlooking Puget Sound. The only way off the island is by boat or plane, so it has a rustic appeal. You might think I'm going a little crazy, but I've been toying with the idea of raising llamas."

"Llamas?" Cain swallowed his surprise. "You mean those South American creatures with long necks? Don't they look like a sheep on stilts?" Mallory playing nursemaid to a bunch of cantankerous billy goat types! The picture just didn't fit.

Mallory chuckled. "Those are the ones. I've served my time, Cain. I always said I'd soldier until I got tired of it. I never thought it'd happen, but it has. I want out."

Cain had always been uncomfortable with sentiment. He didn't want to lose Mallory. They'd been friends, good friends. Mallory had covered his backside on more than one occasion. But caring deeply about someone, whether it was Mallory or Linette, meant giving that person the freedom to walk away. It seemed he was going to be asked to do it a second time in as many months.

"You can't tell me the others will be sorry to see me go," Mallory said with a soft, mocking laugh.

"I'll be sorry," Cain admitted hoarsely. "When do you intend to leave?"

"If you have no objection, I'd like to go as soon as I can arrange a flight."

Reluctantly Cain nodded. He stood, walked around

his desk, and offered Mallory his hand. The other man stood, gripped Cain's shoulders, and hugged him tight.

Neither spoke for several moments. Cain sat back down at his desk, unwilling to watch another person walk out of his life. Unwilling to say good-bye again.

"One thing more," Mallory said when he reached the door.

"Anything."

"I never thanked you for saving my sorry ass. I owe you, McClellan. Someday I might be able to repay the favor."

$\mathcal{I}$T was another one of those days when nothing seemed to go right. Francine's car had been stopped in heavy traffic because of an accident a mile away. Although she'd given herself plenty of time, there was nothing she could do but sit and wait as the frustrating minutes ticked endlessly by. Just when the road cleared and cars started to move again, she heard the distinctive thump-thump-thump of her wheel.

She had a flat tire.

By the time she'd arrived for the interview, she was thirty minutes late and so flustered she was sure the agency would never hire her. She didn't blame them.

Her mother had told her that if it was meant to be, Tim would return to her. In two months it hadn't happened. As for the decision she'd made not to sleep with him, well, she'd vacillated back and forth on that. One day she regretted having cheated herself out of the experience. The next day, like clockwork, she was convinced beyond any doubt that she'd made a prudent choice. If she'd given her body to Tim, she would have set herself up for a lose-lose situation. She'd done the smart thing.

Depending on the day, she was either a frustrated virgin or a wise and discerning woman.

Today she was a little of both. She was thirty-six years old and sick to death of waiting for her life to start. Sick to death of well-meaning friends and family smothering her with advice. So she was looking to make a change. A new job, a new city, a new circle of friends.

Her mother claimed she sought a geographical cure, and Francine suspected her parent was right. But a cure was a cure, and she was desperate.

The doorbell rang, and Francine cast an irritated glance in the direction of her living room. Word had circulated among her brothers about her imminent move. Twice now one of her younger siblings had made an effort to persuade her to stay in California.

After the rotten day she'd had, Francine didn't have the patience to sit through yet another "don't do anything rash" lecture.

She was all prepared to make some flimsy excuse—washing her hair or something equally stupid—when she opened the door.

She didn't get the chance. Her mouth froze in a half-open position. Her heart stopped cold, then jolted back, beating hard and quick.

Tim Mallory stood on the other side of the screen door, bigger than life. He was taller than she remembered and as handsome as the devil himself.

His eyes met hers, as daring and reckless as his smile.

"Tim." His name was little more than a wisp of breath. For one desperate moment she was convinced he was a figment of her imagination. Until he spoke.

"Hello, sweetheart."

"No one calls me that," she reminded him emotionally.

"I do," he told her. "I intend to for the rest of our lives." With that he opened the screen door and with a rough groan hauled her into his arms.

Francine buried her face in his neck and wrapped her arms tightly around him. His breath fell unevenly against the side of her face, as if he'd traveled a long way to reach her. As if a knot of emotion had blocked his lungs from breathing properly.

If there were words to be spoken, it wouldn't happen then. The pure, unadulterated pleasure of holding each other took precedence.

Francine didn't know how long they clung to one another. When her head cleared enough for her to think, she asked, "What are you doing here?"

"I'll explain later," he said tenderly. She felt his gaze like a warm caress and knew he intended to kiss her.

She intended to let him. Smiling up at him, she noticed how dark his eyes were and how full of promise.

"I'm serious. What are you—"

His mouth brushed hers.

It was a struggle not to surrender then and there. Surely he wouldn't be so cruel as to walk back into her life only to leave again.

"We've already been through this once before. Don't play with me, Tim Mallory."

His mouth was poised over hers, and just before he claimed her lips, he whispered, "Ah, sweetheart, that's exactly what I intend to do, for a very long time."

Her resolve melted away.

Tim led her to the sofa and sat her down, then joined her.

"Can we talk now?" she asked.

"In a minute," he promised. He wrapped his arms

around her and directed her mouth back to his. While his lips worked over hers, he pulled her blouse free and expertly unfastened the small buttons.

"Tim." Her protest was weak.

"Let me look at you," he said. "I've dreamed of this, Francine, of watching your eyes."

"This is all fine and dandy, but—"

"You want to know my intentions."

It was an old-fashioned way of putting it, but basically he had it right. "Yes." She swallowed tightly. "Are you here on some mission? Here today, gone tomorrow?"

"Something like that."

Her heart sank like a concrete brick. "I see. And you thought you'd drop by with your case of condoms and put them to good use while you're in town. No use letting them go to waste, is there, when you can seduce me into giving you what you want?"

His grin was as broad as the Grand Canyon. "We're going to use that case, dahlin'. Every last one of them."

This was the classic example of how dangerous love could be. He knew how empty she'd felt, how she'd suffered the last weeks without him. He was all too aware of her loneliness.

She covered her face with her hands. "Just go, Tim Mallory."

"Go?" He sounded shocked.

"Yes. Before I throw you out." She'd be roasted over a barbecue before she'd allow this man to toy with her heart one more time.

He looked confused and uncertain, then laughed and said, "You and what army?"

She didn't have an answer for him.

"It's going to take a hell of a lot more than a threat to

keep me away from you. I made a mistake leaving you the first time. I'm not going to repeat it."

"A mistake?"

"I've come to finish what we started," he told her.

"So you think you can sweet-talk me into your bed."

"I'm sure gonna try," he said, grinning broadly once more.

"Tell me one good reason why I should let you make love to me," she said, crossing her arms, steeling herself.

His eyes glinted as if he looked forward to the challenge. "I'm crazy about you."

Francine laughed without humor. "My current patient is crazy about me, too, but I wouldn't sleep with him."

"Him?" Tim's eyes narrowed.

"His name's Peter McWilliams, and he's eight."

Tim leaned back and braced his ankle over his knee. "You're right. Being crazy doesn't count." He inhaled a deep breath as though this would aid the thinking process. "I could tell you I loved you." He exhaled in a long-drawn-out breath. "All right, if you must know, I do love you."

"Just how much do you know about love?"

"You mean I have to bring references?"

"Don't be ridiculous."

He tipped back his head. "How do I love you?" He pointed his index finger toward the ceiling. "Let me count the ways. One. I'm here, aren't I? Two. I love you enough to resign my position from Deliverance Company. Three . . ." He paused and studied her. "I hoped one and two would convince you."

Her heart started to pound faster, but she wasn't sure yet if she should trust him. "Resign from Deliverance

Company? For how long?" she asked, her voice barely above a whisper.

"Forever. But there's a condition."

"Condition?"

"Yeah. Soldiering's the only thing I know. If I'm going to give it up, then I'm going to need something to keep my hands occupied." He pointedly examined her breasts.

"Tim!"

His laugh was full and rowdy.

Embarrassed, Francine quickly adjusted her clothing.

"I believe I have the answer."

Once again her heart filled with eager anticipation.

"Llamas."

Her shoulders sank, and so did her spirits.

"Believe it or not, I'm fairly good at this sort of thing. I've got a green thumb and a certain way with animals. It seems to me that if I'm going to take on this project, it wouldn't hurt to throw in a wife and a couple of babies."

Francine wondered if she dared believe what she heard. "A wife?"

"Only one."

"That's a smart idea."

"I could always move to one of the Arab countries and take on two or three. However, the wife I have in mind is sure to demand all my time and attention."

"Are you toying with me again?" she asked, not sure she could bear it if he was.

The teasing light left his eyes. "No, Francine." He reached for her hand and clasped it between his own much larger ones.

"I've never asked a woman to marry me before. I'm

not entirely sure how these things are done." He scooted off the sofa and knelt down on one knee in front of her. Slowly he raised his eyes to meet hers. "I love you, Francine Holden. There's no one I want more than you in my life. Would you do me the supreme honor of being my wife?"

She would have answered him with words if her throat hadn't been suddenly blocked shut. Instead she nodded repeatedly.

"Is that a yes?"

"Yes." The lone word squeezed through the tightness in her throat, high-pitched and discordant.

As if he were looking for something, Tim patted his pockets. Francine was sure he was searching for a ring. "You bought me a ring?" she asked, so excited that it was difficult to think coherently.

His eyes grew big and round. "I was supposed to buy you a ring? I have the feeling a wife is going to be expensive."

"No, it doesn't matter," she was quick to assure him, sorry now that she'd said anything.

"As it happens, I do have one with me." Having said that, he withdrew from his coat pocket the most exquisite solitaire diamond she'd ever seen. "I hope it fits. I don't think Cracker Jack will size it."

Francine hugged his head. Tim buried his face between her breasts. "A man could get used to this." Unexpectedly he pushed her back against the sofa and kissed her with a desire so hot, it sizzled.

"When are you going to make love to me, Tim Mallory?" she whispered, and spread a row of nibbling kisses along the underside of his jaw. "Might I suggest right now?"

Tim tensed, inhaled sharply, and raised his head. "Don't ask me why I feel it's important, but if you don't object, I'd like to wait until after we're married."

After weeks of chasing her, teasing her, tempting her into his bed, he wanted to wait until after the wedding! "You're joking?"

He shook his head. "I want everything to be right for you, Francine."

She remembered what her mother had told her about her father, and she nodded. If she'd ever needed confirmation that he did indeed love her, this was it.

"We've waited this long. What's another few days?"

"A few days?" she cried. "Why, that's impossible—" She stopped abruptly. Only a fool would argue with a man she loved when he wanted to marry her. "Then again, I might be able to arrange it."

"Good." He wrapped his arms around her waist. "Don't take time buying a trousseau, either. You won't be needing many clothes."

Francine threw back her head and laughed. "Llamas?" she questioned.

"Llamas," he repeated, "and a couple of kids, the human variety."

SOMETHING wasn't right. Cain could feel it in his bones as clearly now as the day Mallory stepped on the land mine. The threat of danger swirled around him, clinging to his skin in the humid jungle heat. The thick foliage crawled with vermin and fear.

Word had come a week earlier that Carl Lindman, a captured CEO from a major American conglomerate, would be transported that afternoon from one location to another. The informant had been reliable before, but that didn't mean Cain trusted him. The man would sell his children for a snort of cocaine.

Cain and his men had carefully planned the ambush, and Deliverance Company were positioned in several key locations.

The waiting was always hard, especially in the jungle heat. Nervous. Ready. Uncomfortable. It was times like these, when the minutes dragged and the humidity clung to him like a second skin, that Cain fought to banish the image of a beautiful young widow from his thoughts. She was a world away from him, a world that consisted of more than just time and distance.

The distinct whopping sound of an approaching helicopter could be heard faintly in the distance. Cain and his men were camouflaged by brush and verdant growth, so there was virtually no chance the men aboard the helicopter would see them.

The sound of the chopper intensified to deafening proportions. After surveying the area, the pilot settled into the clearing as gently as if a mother were tucking her infant in a bassinet.

Two men toting Uzis leapt onto the jungle floor, their weapons poised and ready. Their gazes scanned the area, looking for anything out of the ordinary.

The two were sloppy, Cain noticed, and was grateful.

The team of men scheduled to rendezvous with the chopper wouldn't be coming. But these guys didn't know that.

Lindman was half dragged, half shoved out of the chopper. It was for this moment that Cain and his men had been waiting.

Another man climbed out of the chopper. He was clean, suave, and clearly disgruntled by the delay. Cain didn't recognize him, but that pretty face of his could have been displayed on a boy-toy calendar.

When Cain gave the signal, his men rose from their positions and attacked. Weapons were fired in rapid succession. The rat-a-tat sounds burst into the serenity of the jungle.

The CEO, not understanding what was happening, hunched his shoulders and whirled around like a top. Cain screamed for the man to hit the ground. The sound of his voice must have reached through Lindman's panic because the CEO dropped face first to the jungle floor.

However, in instructing Lindman, Cain gave away his position. The two men with the Uzis, protected now by the belly of the chopper, trained their weapons on him. The ground around Cain was sprayed with bullets.

Cain returned the fire, rolling over and over, the roar of his own weapon bursting like firecrackers in his ears. He took out the first soldier and heard Pretty Boy scream. Murphy got the second.

The blades picked up speed slowly. Pretty Boy leapt inside, firing crazily as he went. As soon as he was on board, the chopper lifted from the ground. Elevated no more than a few feet, the gunman scanned the ground with the tip of his weapon, looking for his captive. If Cain didn't act fast, Lindman would soon be dead.

Rearing back on his haunches and siting his weapon, Cain fired into the opening of the helicopter. His first shot went wild.

Distracted by the sudden burst of gunfire, Pretty Boy lifted his weapon and fired at Cain.

The bullet hit him. The force of it propelled him backward, knocking him to the ground. Blood gushed down his face and soaked through his clothes. Cain felt nothing. No pain. No stinging. No fear.

The chopper was gone, and Cain stared into the deep blue sky. He placed his hand over his head and felt the blood pump against his palm.

"McClellan." Murphy was at his side. "Take it easy, man. Take it easy. You're going to be all right."

"Crap." This was Jack, ever eloquent. He certainly had a way with words.

"He's going to be fine." Murphy again, with a complete lack of conviction.

Bailey was the last one to arrive with Unit One, the first-aid bag. Not that there was anything anyone would be able to do.

"You're going to make it," Murphy assured him again.

"Liar," Cain murmured, and closed his eyes. He was going to die out here in this godforsaken jungle. He didn't want the last thing he saw to be the anxious faces of his friends.

Instead he concentrated on Linette. He pictured her standing on the end of the pier at Fisherman's Wharf, the wind tousling her hair, her eyes bright as she smiled at him. He could almost hear the sound of her laughter, and he found it more lovely than a song.

He coughed, and pain seared through him like a white-hot poker. His breathing became shallow and difficult, and it seemed that his heart labored with each beat.

"Cain." The voice sounded as if it came from the inside of a tunnel.

He struggled to open his eyes but couldn't make them do anything more than flutter. "Linette," he said.

"He's asking for someone."

"Lynn Something or other? Who's that?"

"Hell if I know."

Consciousness began to fade, but Cain hadn't the strength to cling to it. He hadn't the will to fight any longer. Hadn't any reason to live.

$\mathcal{L}$INETTE was busy baking chocolate-chip cookies for Jesse and Steve's visit when her doorbell chimed. She checked her watch, thinking it might be Charles. If so, he was several hours early.

She opened the door to one of the largest men she could ever remember seeing. He must have stood six five and had shoulders as broad as a Mack truck. Although he was large, she didn't find him intimidating. He appeared equally curious about her and seemed to be trying to place her. He didn't say anything for a couple of moments.

"Can I help you?" she asked.

"Are you Linette Collins?"

"Yes."

"You don't know me. My name's Tim Mallory, and I'm a friend of Cain McClellan."

Linette could think of only one reason one of Cain's men would come to visit her. Something had happened to Cain.

"Please come in," she said, and realized her voice trembled.

Tim stepped inside her living room, holding himself stiffly.

"Would you like to sit down?" She gestured toward the davenport.

"Thank you."

They both sat, one across from the other. Both nervous and struggling to hide it. Tim planted his hands on his knees and cleared his throat. "I hope I'm not intruding."

"No," she said nervously. "Not at all." Then, gathering her courage, she continued, speaking so fast that the words ran together. "What's happened to Cain?"

Tim lowered his head.

"Is he dead? Please, just tell me if he's dead."

"I'm sorry, ma'am. I shouldn't have come here like this without warning. It's just that Murphy and the others didn't know about you. Apparently Cain never mentioned you."

"How'd you find me?"

"Cain left instructions that if anything ever happened to him, you were to be contacted. Your name and address are listed in his will. He must have had it revised recently.

"Keller found a copy of it in the mail when he arrived back from South America."

The room swayed. "Oh, dear God."

"Ma'am? . . . Ma'am, are you all right? . . . Damn, I knew I should've brought Francine with me."

13 🎋

"C an I get you anything? Water?" The big man leapt to his feet and headed toward the kitchen.

A terrible tightness gripped her chest and heart. "How did it happen?" she asked, her voice a thin, emotionless thread of sound.

"During a rescue." Tim held a half-filled glass in his hand. A wide swath of water followed him out from the kitchen.

Linette closed her eyes and bit into her lower lip.

"Do you want me to get you something more? Aspirin?" Mallory suggested awkwardly. "I really should have brought my fiancée. As you can see, I'm not much good at this sort of thing."

"I'll be fine," Linette whispered in an effort to relieve his distress.

"I knew you'd be upset. I figured you'd want to know. Cain would want you to know. He listed you as his beneficiary. It's obvious he holds strong feelings for you." Cain's friend wiped his face. "Francine suggested I come and tell you personally rather than have someone phone."

"I appreciate your letting me know."

"If you want, I can make arrangements for someone to meet you in Grenada."

"Grenada?"

"That's where Cain is now. The backup medical team stabilized him in Venezuela—"

Linette's eyes flew open. "Stabilized him?"

Mallory nodded. "They were able to med-evac him to Grenada. Be assured he's getting absolutely the best medical attention available. Of course, he's listed in critical condition, and has been for several days, but—"

"He's alive?" Had her ears deceived her? Linette feared she was so desperate to believe Cain had survived that her mind was playing her for a fool.

"Yes, of course he's alive. You thought . . . you mean to say you thought he was dead? Hell, I'm sorry. I guess I was trying so hard to protect you from the bad news that I led you to think worse."

"But his will . . ."

"That's where we got your name and address. Murphy said Cain whispered your name just before he lost consciousness. When he called to tell me Cain'd been shot, he asked if I knew anything about you."

"I see."

"Believe me, I couldn't be more sorry."

She shook her head, her relief so great that it was all she could do not to hurl herself into his arms and thank him. "I assumed he was dead."

"No wonder, me talking about wills and all."

"What happened?" she asked in a rush, all at once, needing to know. She felt euphoric and struggled to hold back the sudden need to laugh. The sudden need to cry.

"Not being there myself, I can't really say. When I talked to Murphy and Jack, they only gave me sketchy details, other than . . ."

"Yes," she coaxed.

"They said Cain put himself in the line of fire in order to save someone else."

Cain close to death. Cain dying alone in a foreign hospital. All at once Linette was tired. Tired of pretending she didn't love him. Tired of fearing the worst. Tired of insulating her heart.

"You can arrange a flight for me to Grenada," she said, her voice gaining conviction. "When?"

"There's one leaving this evening."

"I'll take it."

"How'd it go?" Francine met Tim at the front door of her parents' house. He'd been nervous about meeting Linette Collins and telling her of Cain's mishap.

Tim pulled her into his arms and kissed her. "I wish you'd gone with me," he said. "I'm afraid I made everything sound much worse than it is."

"Sound worse? It doesn't get much worse than this. From what Murphy said, Cain's holding on to his life by a thread."

"He'll live," Tim said with such confidence that Francine eased her head back to meet his eyes.

"How can you be so sure?"

"He's made it this far, hasn't he?"

"Yes, but that's no guarantee." Although Tim had trouble expressing his emotions, Francine knew he was thoroughly shaken by Cain's injury. She feared he was painting a rosy picture in his mind of his friend's condition rather than dealing with harsh reality.

"Linette's flying into Grenada this evening. She'll give him the incentive he needs to stay alive," Tim said matter-of-factly.

Francine walked into the kitchen and poured herself a glass of iced tea. She noticed when she lifted the pitcher that her hand shook. She set it down with a clunk and closed her eyes before voicing the concerns that plagued her. "Are you sorry you weren't with him when it happened?" she asked, doing her best to keep her voice even and detached. "Do you think if you'd been there, things might have turned out differently?"

Tim stepped behind her and cupped her shoulders, his touch gentle and reassuring. "I don't have any regrets, if that's what you're asking me. That portion of my life is over. I'll never go back to soldiering."

Francine trembled with relief. "Don't say it if you don't mean it. That would be even more cruel than to marry me and then leave me."

Tenderly he kissed the side of her neck. "I wouldn't have asked you to be my wife if I wasn't sure about this."

The kitchen door opened and Francine's mother walked into the room, her arms full with two bags of groceries.

"Timothy Mallory, what are you doing here?" she demanded. "Tradition says you're not supposed to see the bride the day of the wedding."

"But the ceremony isn't for hours yet," he protested as if staying away from Francine were too much to ask of him. "You can't expect me to wait that long."

"Of course I do. Shoo. We've got a million things to

do before this evening." Martha Holden all but booted him out of the room.

Tim cast Francine a pleading glance on his way out the door.

"Really, Mom," she protested on his behalf. "Don't you think you're going to extremes?"

"Perhaps. But that's my prerogative as his future mother-in-law. I take my duty as mother of the bride seriously." She laughed, her eyes gleaming with pride and happiness.

"You like Tim, don't you?"

"You love him. That's enough for me, but as it happens, I find him endearing. He reminds me a good deal of your father years ago. He's got that same brash nature, with an appreciation for the mischievous. You're going to be happy with this man, Francine. I couldn't have chosen a husband better suited to you had I gone out and searched myself."

Francine unloaded the first grocery sack. "I love him so much. I've been so afraid, ever since Murphy phoned with the news about Cain McClellan."

"Afraid?"

Francine nodded. "I worried that Tim would somehow feel responsible for what happened. That his being there might have changed everything."

"So that was what you were talking about when I interrupted you."

"I was afraid to bring up the subject until now, then I decided I had to know. If Tim did feel that way, I don't know what I would have done."

"Does he?" her mother asked gently.

Francine shook her head. "He assured me that part of

his life is over. He means it, Mom. He really means it. I'm not a passing fancy to him, he honestly loves me."

"He had the chance to learn that on his own," her mother said gently. "He's confident in his decision. But he might not have been that way had you pressured him into not going back to Florida. My heart ached for you when he left."

"But he came back, Mom, and this time he's going to stay."

Knowing Tim was truly hers went through her mind as Francine walked down the aisle on her father's arm later that evening.

The wedding was a simple affair, held in the church Francine had attended from the time she was a toddler. Her immediate family was there, along with several aunts, uncles, cousins, and longtime family friends. It amazed Francine that her mother had been able to arrange a wedding on such short notice.

Her wedding gown was made of antique white satin with a lace-and-pearl overlay. When she first saw Tim in his black tuxedo with tails, she didn't recognize him. But when he winked and pointed to the jacket pocket, she knew it could be no other. He'd carried a condom with him to his own wedding.

Francine was sure her face turned a bright, fire-engine red.

When they spoke their vows, Tim's voice boomed proudly as he pledged his life to hers. Apparently he felt he needed to convince her family of his sincerity by shouting out his promises. Francine's own voice trembled with emotion and love.

The reception followed in the church hall. Her sisters-in-law stood ready to serve the cake and punch. The lace-covered table was stacked with an array of beauti-fully wrapped gifts. Francine was touched by such an abundant display of generosity, and Tim, too, repeatedly asked if all those gifts could possibly be for them.

"How soon can we escape?" her husband asked out of the corner of his mouth.

They'd barely arrived, and the reception line was just now getting started.

"Not yet," she whispered, flustered by his question.

"This condom is burning a hole in my pocket," he said as Francine's eighty-year-old great-aunt approached. Fortunately Aunt Emma was hard of hearing.

"Tim!" Francine said.

"It's the truth," he muttered.

"I'm eager, too," she assured him, and introduced him to Aunt Emma.

It didn't take long for her family and friends to pro-gress through the line. Afterward, Francine hurried the cake-cutting ceremony.

Before she knew where the time had gone, they'd ar-rived at the hotel. Tim carried her into the plush suite at the St. Francis in the heart of San Francisco. Instead of putting her down after crossing the threshold, as she expected, he went into each of the three rooms, giving her a walking tour. Only he was the one who did the walking.

He made her feel that she weighed no more than a bird, and she fretted about his bad leg. He silenced her worries with one deep kiss.

He had a bottle of French champagne on ice, and af-ter laying her on top of the king-size mattress, he ex-pertly opened the bottle.

He poured them each a glass, insisted she drink from

his goblet, and when some dribbled down her chin, licked it from her face. His mouth trailed the slim column of her neck, dipping at the hollow of her throat.

Francine rolled back her head and sighed. Already she felt dizzy, and it wasn't from her one sip of champagne, either.

"Tim."

"Humm?"

"Make love to me."

"I am."

"I mean really make love to me."

He paused and lifted his head to look her in the eye. "You mean you're ready now?"

She laughed softly. "In case you hadn't noticed, I've been ready for weeks."

"But what about dinner? I thought we'd order room service."

"We will," she promised, so much in love with her husband, she felt as if she were about to burst. "But later. Okay?"

He stood and shucked off his suit jacket so fast, it was still in the air by the time he'd pulled the shirt over his head. He carelessly flung the shirt aside. As if he'd been too long away from her, he knelt on the edge of the mattress and kissed her once more. If he feared she was about to change her mind, he had no reason to worry.

One kiss, and in that time she felt seduced and wooed and deeply cherished. Francine opened her mouth to him and kissed him back.

He broke off the kiss roughly and centered his attention on her neck, blazing a trail of hot kisses over her throat and back to the scented hollow.

"I intended to go much slower than this," he whispered, and Francine could hear the apprehension in his voice.

"Next time we'll go slow," she promised. She sat up and lifted her hands behind her back in an effort to unfasten the row of pearl buttons that stretched down the length of the wedding dress. Her hair, which she'd worn unplaited, continued to get in the way.

Tim walked on his knees across the mattress to assist her. Francine held her hair up and out of the way.

"I didn't know virgins were this red hot."

"Do you want me to be shy and retiring?"

"No," he muttered, cursing under his breath at the difficulty the buttons gave him. "This damned dress is worse than a chastity belt."

Francine giggled and reached for her wineglass, sipping champagne. "Want me to help you undress?" she asked.

"Not when it's going to take the two of us all night to get you out of this contraption."

Francine couldn't remember a time she'd been happier. "We can cut it off me."

He cursed again. "It might come to that."

He made progress, but it was agonizingly slow.

"I could always lift my skirts and let you have your way with me." With that she sighed dramatically.

"I've waited too long to get you in that position to be outsmarted by a blasted wedding dress. Who designed this thing, anyway? The Sisters of Perpetual Frustration?"

Francine smiled, and as he freed the bodice, she worked her arms free and peeled off the upper half. When he'd progressed sufficiently, she stood and slipped the material over her hips, letting the gown pool at her feet.

When she looked up, she found Tim staring at her.

"Is something wrong?" she asked.

"I had no idea a woman wore so many underthings. Are these going to be as difficult to remove?"

"Not at all." She proved it by stripping them off one by one with what she hoped was a maddening lack of haste. It gave her a certain pleasure to watch her husband's eyes widen with admiration.

Until she'd met Tim, Francine had always been self-conscious of her body. She was tall and thick waisted and built more like a lumberjack than a beauty queen. Yet Tim made her feel delicate and beautiful.

His eyes feasted on her. When she'd finished, he reached for her and took her back to the bed. She stood before him while he sat at the edge of the mattress. A slow smile brightened his features.

"How is it a woman so beautiful would ever marry a man like me?"

"You're just lucky, I guess," she told him, and reached for this man who was her husband.

CAIN felt as if he were lost in a tunnel of pain. Drugged pain. The agony was there, but not the white-hot, searing agony he'd experienced soon after being wounded. This pain was chilling. As cold as a grave.

The drugs smothered the worst of it. He didn't fight it—he hadn't the strength. Instead he waited impatiently for the angel of death to arrive. The will to resist was gone, the will to live tenuous.

"Cain?"

Linette's voice came to him on a cloud, sounding ethereal, celestial. An angel of life when he'd expected the Grim Reaper to come swooping down to claim his soul.

He struggled to open his eyes but discovered he hadn't the strength. Linette, here? It wasn't possible. Perhaps he was already dead and didn't realize it. But if that were the case, he didn't understand why he should continue to hurt this way. Was this hell, to be trapped within earshot of the woman he loved? Already he'd been cursed never to hold her or love her again. He was sentenced to hear her call to him from another world and helpless to respond. Cursed to love her until his heart felt as if it would burst wide open and be unable to give her the assurance of his caring.

Perhaps this was all some part of a drug-induced dream. He must be dreaming, and yet . . . and yet, he felt her hand pressed over his, heard her soft voice, trembling with anxiety.

He'd never mentioned Linette to any of the men of Deliverance Company. Not even Mallory. He'd wanted to protect her from who he was and what he did. She was honest and pure, and he didn't want to taint her goodness.

"Oh, Cain," Linette said breathily. She must be close, because he could feel her soft breath fan his face. "Listen carefully, my darling. I love you. I'm here."

With every ounce of strength he possessed, Cain tried to respond, but the effort quickly drained what reservoir of energy he possessed.

"I'm praying," Linette continued, her voice trembling with emotion, "that you'll feel my love for you. Feel it, Cain. Let it be your shelter."

His shelter.

It was as if he'd walked out of the freezing cold into a room with a fire burning in the fireplace.

"I'm sorry, miss, you'll have to leave now."

The authoritative female voice sounded from behind Linette. Cain tried to protest but once more found it impossible to so much as flutter his eyelids.

"So soon?" Linette protested.

"I'm sorry," the other woman said, sounding sympathetic. "But you can only spend five minutes every hour with your friend. Those are the rules."

To hell with the rules! Cain screamed in his mind. He needed Linette.

"I'll be back," Linette promised. Her lips brushed his brow, and her fingers squeezed his. "Just remember what I said," she whispered in parting. "Let my love be your shelter."

A crushing pain filled his chest when she walked away. The agony was familiar. This was how it had felt without love in his life. This emptiness. This loneliness.

Before he was aware of time passing, Linette was back.

"Hello, my darling," she whispered. She spoke to him in soothing tones, and he felt it again—the warmth he'd experienced when she'd first arrived. It was as though a heated blanket had been wrapped about his shoulders. Around his heart.

"I met your friends," she whispered. "They love you, too."

If he'd had the strength, Cain would have laughed out loud. He'd never thought of Murphy as the loving type. He was well aware his men respected him. Leave it to a woman to confuse regard with love.

"I'll be back soon," Linette promised.

He heard her footsteps against the floor as she walked out of the room. This time the warmth didn't go with her. It stayed, and for the first time since he'd been shot Cain realized he was going to live.

He knew this with a certainty he didn't question.

Linette was with him.

Linette loved him. He had a reason to fight.

14 🦎

*C*ain's men didn't like her. In the beginning, Linette thought it might have been her imagination, but the resentment was far too real to ignore. At times it seemed to come at her in waves, as though she were responsible for what had happened to their leader, their friend.

The man called Murphy was the worst. He acted as if she were an intruder. He made it plain that he didn't want her at the hospital. She could feel his indignation every time she returned from her hourly five minutes with Cain. Murphy seemed to believe he should be the one to linger at Cain's bedside. Yet when Linette had offered to let him visit Cain instead of her, he'd gruffly insisted she be the one.

"How's Cain doing?" Keller asked when she stepped back into the waiting area. She'd been in Grenada a week now. In that time Cain had revealed only a few visible signs of improvement. Linette celebrated each one. The doctors weren't making predictions on his chances of survival. They claimed Cain had hung on far longer than the experts had anticipated. If anyone would break the record, it would be him.

Those brief five-minute sessions with Cain drained Linette's energy. It was as if he demanded every ounce of strength she possessed, as though her being with him was what gave him the energy to live.

She frequently returned to the waiting area exhausted and literally collapsed onto the chair. More often than not, Murphy, Keller, or one of the other men would be waiting for her, eager for word of Cain's condition.

Although he hadn't spoken, Cain knew she was there. He'd squeezed her hand the day before, the action so weak that Linette had nearly wept. First with joy and relief and then with despair that he'd stepped so close to death's door—that she'd come so close to losing him.

"Cain's better, I think," she answered Keller's question. Of the men of Deliverance Company whom she'd met, Linette liked Keller the best. He was a no-nonsense sort of person, a little rough around the edges, with a hard-as-tacks exterior, but he cared deeply about Cain.

Keller—she never had learned any of the men's first names—was a pacer. In the week she'd been in Grenada, Linette had watched the gruff-looking man make deep grooves in the carpet with his constant pacing.

Murphy was the dark, silent type. Exactly why he didn't want her in Grenada Linette couldn't fathom. It was as if she were trespassing over territory he considered sacred.

"You think Cain's better?" Murphy's low voice mocked her. He looked her way, and his gaze narrowed with dislike he didn't bother to disguise.

"Have I done something to offend you?" Linette asked.

She hated confrontation, avoided it whenever possible, but she'd had about all she could take of this man's attitude.

"Not me, you haven't," Murphy returned.

"Who, then?"

"Cain."

"Cain?" Linette felt at a loss to understand this sullen man. "How have I hurt Cain?" If they were going to keep tabs, she could name a few infractions he'd committed against her, beginning with concealing the truth about himself.

"You messed up his head," Murphy said, glaring at her. "We all knew something wasn't right with Cain, and hasn't been for months. What we should have guessed was that it involved a woman."

"You can't blame me for what happened to Cain."

"You messed up his thinking," Murphy shot back. "Cain was willing to sacrifice his life, and now I know why. He couldn't think straight anymore."

Linette found she was shaking—not because of what Murphy told her; she'd guessed as much herself—but because she was tired and worried and afraid. Afraid what he said was true, that Cain had taken unnecessary chances because his mind had been on her instead of the mission.

"Lay off her," Keller snarled at Murphy. "Can't you see she's had about all she can take already?"

"See what I mean?" Murphy flared. "We barely know her, and already she's causing dissension between us. Women are nothing but trouble."

"You didn't have to tell me about Cain," Linette said, fast losing her patience. "I'd never have known if Tim Mallory hadn't contacted me."

"Mallory's a prime example of what a woman can do to ruin a decent fighting man."

"I beg your pardon?"

"It's true," Murphy insisted. "Mallory used to be one of us. He was as good a man as any I've known, then he had to go and fall in love. Look what's happened to him since." He rammed his fingers through his short hair and pinched his lips as if to bite back a curse.

"Within a week of his return to Deliverance Company, there wasn't a one of us could bear the sight of him. He was rude, cantankerous, and miserable, and all because of a woman."

Linette briefly remembered Tim Mallory mentioning his fiancée.

"From what I understand, Mallory's got a ring looped through his nose and is being led around some pasture in Washington State. Mallory married. I never thought I'd see the day."

"I heard he was raising llamas," Keller inserted, shaking his head in wonder.

"Llamas?" Murphy cried. From the way he said it, one would have thought his cohort had desecrated a national monument. The mercenary slapped his hands against his thighs. "I rest my case."

"It's not fair to blame Linette for what happened to Cain," Keller mumbled, not sounding any too sure.

"You're damn right I blame her." Murphy tossed Linette another of his menacing looks. "Now that I think about it, Cain hasn't been himself for a good long time. Next thing we know, he'll be applying for a regular job just so he can keep his sweetie-pie happy: Women and mercenaries simply don't mix."

"The nurse told me she thinks Cain's made a turn for

the better since Linette's arrival." It was Keller again, looking slightly embarrassed at Murphy's accusations.

"Who's to say that Linette had anything to do with it?" Murphy argued. "Cain's got the best medical team in the world working on him. You might credit the doctors."

"He was as good as dead, and we both know it."

The two men faced off, glaring at each other. "I say it was Linette," Keller returned heatedly.

"Please, don't," Linette pleaded. She placed herself between the two of them. Each man was many inches taller than her. Linette braced her hands against their chests, feeling a little like Samson between two giant pillars. Samson without hair, weakened and blind.

"The last thing you should be doing is fighting," she told them, struggling to remain calm herself.

"Then leave," Murphy told her.

"No," she returned evenly, although her heart was in turmoil.

"She has every right to stay if she wants," Keller insisted. "Cain needs her."

"The hell he does. Deliverance Company is Cain's life. He doesn't need anything more than that."

What Murphy said was true. The message had been delivered by Cain personally months earlier. "All right. All right, I'll leave," she said, shocking both men.

They diverted their attention to her. Keller's eyes were filled with what looked like disappointment, and Murphy's shone with intense satisfaction. He'd gotten what he wanted.

"But in my own time," she amended. "When I'm sure Cain will recover."

She'd leave, she decided, when her heart had the

strength to walk away from him. Again. But this would be the last time.

"When?" The question came from Murphy and was no surprise.

"Soon," she promised.

"Not soon enough," Murphy muttered, then turned and walked away.

CAIN sensed a difference in Linette. She was gentle and encouraging as always, yet it felt as if she were miles away emotionally. She'd erected a roadblock between the two of them. It wasn't what she said or how she behaved; it was mental, and it confused the hell out of him.

The effort demanded to open his mouth was beyond comprehension. Saying her name proved to be a test of sheer physical endurance. The lone word worked its way up his throat, catching on emotion and gratitude.

"L-in—ette."

"Cain?" Her voice elevated with joy. "I'm here." She lifted his hand to her lips and kissed his knuckles repeatedly. He felt moisture against the back of his hand and knew she wept silently.

He wanted to tell her so many things and struggled valiantly to remain conscious. No longer did the cold plague him. He was warm and comfortable and within minutes fighting the lull of sleep.

Days blended one into the other with barely a notice. Cain was able to calculate the time by which nurse was on duty. The older nurse with white hair and angel eyes worked the graveyard shift. The pert brunette was with him from three to eleven. One named Hazel who arrived early in his day. Days of the week were more difficult to figure.

None of it mattered as long as Linette was with him. Each day was a gift to be cherished.

Then, when he'd mastered the ability to remain conscious for more than three or four minutes at a time, Linette left him. It might have taken him some time to realize she was gone if it hadn't been for Murphy.

"Where's Linette?" he asked his friend.

"Gone."

Cain felt as though someone had knifed him. "Gone?"

"You don't need her."

"What made her go?" Cain demanded, his voice shockingly weak.

"She has responsibilities. It's better this way, don't you think?"

Cain rolled his head to one side, unwilling to answer. Better for whom? Him? Not likely. It would have been a kindness to let him die rather than nurse him back from the brink of death and then doom him to a fate of loneliness.

He hadn't asked her to come, Cain reminded himself. He wasn't entirely sure who had told her he'd been injured. Mallory, most likely, but how he ever found out about her, Cain couldn't guess.

"You don't need her," Murphy went on to say.

Once more Cain didn't respond.

"There's nothing like a woman to screw up a man's thinking. I'm right, aren't I?"

Cain forced a nod. He might as well admit the truth. Murphy was right. He'd proved he could make it without Linette, and she sure didn't need the likes of him.

"She's beautiful." Linette sat in Nancy's living room and gently cradled her sister-in-law's newborn baby daughter in her arms. A wealth of emotion filled her as she studied this perfect child. "Welcome, little Michelle," she whispered, her voice soft and low.

"We named her after Michael," Nancy said, studying Linette. Home from the hospital for only two days, the other woman looked fabulous. "You don't mind, do you?"

"Michael would be so pleased and proud," Linette whispered. "He'd consider it a great honor. I do, too." It came to Linette then how freely she could speak of her dead husband these days. Generally when his name cropped up, she experienced a sudden, crushing sense of loss. She wasn't sure when this had changed, but she was grateful.

With her index finger, Linette outlined Michelle's plump, pink face. The infant smelled of baby powder and summer and was precious beyond words. The love Linette experienced for this new life flooded her heart.

"Mom and Dad came to visit me while I was in the hospital," Nancy said casually, but it seemed to Linette that her sister-in-law was studying her, waiting for some response.

"I imagine they were thrilled to death with Michelle." Linette knew Nancy's relationship with her parents had been strained since the Christmas holidays. She hoped that this birth in their family would bridge their differences.

"They were very pleased we named her after Michael." Linette nodded. That much was understood.

"They asked about you," Nancy said. "They wanted to know if you were still involved with Cain."

"What did you tell them?" It grieved Linette that her last meeting with Michael's parents had ended so badly.

"I thought you were dating Charles Garner, but when I called to tell you about the baby, Bonnie told me you were on some Caribbean island, and that Cain McClellan had been badly injured."

"I was with Cain," she admitted reluctantly. "It didn't look like he was going to live."

"I see."

Perhaps Nancy did. At their last conversation, Linette had claimed it was over between her and Cain and that she was dating someone else.

Charles. If she were suffering regrets, it was over her brief relationship with the attorney. She hadn't phoned him since her return, and she wouldn't now. Their last conversation had gone poorly. She'd tried to explain why she was leaving for Grenada so abruptly. She'd told him about Cain's injuries and that it was a matter of life and death.

Charles had grown cold and angry and insisted she stay in San Francisco. Linette had never seen this side of him and pointed out that he had no right to demand anything of her. He'd called her a fool, and perhaps she was, but then so be it. She refused to allow him to make decisions for her.

Later, when she'd had time to think over their heated conversation, Linette decided it was best not to see Charles again. Clearly he expected more from her than she was willing to give.

"What about Charles?" Nancy asked, disrupting Linette's thoughts.

Linette answered with a short shake of her head.

"But I thought you liked him?"

"I was crazy about his boys," Linette admitted, and

experienced a deep twinge of regret. "Unfortunately their father isn't nearly as appealing."

"What about Cain?" The question was low, as if Nancy were afraid of asking. "Oh, Linette, I've been so worried about you."

"There's no need. I sincerely doubt that I'll be seeing Cain again, either."

"But you'd like to?"

Linette didn't need long to think over her reply. "Yes."

"How can you say that, knowing what he does?"

Linette laughed softly and pressed her lips against the sleeping infant's brow. "I suppose I should have learned my lesson a long time ago," she admitted, but it was all wishful thinking, and she knew it. She expected never to see Cain again, but that didn't mean she would stop loving him.

The doorbell chimed. Eight-year-old Christopher darted across the living room carpet as if he expected to find Santa Claus on the other side. Before Nancy could stand or Linette could place Michelle inside the ruffle-laden bassinet, Christopher had thrown open the door.

"Grandma," the boy cried with delight.

"How's the big brother doing?" Jake Collins asked, ruffling Christopher's hair.

"I hope you don't mind us dropping by unexpectedly like this," Janet said, walking into the room. She hesitated, looking uncertain when she saw Linette.

"Hello, Janet," Linette greeted them, wanting to put her mother-in-law at ease.

"Hello, Linette." Michael's mother's voice stiffened, and she glanced toward her husband as if she weren't sure what she should do next.

"It's good to see you again," Jake said, and walked over to study his newest grandchild. "Isn't she the most beautiful baby you've ever seen?"

"Daddy, I think you might be considered prejudiced!" Nancy chided him.

"She's the most beautiful little girl in the world to me," her father protested. "The spitting image of you at that age."

Janet sat down across the room from Linette. "How are you feeling, Nancy?"

"Absolutely wonderful."

"She had the baby naturally, you know." This comment was directed with pride at Linette.

"No, I didn't. Congratulations, Nancy."

"I couldn't have done it without Rob. He was a great coach, and the difference between Christopher's birth and Michelle's is like night and day. I feel great."

"Would you like to hold Michelle?" Linette asked Janet.

Janet smiled and nodded.

Careful, so as not to disturb the baby, Linette stood and gently placed the tiny bundle in Michael's mother's arms. It seemed the austere features softened when she received her granddaughter.

"If this keeps up much longer, Michelle will expect to be held all the time," Nancy protested, but without conviction.

"I'll hold her whenever you need," Janet volunteered, and cooed at the infant. "That's my job. What good is it to be a grandmother if I can't spoil my grandchildren?"

Christopher found it imperative to show his grandfather something in his room, and soon afterward Nancy went to place the freshly washed diapers in the dryer. Unexpectedly, Linette was left alone with Janet.

The silence was heavy between them. Linette worked to formulate the words to show her regret over their last meeting, but before she could begin, Janet spoke.

"I'm pleased we have this opportunity alone," she said, her voice barely above a whisper. "I've done a good deal of thinking in the months since January. I don't agree with everything you said, but I concede that you might have a point." She lowered her head slightly. "Losing Michael, well . . . you of all people can appreciate how difficult it was. Although it's been nearly three years now . . ." She hesitated and bit into her lower lip. "I loved my son. . . ."

"I loved him, too," Linette said gently. She walked across the room and sat on the sofa next to Janet. She'd forgotten how small her mother-in-law was and looped her arm around her fragile shoulders.

"You don't know how many times I've thought about you in the past several months," Janet said. "Jake and I've missed you terribly. When Michael died we felt we still had you, and then . . . There's no need to rehash our disagreement, but since New Year's Day, Jake and I've had a number of talks, and he's helped me realize how wrong I've been. I had no right to expect you to dedicate your life to Michael's memory."

"I regret our disagreement, too," Linette said, and gently squeezed her mother-in-law's shoulders.

"I didn't mean what I said about doubting your love for Michael. You were the best thing that ever happened to my son. He told me that himself just before he died. You seemed so strong, and it was far easier to lean on your strength, yours and Jake's, than accept the fact my son was forever gone from me."

Linette hadn't felt strong, especially in the first few weeks and months following Michael's passing. She didn't now.

"I know that you're dating other men these days, and I've accepted that you'll probably remarry. Both Jake and I want you to be happy, Linette. You deserve that much."

"Thank you." Her words teetered with emotion.

"I know I don't have any right to ask this of you, but when you do remarry, would you allow Jake and me to be grandparents to your children?"

"Oh, Janet." Tears filled Linette's eyes, and she found it impossible to speak for the lump in her throat.

"I promise you that I won't pretend the children are yours and Michael's family. It's just that Jake and I have come to think of you as our daughter. We love you, Linette, and are truly sorry for the way we behaved."

"I think my children would be fortunate to have you and Jake as their grandparents." A husband and family seemed impossible just then, and Janet's words produced a soft ache. She longed for a child. Holding Michelle was both a joy and a trial.

"For weeks I've been promising Jake I'd phone you. My heart nearly stopped when I saw you with Nancy, but I knew it was time to make amends. Long past time."

"I'm pleased we talked." She drew in a deep breath at the emotion that hovered so close to the surface. "Michael was blessed to have you and Jake for parents, and I feel the same way to have you as my in-laws."

"I still miss him."

"I know," Linette whispered. "I do, too, but it won't hurt as much with time. I'll never stop loving Michael, but I don't desperately cling to my memories of him.

They're a part of me now. Some of the happiest days of my life were spent with him. I'm content now. My frustration and anger are gone, and the pain isn't as sharp. For the first time in more years than I can remember, I'm looking forward to the future."

A tear ran down the side of Janet's face. "I am, too."

As best they could, with Nancy's infant daughter between them, the two women hugged. That was how Nancy found them—hugging, laughing, and weeping.

"Hey, you two. If you're going to have a party, the least you could do is invite me."

15 🦎

Francine saw the dust rising from the driveway long before the car came into view. Standing on the back porch, she wrapped her coat about her and pressed her hand against the small of her back. The other hand rested on her stomach, which protruded between the coat's opening. With three months left before her baby was due, she couldn't imagine getting any bigger. Already it was difficult to climb in and out of a chair and do the things she was accustomed to.

"We've got company," she called out to Tim, who was working with Bubba, the most cantankerous of the llamas they owned.

"I'm not expecting anyone," Tim answered. She noted that he didn't take his eyes off Bubba, and with good reason. He'd learned his lesson the first time.

"I'm not expecting anyone, either."

"Do you recognize the car?"

"No," she called back. The vehicle slowed as it rounded the last curve and pulled into the yard.

Tim stepped out of the corral, removed his hat, and wiped his brow with the back of his forearm.

"It's Cain McClellan," Francine announced excitedly, and hurried down the steps—"hurried" being the operative word. Francine didn't move all that speedily these days.

Tim moved to the car, and after Cain climbed out, the two men shook hands, then hugged briefly, slapping each other several times across the back.

"This is a pleasant surprise," Tim said.

"I just happened to be in the neighborhood," Cain said.

Francine watched, smiling, as the two men laughed at the blatant lie. Vashon Island was its own neighborhood. It had taken some getting used to, living her life according to a ferry schedule. Tim worried about her delivering the baby, but she was confident they'd have plenty of time to get to a hospital.

Cain's gaze scanned Francine and lingered at her abdomen. "I see you two have been busy."

Tim chuckled. "As best we can figure, I got her pregnant on our wedding night." His eyes connected with Francine's. "It's something of a family tradition."

"How are you, Cain?" Francine asked. She knew Tim and his friend frequently exchanged e-mails and talked occasionally on the phone, but this was the first she'd heard of Cain traveling.

"Much better, thanks."

"Come inside. There's no need to talk out here in the cold." Francine led the way into the family-size kitchen. She assembled a pot of coffee while the two men pulled out chairs and sat themselves down at the round oak table.

"You're a sight for sore eyes," Tim said, studying his friend. "Damn, but it's good to see you."

"It's good to be here," Cain returned.

"How's everyone?"

Francine watched her husband, looking for any telltale signs that he missed his former life. They rarely discussed Deliverance Company. When she questioned him about the missions, he was tight-lipped. It was as if that part of his life was over and he had to struggle to remember what it was he'd done before they'd been married.

Although she was crazy in love with Tim, Francine couldn't help wondering about the adjustment in both their lives. It hadn't been easy for either one of them. They were both independent people with strong personalities. In addition, Francine missed her family dreadfully. The little things about island living continued to irritate her, but she was learning.

Tim seemed to have made the transition effortlessly, but there were times when she wondered. As she did now. Her fear was that Cain had returned to talk Tim into going back for one last mission. The very thought caused her blood to run cold.

"Murphy, Keller, and Bailey all send their best. They're doing great."

"And you?" Tim asked.

"I'm getting stronger every day."

"I'm glad to hear it."

Francine poured coffee into two mugs and carried them over to the table. Tim snaked his arm around her waist and held her against his side. "We've been married six months now, and I swear I still get goo-goo-eyed every time I look at her."

"Tim!" Francine dared not look at Cain. Her cheeks burned with embarrassment.

Tim laughed and, after bouncing a kiss off her tummy, released her. Francine brought her tea to the table and joined the two men. She studied Cain and realized how thin and pale he was. From what she understood, he was lucky to be alive.

"I'm thinking of selling Deliverance Company," Cain announced out of the blue.

Francine tensed, thinking Cain was giving Tim first crack at buying the business. Tim must have assumed the same thing, because his eyes found hers. It wasn't necessary to voice her objection. One look assured her that her fears were unsubstantiated.

Tim reached for her hand and laced his fingers through hers. "If you're offering it to me—"

"I'm not." Cain cut in. "At this point, Murphy's the one most interested, but I haven't completely made up my mind. I wanted to talk to the two of you first."

Tim and Francine looked at each other. "Us?" Tim asked, clearly puzzled.

"I wanted to see for myself if you were as happy as Mallory implies in his letters. I'll admit that when I learned you two were marrying, I didn't give the union much of a chance. I know Mallory too well. I wasn't sure he was the type to settle down and raise llamas."

"The hell I'm not," Tim protested.

"You've proved me wrong," Cain said, and he looked pleased to admit the fault. "You've beaten the odds. It gives me hope."

"What would you do without Deliverance Company?" Tim asked.

"I'm not sure yet," Cain said after a short hesitation.

"I'd probably move to Montana. I've got a spread there, but what I know about cattle ranching would fit inside the eye of a needle."

"You learn fast," Tim said, "trust me. Cattle can't be all that different from llamas. Besides, don't you have the world's best foreman? I remember you bragging about him a couple of years back."

"John Stamp and his family are the salt of the earth."

"Are you going to wait to see if you get some nibbles on Deliverance Company before you make up your mind?" Francine asked.

"No," Cain said, surprising them both. "Everything depends on a certain woman who owns a yarn shop. If she hasn't already decided she never wants to see me again."

"Linette?" Francine guessed.

Cain nodded. "I can't give her one good reason to marry me."

"She won't need any reasons," Francine said with unshakable confidence. "I didn't when I married Tim. Loving him was enough, and Linette loves you."

CAIN certainly hoped what Francine said was true, and that Linette still loved him. It had been over six months since he'd last seen her. A whole lot could have changed in that time.

Cain arrived in San Francisco and checked into a hotel room. Slipping the room key into his pocket, he sat on the side of the mattress and closed his eyes. He'd thought about this day, lived for this day, for months.

He checked his watch, debating if he should phone her first. After a moment he decided it would be harder for her to close the door in his face than to hang up on him.

He caught a cab to her apartment building and took the stairs. A year earlier he'd raced up the three flights, taking two and three steps at a time. This year he walked up one step at a time and was shaky and weak before he reached the third floor. If Linette did agree to marry him, she should know she wasn't getting any bargain.

Straightening his shoulders, he pushed the doorbell and waited. An eternity passed before he heard the lock turn. The door opened, and all at once she was there. They stared at each other, breathless and stunned.

Cain didn't think she could be any more beautiful than the way he remembered her. But she was. She wore a winter rose silk dress, and her hair was pulled back from her face and held in place with pearl-edged combs.

She whispered, "Cain."

"Hello, Linette."

As if unaware of what she was doing, she raised her hands to his face and gently flattened them against his cheeks. Her touch was light and uncertain.

He briefly closed his eyes and smiled. "I'm real," he assured her.

All at once she was crying. Of all the responses Cain had anticipated, he hadn't thought she'd break down and weep. He held her against him. Once they were inside her apartment, he closed the door with his foot.

Cain felt as if he'd die if he didn't kiss her soon. He brought her close to him, and it was like stumbling through the gate of paradise. His heart swelled with a love so strong, so potent, he feared it couldn't withstand the pressure.

Sobbing, her tears moistening his face, Linette kissed him again and again and again as if she couldn't get enough of him.

That was what broke him. Cain's arms tightened around her waist, and he lifted her from the floor. All the weeks of lying in the hospital, of dreaming of this moment, praying she still loved him, that he still had a chance with her. He'd been to hell and back, and he'd gladly retrace his steps if it meant he hadn't lost her.

"I love you," he chanted between long, deep, desperate kisses. "Marry me, Linette." He hadn't meant to propose like this, first thing. He'd thought long and hard about how he planned to ask her.

She lifted her face from his and stared down on him as if afraid she hadn't heard him correctly.

"You heard me right," he said. "I'm asking you to be my wife."

"What about—"

"I'm selling it to Murphy."

"You're sure?"

He smiled and nodded. "Positive."

The doorbell chimed, and Linette sighed and braced her forehead against his shoulder.

"Who's that?" Cain asked.

It took her a long moment to answer. "A . . . friend."

"Male or female?"

Again Linette hesitated. "Male."

Cain didn't have a single reason to be jealous. Linette's eager kisses convinced him she loved him. Nevertheless the green monster ate at Cain's confidence like a hungry rabbit devouring fresh garden lettuce.

The doorbell chimed again, and Cain stopped her from answering. "Is it that attorney you were seeing earlier in the year?"

"No. His name's Phil." She bit into her lower lip and

moved toward the door. As if reading his thoughts, she offered Cain a weak smile. "He's just a friend."

A tall, attractive man stepped into the apartment, looking bright and cheerful. His gaze immediately connected with Cain's and narrowed. The laughter drained from his eyes.

"Hello," Cain said, and held out his hand. "It seems we have a bit of a problem."

"Phil Duncan, meet Cain McClellan," Linette murmured.

As Cain moved forward to exchange handshakes with Linette's date, he noticed how flustered she looked. It would have been better if he'd phoned first, he realized now, instead of placing her in this awkward position.

"Linette's mentioned you before," Phil said thoughtfully, and following the brief introduction, he sat on the sofa. It seemed to Cain that the other man went to lengths to make himself comfortable, or at least give the appearance of being so. "How long are you in town for this time?"

The censure was too thick to ignore. "As long as Linette will have me. I've asked her to be my wife."

His words were met with a strained silence. Then, "She'd be crazy to accept." Phil looked to Linette for a response. "You haven't, have you?"

"Not yet," Cain answered on her behalf, and sat across from the other man. He was on the edge of the cushion, and their eyes were level. It was a matter of male pride, but Cain didn't want her answering to anyone but him.

"Linette?" Phil looked directly at her, waiting. She was the only one left standing, and frankly Cain wished she'd sit down.

"I . . . I . . ." She hesitated. "I have a few questions I need Cain to answer first."

"Great, ask away," Phil instructed, showing enthusiasm. He leaned forward and pressed his elbows to his knees. "While we're at it, let me throw my hat in the ring."

"Throw your hat in the ring?" Linette echoed, frowning.

"Right. We've been dating how long now? Three, four months?"

Linette opened and closed her mouth before casting Cain an apologetic look.

"Four. Actually, now that I think about it, it's closer to five," Phil answered for her.

Cain hadn't expected her to keep a silent vigil awaiting his return, but it pricked at his pride that she had gotten involved with another man so soon after her return from Grenada.

"We were friends a long time before we ever started dating, isn't that right?"

"Yes," Linette admitted reluctantly.

"I'm not willing to do the gentlemanly thing and step aside because you're infatuated with your soldier friend here. He's moved in and out of your life like a bad storm for the last year."

"I'm here to stay," Cain said forcefully. It was apparent that buddy boy wasn't going to surrender without a fight. What the man apparently didn't realize was that when it came to war, Cain was the expert. He'd make mincemeat of Phil Duncan in seconds.

But at what price? Cain asked himself. He studied the other man and found him to be clean-cut, successful from the looks of him, a decent sort. As much as it irked him, Cain experienced a grudging respect for Linette's *friend*.

"I'd like to marry Linette as well," Phil announced. Silence fell like a butcher's cleaver into the middle of the room.

"Phil." Looking shocked, Linette pressed the tips of her fingers to her lips.

"Exactly how long have you two known each other?"

Cain directed the question to Linette, but it was Phil who answered. "Long enough. I was a friend of Michael's."

"I see," Cain murmured.

"Phil and Laura are . . . were good friends of ours," Linette explained.

"Our divorce was final this summer," Phil went on to explain in that nonchalant way of his. He spoke of the end of his marriage as he would report the stock market averages, revealing little emotion.

It certainly hadn't taken good ol' Phil long to seek out greener pastures, Cain noted.

"It's apparent I can give Linette what's important in life," the other man went on to say. "Love, security, and a solid future." Leaning back, balancing his ankle on his knee, Duncan appeared cocky and sure of himself. "What is it you intend to offer her?"

Cain weighed his response carefully, knowing it could well sway her decision. "My heart. Children. As for the future, it doesn't come with any guarantees. Linette's probably more aware of that than either of us. So I can't and won't predict what could happen there."

Buddy boy frowned. "Frankly, that doesn't sound like much."

"It isn't," Cain agreed readily enough. "All I can offer her is my love. It's taken me nearly twelve months to figure out what I should have recognized from the first. I need her. You're right, I'm no prize. Linette would be a fool to marry me and move to some cattle ranch with a man who doesn't know a bloody thing about being a rancher."

"We'd live in Montana?" she asked.

He nodded.

"Children?" This word quivered as it left her lips.

"As many as you want, but you should realize I don't know any more about being a husband and a father than I do about ranching."

"You'll learn," she said confidently, and then frowned. "What about Deliverance Company? You're through with fighting?"

"Never again."

Linette laughed softly and kissed Phil Duncan on the cheek. "You really ought to take up acting, Phil. You gave an Academy Award performance. Thank you."

"Who said I was acting?"

"Laura might take exception to your becoming a bigamist."

Cain frowned and looked from one to the other. "What's going on here? I thought you said you were divorced."

The other man grinned broadly. "I lied, but you know what they say about love and war. I figured this was as good a way as any to have you spell out your intentions."

Frankly Cain didn't appreciate Phil's efforts and told him so with a menacing look.

"Be good to her, McClellan, she deserves a man who appreciates her."

This was exactly what Cain intended to do. "I will," he promised.

Phil stood and addressed Linette. "I suppose this means you won't be joining Laura and me for dinner?"

Linette laughed and nodded. "You'll forgive me?"

Phil answered her with a dramatic sigh. "I suppose. Just make sure we get an invitation to the wedding, understand?"

"You've got it," Cain promised. The men shook hands a second time, and Phil left shortly afterward.

No sooner had the door closed than Linette was back in Cain's embrace. "Did you mean what you said about children?"

"Every word."

"How soon can we be married?" Linette wanted to know. She asked this as if she were afraid he would change his mind. Quickly she added, "Soon, I hope. I've waited a long time for this moment."

"I'm not going to change my mind." He felt as though her love would heal him faster than any doctor. The emotional wounds had marked him far more intensely than the physical ones.

His arms linked around her waist, Cain pulled her close. "We can apply for the license first thing in the morning. Where would you like to spend our honeymoon?"

A twinkle came into her eyes as she lifted her mouth to his. "Bed."

𝒩ANCY and Rob agreed to stand up for them, and Linette was grateful for their love and friendship. If it hadn't been for her brother- and sister-in-law, Linette would never have met Cain McClellan.

Linette knew Nancy had her doubts. Perhaps Rob did, too, but neither voiced them. It was hard for Nancy to hold her tongue. All Linette wanted was for her former sister-in-law to be happy for her. Marrying Cain was what she wanted, what she'd dreamed would happen. She might be a fool, but she was grabbing this opportunity for happiness with both hands and holding on as though her life depended on it.

Bonnie was a godsend in the days before the wedding. Linette swore she was more nervous as a bride the second time than she had been with Michael.

When the time arrived, the church was filled with a party of nearly fifty people. Her own family and Michael's parents were there. Linette was touched to find that Cain's foreman and wife, John and Patty Stamp, had flown in for the ceremony from Cain's cattle ranch in Montana.

Linette held a bouquet of pink rosebuds and proudly took her place next to Cain at the altar. In her heart she recognized that she would be content to spend the next fifty years beside this man. Love was like that.

Following the short reception, they left in Cain's vehicle, heading north.

"Where are we going?" she asked, her head resting against his shoulder.

"To bed," Cain teased, and kissed the crown of her head. "That was where you said you wanted to spend our honeymoon, but you omitted saying exactly where that would be, so I took matters into my own hands."

"Frankly, I wouldn't care if it was on the moon as long as I could be with you."

"Wife," Cain said, as if testing the word on his tongue. "It has a nice sound to it."

"So does husband."

For a long time they rode in silence, content to be close to each other, eager to be closer and more intimate. After a while Linette traced her fingertips down the side of his face and over the rigid line of his jaw. She swore Cain stopped breathing.

Linette experienced a rush of love at the sensual power she had over him. No more than a moment passed before he captured her hand and entwined his fingers with hers.

"You're making it difficult to concentrate on driving."

"How far do we have to go yet?"

"Too far if you continue touching me."

"I was hoping on doing more than that."

"So was I." He mumbled something more under his breath that she didn't understand. "Fifty miles," he said. "I promise to make it worth the wait."

"I should hope so," she said, loving the freedom to be close to him. She placed her hand on his thigh and gently dug her nails into the hard muscle of his leg.

"Linette," he said between his teeth. "You're playing with fire."

She laughed softly. "Fire always did intrigue me."

Cain pulled off to the side of the road, and the tires spat up dirt and gravel. He set the car into park and reached for her. Linette barely had time to recover before his mouth swooped down on hers. He kissed her deep and hard.

She moaned softly.

"Do you have a clue of how difficult it's been not to make love to you these last few days?" he asked, trailing kisses along the side of her neck.

"Yes." She knew exactly how hard it had been on

them both, but she felt cherished and adored that he'd insisted they wait until after the wedding. She loved him all the more for his patience.

He kissed her again slowly, with restraint, using his tongue to show her what he'd like to be doing to her body. What he would soon be doing.

When he dragged his mouth from hers, he rested his chin on the top of her head. "Much more of this and we could be arrested."

Linette smiled softly to herself. "The way I feel right now, it would almost be worth it."

Cain drove fifteen miles over the speed limit for the rest of the trip, then stopped in a small seaside town. Apparently he was familiar with the area because he drove directly to a house perched against a windswept hillside that overlooked the Pacific Ocean.

"Is anyone home?" Linette asked, noticing the light shining from inside the huge house.

"I certainly hope not," was all Cain would say. He helped her out of the car, lifted the suitcase from the trunk, and led the way up a brick-lined pathway. "This place belongs to a friend of mine."

"Have I met him?"

"No. Fact is, until just a few days ago, I hadn't talked to him in over ten years. He told me that if I ever needed a retreat, I should give him a call. I phoned last week."

"Ten years, and he still remembered you?"

"He remembered. I saved his life." After digging the key out of his side pocket, Cain inserted it into the lock and pushed open the door. He propped the suitcases against the door to hold it open and then effortlessly lifted Linette into his arms. Their eyes met, and he smiled meaningfully.

Linette linked her arms around his neck as he carried her over the threshold. They kissed long and passionately. The wind howled behind them, and reluctantly Cain set her feet back on the floor and dealt with the luggage.

While he was tucking away their suitcases in the back bedroom, Linette explored the house. Huge picture windows looked out over the churning Pacific Ocean, but night blocked out the majority of the view.

Hearing movement behind her, Linette turned to discover Cain standing on the opposite side of the room. His hands were buried in his pants pockets.

"I imagine the view's lovely in daylight," he said.

If Linette hadn't known better, she would have thought her husband of less than four hours was nervous.

"I'm sure it is."

"Are you hungry?" he asked, glancing toward the kitchen. "The refrigerator's stocked with enough food to last us a week or longer."

"I'm famished."

"Great." Cain moved eagerly toward the other room. "I'll see to dinner."

"My appetite isn't for food, Cain McClellan," she chided him, her voice low and breathless. "It's being your wife that strongly appeals to me." Anxious herself, Linette could have sworn her heart beat like cymbals crashing against each other.

Cain smiled, and Linette was certain she'd never seen a man look more relieved. "I wondered how I was going to manage to sit through a meal and not ravish you." He ate up the distance between them in two giant strides. He reached for her and brought her into his arms.

CAIN swore he'd never known pleasure this profound. Over the course of their wedding night, they'd made love twice. Linette had wept when she'd viewed the thick, still pink scars that marked his body. Not wanting anything to distract her, he'd turned out the light.

Cain glanced toward the digital clock on the nightstand. It was almost four. Dawn was hours away yet. Linette breathed evenly and snuggled up against his side. He urged her head onto his shoulder, and she draped her hand over his abdomen. In that moment Cain would have rather died than move.

He'd never experienced contentment like this. Physically he was sated, but it was his emotions that he found himself analyzing. So this was what it meant to love someone so much that it brought a physical ache just thinking about it. So this was what it meant to give your heart completely to another.

Cain had been afraid. He'd been terrified commitment to Linette would mean surrendering a part of himself. He'd been wrong, very wrong. Only now did he realize how deeply he'd cheated himself in the last year. In loving Linette, he'd realized he was the receiver. Her love had made him whole. Her tenderness had wiped away the pain of a bitter childhood, the need to prove himself, the drive to gain the attention and approval of an alcoholic father—a man incapable of giving either. A father long dead and long buried.

"What time is it?" Linette asked in a husky whisper.

"You're awake?"

"Not really. I'm just curious about the time." She remained exactly as she was, her ear pressed over his heart, her arm draped over his middle.

Cain grinned. "About four."

"You couldn't sleep?"

"I woke up."

She started to pull away. "You're not accustomed to sleeping with anyone, and I—"

"No," he interrupted, stopping her. "Don't move."

Linette went still. "So you are accustomed to sleeping with someone?"

He chuckled. "No. You sound jealous."

"Should I be?"

He weighed his words carefully. Heaven would vouch he was no saint. Never had been and probably never would be. "There hasn't been another woman from the moment I met you, and there never will be."

Linette's body relaxed against his. "I love you, Cain McClellan."

He closed his eyes and kissed the crown of her head. "And I love you." He stroked her bare back and was surprised at the ready way his body fired to life. His one concern before he'd asked Linette to marry him had been his health. The doctors had claimed it would take a good deal of time to recover from the gunshot wound. It embarrassed him to inquire about his sexual stamina, but his questions had been greeted with professional ease. The doctor didn't know for certain, but he speculated that in light of Cain's injuries, his physical endurance would be limited.

His physician, however, wasn't married to Linette. To Cain's relief and delight, he discovered his recovery time from lovemaking was amazingly quick.

His hand descended lower and cupped her bare buttock. "Linette?" he quizzed softly.

"Humm?"

"Just how asleep are you?"

He felt her smile against his bare chest. "What makes you ask?"

"I don't know," he hedged. "Idle curiosity, I guess, and the fact I can't seem to keep my hands off you."

"I like your hands on me," she assured him. Edging upward, she slid her glorious body over him, tantalizing him until she located his earlobe and caught it between her teeth.

LINETTE lay beside him quietly, cradled close against his long, muscled length. Their legs were entwined, their arms wrapped around each other. Cain brushed a kiss across her cheek. Her eyes were closed, and she smiled dreamily.

"A woman could become accustomed to this kind of attention," she whispered.

Cain grinned. "I wonder when I'm going to have time to learn about cattle ranching. I'd much rather spend time in bed with you."

Linette smiled lazily. "You'll learn. We both will."

Cain understood what she was saying. This was a change of lifestyle for them both. They'd relinquished the past and grabbed hold of the future without looking back, without regrets. At least not yet. Linette had sold her knitting shop to Bonnie. She hadn't said much about letting go of the business, but Cain recognized the sacrifice it had entailed. Wild and Wooly had given her purpose following Michael's death. She'd funneled her energy into the business. The shop represented the life she'd built stone upon stone, one day at a time, after losing her first husband. Yet she'd freely relinquished this part of herself in order to marry him. It had been no small sacrifice.

Ϛʜᴇ was the prettiest woman in the cantina, and Jack Keller swore she'd been watching him from the moment he'd arrived. He'd come to quench his thirst, but if a saucy señorita was interested in adding a bit of spice to his afternoon, Jack wasn't opposed. He didn't have anything better to do with his time. Killing an hour or two in bed was just the tonic he needed, he mused.

Murphy had sent him on assignment to this godforsaken stinkhole. If Cain had been the one issuing the orders, he wouldn't have minded, but this was Murphy. It didn't seem right to be taking orders from anyone other than Cain.

As far as Jack was concerned, the new owner of Deliverance Company had a lot to learn. It would be a long time before Murphy was the caliber of leader Cain McClellan had been.

Cain married. Mallory, too. Disgusted, Jack shook his head. It didn't sit right with him or the other team members. What was this world coming to, when two of the best fighting men he'd ever known allowed themselves to fall into the worst trap of all? Marriage.

This new lifestyle was inconsistent with everything Jack knew about his colleagues. He couldn't speak for the others, but he was hoping that after a few months of pandering to a wife, Cain would come to his senses and return to Deliverance Company. This was where he belonged. Try as he might, he couldn't picture Cain with a ring through his nose.

Jack took a deep swallow of the cold beer and wiped the back of his hand across his mouth. Carrying the chipped mug with him, he strolled over to where the young lady sat.

"Care if I join you?" he asked her in Spanish.

She fluttered her eyelashes and shrugged one delicate shoulder. "Feel free," she responded.

Jack pulled out a chair, twisted it around, and straddled it. He took another drink of his beer and called for the bartender and ordered two more, one for him and the other for the girl.

"You got a name?" she asked.

"Yeah," he teased. "What about you?"

"Zita."

"Pretty name for a pretty lady." That had to be the oldest line in the book, but one look told him she wasn't interested in his wit.

"Thank you."

The bartender delivered two more mugs, and Jack paid him. Zita reached across the table for the beer, and Jack noticed that she bent low to be sure he received an ample view of her wares. Her breasts were large and lush, the size of cantaloupes. Jack wished more women were inclined to wear blouses with elastic necklines. It made access to their breasts easier than fiddling with all those silly buttons.

"How much?" he asked, getting to the point. There was no need to be coy. He knew what she was.

She cast him a hot look. "You insult me."

He laughed, and wanting her to think he didn't have much time, he checked his watch. "I doubt anyone's capable of offending you."

Keep your pants zipped. That was something Cain had said often enough and loud enough. Only Cain wasn't running the show any longer, Murphy was.

"Another time, then," Jack said, setting aside his beer.

"Wait," Zita said quickly, and slipped her hand across

his thigh, her long nails digging into the hard muscle there. "Don't go. Not yet."

Jack cast her a half smile. "Then give me a reason to stay."

She slid her hand slightly forward toward his crotch and splayed her fingers like a cat flexing its claws. "I'm very good," she said under her breath.

"I believe you." Already Jack could feel the hot blood racing through his veins.

"I don't come cheap."

"I didn't think you did."

"I have a place with a clean bed close by."

He hid a smile. "That's a plus."

"You'll pay me first?"

Jack hesitated. "Half now. Half later."

She grinned and nodded. "Follow me."

Jack stood and followed the woman out of the cantina. Her hips swayed as she hurried across the courtyard. "Hey," Jack said, calling after her, "what's the hurry?"

"No hurry," she assured him, placing a hand on her hip and tossing him a slow, sexual smile.

Impatient to sample her wares, Jack caught her by the shoulder and turned into a nearby alley. Her back was against a wall as she looked up at him with deep chocolate eyes. Slowly Jack lowered his mouth to hers. She tasted of warm beer and passion. He could live without the stale taste of beer, but the passion excited him. Entwining his fingers in her thick dark hair, he kissed her again.

She squirmed against him. "Not here," she said, pushing against him.

"Why not?" He looked around, and not seeing anyone close, he reached under her skirt and slid his hand over her bare buttocks.

"My house is very close," she promised.

The way Jack was feeling just then, "very close" wasn't near enough. Rarely had he been this hot for a woman, but it had been a good long while since he'd given in to his baser needs. Apparently too long.

"Please, Señor," she pleaded softly.

Jack dragged a cooling breath through his lungs. "All right," he mumbled.

She relaxed against him and kissed him long and hard. Then, taking him by the hand, she led him down a narrow side street. Jack was in too much of a rush to notice much about which way they were headed. He was fairly certain he'd find his way back to the cantina without a problem.

Smiling up at him, she unlocked the door and threw it open. Once more Jack reached for her, turned her into his arms, and kissed her lustily. His hands were on her breasts as he eased her through the doorway. His intention was to steer her toward the bedroom and have his way with her. Heaven would testify she was willing enough.

Jack opened his eyes, and it felt as if the breath had been knocked out of him. There, sitting at the rough wood table, was a man, eating casually with one hand. In the other was a pistol pointed directly at Jack's heart.

"Welcome to hell, Jack Keller," he said with a sick laugh, licking the fingertips of his free hand. "You don't remember me, do you?"

Jack backed away from Zita, his blood turning cold. He did recognize the other man. The last time he'd seen this gunman, the desperado had been standing in the belly of a helicopter with his weapon trained on Cain McClellan.

"Trust me. Before the day is over, you will remember everything," the man said. "You will curse God that your friend didn't die the first time."

16 🦎

*I*f you're going to be a real cowboy, I suspect I should teach you the code," John Stamp said casually to Cain.

"Code?" Cain shifted his weight atop the large sorrel and studied the rolling snow-covered hillside, hoping to familiarize himself with the landscape.

"To the best of my knowledge it's nothing that's formally written down. It's a way of thinking and acting. You'd pick it up sooner or later."

"Be easier if you told me outright, wouldn't it?" Cain commented. He'd been working with John every day for the past three weeks, harder, he swore, than he'd ever worked in his life. Each night he returned to Linette with his head crammed full of things he'd learned about his land and his herd of cattle, his head buzzing with the certainty he could work this land for the next fifty years and still be a greenhorn.

"I believe you've already figured out how important it is to close gates."

Cain snickered at the memory of his first day riding with John. "I've got that one down pat."

"Good."

"Also, it's not a good idea to keep someone waiting for you."

Cain eyed the foreman speculatively. "You told the women that? I swear it takes five minutes longer after Linette claims she's ready to leave."

"So the honeymoon's over, is it?" John said teasingly.

Actually it wasn't. Cain had adjusted with little trouble to married life, which surprised him. He'd expected they'd need to adapt more to each other's ways than they had. Naturally, being crazy in love helped. As for the honeymoon part, he felt as frisky as someone fifteen years his junior. Cain had never considered himself especially oversexed, but that had changed since his marriage. It amazed him how frequently he needed his wife.

"What's so funny?" John asked.

"Nothing," Cain said, his hands tightening around the sorrel's reins. "Go on with your list, I'm listening."

John seemed to require a few moments to think. "If Linette hasn't said anything yet, she will. Remember to remove your spurs before going into the house."

"The slang for spurs is 'can openers'?" Cain had heard one of the other hired men say something along those lines recently.

"You got it."

Cain had soon learned that cowboys had their own lingo. He was picking up a few words here and there, but there were several he hadn't quite figured out. The day before, he'd heard Pete, a wiry fellow in his early fifties, talk about a gelding who was cut proud. Cain still hadn't figured out what that meant. Ah, well, he'd learn soon enough.

"Anything more?"

"Plenty," John assured him. "This one's important. Don't ever cuss out another man's dog."

"You make it sound like writing a check without any money in the bank."

"It's worse than that."

"They throw you in jail for bouncing checks."

"You don't want to know what happens to someone who cusses out a neighbor's dog. You can say what you will about his wife, but leave his dog alone."

That wouldn't hold true with Cain, but he didn't want to be teased about being a newlywed, so he kept his mouth closed. Glancing at his watch, he calculated how long it'd be before they'd head back to the house.

The day before, he'd arrived home just as Linette was taking a loaf of freshly baked bread out of the oven, and the earthy scent of yeast had filled the house. Her eyes had lit up when she'd seen him, and his heart had done a little flip-flop just knowing she was his. Cain had never suspected life could be this good.

"Another thing," John said, cutting into Cain's musings. "Always drink upstream from the herd."

Cain chuckled. "I suppose the next thing you're going to tell me is that a horse in the barn is worth two in the bush."

John rubbed his hand down the side of his face as if testing to see whether he needed a shave or not. "You're learning, McClellan. Won't be long now before the creak's out of your saddle."

𝓛INETTE hummed as she polished the cherrywood end table. Soon she was meeting Patty Stamp and the two were driving into town. Generally they made the drive only once a month, and the men tagged along, but this trip was special. Something Cain didn't know about. A surprise of sorts, although it shouldn't have been.

Linette suspected she was pregnant.

She didn't want to say anything until she was positive. The test kit Patty Stamp had provided read positive, but Linette wouldn't believe it until she heard it directly from the physician himself.

Other than missing her period, she suffered none of the obvious symptoms she'd heard about. No morning sickness. Nor was she overly tired. Perhaps it was too soon. They'd been married less than six weeks. From what she'd heard, it wasn't supposed to be this easy.

The sound of an approaching vehicle prompted Linette to set aside her dusting rag and look out the front window. A large oversize pickup barreled down the driveway.

Thinking something must be wrong, Linette reached for her jacket and stepped onto the porch. She wrapped her arms around her to ward off the cold wind, which howled like a stray calf.

Her heart staggered at the sight of Murphy, Cain's former colleague, who leapt down from the cab. He stood with his feet braced apart as if he expected to do battle with her.

"Where's Cain?" he asked, and the wind howled louder behind him.

"On the range."

"Can you reach him?"

A chill raced up Linette's arms. "Would you care to come inside? We may have had our differences in the past, but that isn't any reason to stand here in the cold and shout at each other."

He nodded once, giving the impression he was lowering his standards to do as she requested. Linette gritted her teeth to keep from saying it didn't hurt her any to leave him outside to freeze if that was what he wanted. To her credit, she managed to swallow the sarcastic comment.

Murphy took the porch steps two at a time. "How long will it take to reach Cain?" he demanded.

Linette ignored the command in his voice. The mercenary might be accustomed to issuing orders and having them obeyed, but she wasn't one of his men.

"Would you care for some coffee?" she asked instead.

Murphy glared at her. "I asked about Cain."

"And I asked if you'd like some coffee."

"I don't want coffee, I need to talk to Cain," he said with a decided lack of patience.

"All right." Linette left him and headed for the kitchen but was saved the effort of contacting her husband. Just then Cain walked in the back door, looking dusty, tired, and so loving that it was all she could do to keep herself from running into his arms.

"You're early," she said, forcing a smile.

"Yup." He devoured the short distance between them and took her into his arms. He kissed her before she could tell him about Murphy. Once her husband's mouth was over hers, it demanded every ounce of will she possessed to remember the other man herself.

"How about taking a shower with me?" he whispered close to her ear.

"Cain—"

"How long has it been since we last made love?" he asked, then answered the question himself. "Too long." He kissed her so thoroughly, she felt her knees would go out from under her.

"Cain—"

"I believe she's trying to tell you I'm here," Murphy said from the kitchen doorway. One hand held open the door and the other was braced against his hip, his eyes disapproving.

"Murphy." Cain stepped away from Linette, and the two men exchanged hearty handshakes. "What are you doing here?"

"We've got a problem."

Linette noticed the reference to "we" even if Cain didn't. Her husband had promised her his warring days were over. He'd given her his word of honor. Never again, he'd said.

Linette forced herself to relax. She was leaping to conclusions. Just because Murphy showed up unexpectedly and announced he was in trouble, even if he had prefaced the problem with "we," that didn't mean Cain would become involved.

"What's wrong?" By tacit agreement the two men moved to the kitchen table. Linette took down two mugs and poured them each a cup of coffee. Unwilling to be excluded from the conversation, she pulled out a chair and sat next to Cain.

Murphy hesitated when Linette sat down.

"You can speak freely," Cain assured him.

Murphy began, "Does the name Enrique mean anything to you?"

Cain frowned. "Just the one name?"

Murphy nodded.

"Should I know it?"

"He was the man who shot you."

"Ah, yes. Pretty Boy." He wasn't someone Cain was likely to forget, Linette suspected, although she wasn't sure he'd ever known the other man's name.

"He's back in action," Murphy said, and his mouth thinned just saying the words.

"Another CEO this time?"

As Linette watched her husband, a knot began to form in the lower part of her stomach. His eyes lit up, and a half smile touched his lips.

"No. This time he's got Jack."

"Jack Keller?"

Murphy nodded.

Cain frowned fiercely. "What does he want from Jack?"

"I don't know."

"Has he demanded a ransom?"

"That's the funny part. He hasn't asked for a dime."

"You're sure Jack's alive?"

"No."

"What are your plans?"

"Rescue Jack if I can, then kill Enrique. Either way the bastard's taken his last man. The problem is I'm going to need help."

Linette stiffened. The two men talked about life and death with stark indifference as if neither was of any real consequence.

She wanted to stand up and shout at them to look at themselves, to listen to what they said, to really listen. It might have been her imagination, but it seemed to Linette that Cain, the man she loved, the man she shared a bed with each night, the man who was the father of the child she suspected she carried, became a stranger to her. His heart grew hard and cold before her very eyes.

"When are you leaving?" Cain asked.

"Within the week." The other man's eyes held Cain's. "I want you with me."

Cain hesitated and looked to Linette.

"You promised me never again," she whispered, her voice sounding scratchy and weak.

"This is Jack," Murphy exploded, and stood. "If it wasn't for Jack, Cain wouldn't be here now. None of us would be. Jack's a good man. He doesn't deserve to die friendless. You know damn good and well that if the situation was reversed, he'd be the first one to volunteer to go in after you."

Still Cain hesitated. "Let me talk to Linette."

Murphy glared at her, then turned and walked out of the kitchen, leaving the door to swing in his wake.

For a long moment neither spoke. Linette knew what Cain wanted. He was waiting for her to absolve him from his promise. Waiting for her to tell him that these were extenuating circumstances and it only made sense that he be the one to rescue his buddy.

Linette, however, wasn't willing to be that generous.

"Honey?"

"It doesn't matter what I say. You'll do what you want anyway."

"It does matter," Cain insisted.

"We haven't been married two months and already you've got an excuse to go back into the field."

"This isn't like any other operation. This is for a friend, a man I've worked with for years. This sort of thing has never happened before. It won't again."

"You promised me before we were married that you wouldn't go back."

Cain forcefully expelled a sigh. "Under normal circumstances I wouldn't. But this is for Jack. I owe him my life."

Linette closed her eyes. It might have been paranoid of her, but she wondered if Murphy had his own agenda as far as Cain was concerned. She wouldn't put it past the mercenary to bring Cain back into Deliverance Company little by little.

"Why does it have to be you?" she asked.

"Because I'm good. Jack's chances are better if I'm the one heading the mission. Sweetheart, Jack's a friend, a good friend. And Enrique's the bastard who shot me."

"In other words you want to go?"

It took Cain a long time to answer. "Yes."

Something died inside of Linette.

If it hadn't been for the gunshot wound and his close brush with death, Cain would have been content to leave matters between them as they were. His injuries had reminded him of his mortality. He was lucky to be alive, and given a second chance, he wanted to make the most of it. For a time he'd managed to convince himself he could change his stripes.

"What about your other promises?" she asked, staring straight ahead. She discovered she couldn't look at him and focused instead on an inanimate object on the counter.

"What promises?"

"Love, cherish, the vows we spoke in church. Do you want me to absolve you from those as well?"

"Linette," Cain said on the tail end of a sigh that revealed his exasperation with her. "You're making more out of this than necessary. A friend of mine is in trouble. He needs help, and I'm in a position to rescue him. It doesn't mean I'm going back to Deliverance Company."

"What is it you want from me?"

"I was hoping we could talk about this sensibly."

"You're looking for me to release you from your promise. Admit it, Cain. Be honest enough to own up to the truth."

"All right, if that's what you want me to say, then I will. You're right, I did promise you I wouldn't go back into the field, but then I didn't count on one of my best friends being taken captive, either."

There was a knock at the back door and Patty Stamp stepped into the kitchen. "You ready, Linette?" she asked cheerfully, then hesitated when she saw Cain. "Oh, sorry, I didn't mean to interrupt anything."

"You didn't," Linette said, forcing a smile. "Let me get my coat and purse and I'll be ready."

"I'll wait out in the car," Patty said.

"I'll only be a moment," Linette promised, and headed out of the kitchen.

"Linette." Exasperated, Cain called after her.

"Yes?" she answered lightly as if not understanding why he would delay her.

"What about Jack?"

"I'll tell you what, Cain. I'll leave the decision in your hands."

"No," he said forcefully. "I refuse to accept that."

"Then go," she said without emotion, "but don't kid yourself into thinking this is the last time. There'll always be a good reason. It'll always be just this one time. Always be someone else who needs you more than me."

"You're overreacting," he snapped.

"Maybe," she answered, "but I doubt it." She didn't wait for his answer. With tears blurring her vision, she hurriedly reached for her purse and jacket and raced outside.

Linette joined Patty on the front seat of the minivan and ran her glove-covered hand across her face. Patty glanced at her as if she weren't sure what she should do.

"I'm fine," Linette said with a shaky laugh.

"You don't look so good to me. Did you two have your first spat?"

"You could say that."

"Don't worry, everything will work itself out."

Linette couldn't help but wonder. Patty eased the car into drive and headed down the long dirt driveway that led to the main road.

"I didn't know you had company," Patty said when she spied Murphy's truck.

"It's a friend of Cain's."

"Don't you fret," Patty said a second time. "By the time you get home, Cain will be so pleased to see you, he'll want to kiss and make up soon enough."

"Cain won't be here."

"Nonsense. Where else would he be?"

"God only knows," she said chokingly.

Several hours later the physician had confirmed what a test kit and nature had already told her: Linette was pregnant. The certainty that Cain's child grew beneath her heart was what helped her through the long drive back to the ranch.

"Wait until Cain hears this," Patty said. "Boy, would I love to be a fly on the wall when he learns you're going to have a baby."

Linette knew Patty was trying to lift her spirits, but she didn't try to kid herself into thinking Cain would be waiting for her when she arrived home. Yet she couldn't help hoping.

It was dark by the time they arrived at the ranch.

"See, what did I tell you?" Patty said, sounding wise and smug. "Cain's home."

Murphy was there as well.

Patty dropped her off, and Linette walked in the back door off the kitchen. Cain and Murphy were sitting at the table, going over some papers.

Cain's eyes held hers. "Where'd you go?"

"Town," she said, going over to the oven to check on the roast she'd left slow cooking there. "I had some errands to run." She wouldn't tell him about the pregnancy now. She refused to use their child as a weapon.

"Murphy and I've been talking, and I've made up my mind. I'm going with him after Jack." He announced his decision as if he expected her to argue.

There was no fight left in her. "I figured you would."

"We leave at first light."

Her hand tightened around the pot holder, and she nodded.

That evening Cain and Murphy talked long after dinner. Linette finished the dishes, put a load of wash into the machine, and casually announced she was going up to bed.

"If I don't see you in the morning, Murphy," she said smoothly, "have a safe trip."

He eyed her as if he weren't sure he should believe her. "I'll do my damnedest."

"Take care of Cain for me." Her eyes held his for a lengthy moment before he nodded.

"Thank you," she said, and, turning, walked slowly up the stairs.

Linette was asleep when Cain joined her several hours later in the large king-size bed. She sighed when he started to nibble on her earlobe.

"Wake up, sleepyhead," he whispered, his voice low and seductive. His hand massaged her gently.

"Is it morning already?" Her eyes burned, and she felt as if she hadn't slept more than a hour. It seemed impossible that it was time to wake up.

"Don't worry. We've got four or five hours. But I didn't want to waste our last bit of time together sleeping," Cain told her, expertly unfastening the buttons to open the front of her pajamas.

"You want to talk?" she asked, and yawned loudly.

"No," he said, gently rolling her onto her back. "I want to make sure you miss me as much as I'm going to miss you."

Her response to her husband was instinctive. He helped her out of her pajamas, then shucked off his own.

"Baby, I promise—"

Linette stopped him. "Don't make me any more promises," she told him.

It was over almost before it started, their need was so great. They were both too exhausted to speak afterward, for which Linette was grateful. As a result Linette fell asleep tucked securely against her husband, his arms around her.

His kiss against the side of her neck woke her.

"Again?" she asked groggily, thinking he wanted to make love a second time, an occurrence that wasn't uncommon in the weeks since their marriage.

Cain chuckled and kissed her again. "I don't have time. Murphy and I are about to leave."

Linette's eyes flew open and she sat up on the bed, her heart pounding hard and fast. "Already?" A glance at the clock radio told her it was barely three.

"We've got a flight to catch."

She nodded and swallowed against the constriction blocking her throat. It came to her to tell Cain that within a few short months he'd be a father, but it didn't seem right under these circumstances.

"I'll be back before you know it," he assured her.

Linette did her best to smile.

"Don't ever doubt my love for you," he said.

Murphy's shout came from below.

"I'll be there in a minute," Cain called back. He walked across the room, then hesitated as if he weren't certain yet he had the strength to leave her.

Linette cradled her arms around her middle. "Don't do anything stupid."

He stood in the doorway. "I won't."

Linette closed her eyes, unwilling for him to see how close she was to tears. "Good-bye."

"Good-bye."

She scooted back down into the warm blankets and waited for the man she'd married to calmly walk out of her life.

"WHAT have you learned about Enrique?" Cain asked Matt Morrissey, the newest member of Deliverance Company.

"Nothing we didn't already know," Matt said.

"The girl? Zita, wasn't it?"

Matt nodded. "She says she'll only talk to you. My guess is that Enrique paid her handsomely to lure Jack into her place, and now she's looking for a handout from us as well. I doubt she'll be able to help us."

"You're sure of that?" The first communications from Enrique had been addressed to Cain, which was one of the reasons Murphy had initially contacted him at the ranch. Apparently the drug lord didn't know Cain had sold Deliverance Company. Cain was beginning to think there was more to the kidnapping than met the eye.

"I'm not sure of anything," Matt Morrissey said, "but she looks like the type who would gladly cut out her grandmother's liver for five extra dollars."

"You have her with you?"

"She's waiting outside."

"Bring her in." The information phase of this rescue wasn't going well. They'd expected a ransom or other demands long before now, which led to speculation that Jack might no longer be alive. The prospect left those who knew and worked with Jack Keller depressed and short-tempered.

A few moments later Morrissey returned with a beautiful young woman with eyes as round and dark as a fawn's. "Hello," Cain greeted her in her mother language.

The woman eyed him without emotion. "You're Cain McClellan?" she asked.

Cain nodded.

"He wants you dead, you know?" She said this as if it gave her a good deal of pleasure to be the one to tell him the news.

"Many men want me dead."

"Enrique wants more than for you to die."

Cain yawned. He'd heard this and more from several men.

"You killed his favorite brother, and now he wants to return the favor."

"Jack isn't my brother."

"No, he is your friend." This was said smugly, as if she expected a reaction. She laughed then, and the eerie sound of it echoed against the bare walls. "You are a good friend to this Jack, aren't you?"

Cain's gaze narrowed, and he said nothing.

She laughed again and leaned forward, exposing her breasts. "Are my breasts as beautiful as your wife's?"

Cain discovered he was fast losing his patience. "What does Enrique want?" he demanded brusquely.

Dramatically she tossed her hands into the air. "Nothing. He has everything he needs. He wishes me to thank you for your quick response."

The woman spoke in riddles. Cain could think of nothing more to ask her. Matt returned and took her away, and Murphy joined Cain shortly afterward.

"It makes no sense," Cain told his friend.

"What doesn't?" Murphy inquired. "Apparently I killed Enrique's brother and he's after revenge."

"That's why he has Jack."

"That's what he wants us to think, but I don't buy it. Jack's a friend, but he isn't my brother. I'd feel bad if anything happened to Jack, but it wouldn't change my life. Jack readily put his life on the line with every mission."

Cain was packing now, his mind working fast. "How many people know I'm married?"

Murphy shrugged as if he found the question of little consequence.

"Zita knows," Cain snapped. "Enrique knows."

"It isn't like you were planning on keeping it a secret, is it?"

"No, but if Pretty Boy was looking for revenge, just where do you think he'd start?" Cain couldn't believe how stupid he'd been. He'd walked right into Enrique's trap. The drug lord had lured him away from the ranch, away from Linette, with Jack's kidnapping.

"You don't think he'd actually do anything to Linette, do you?" Murphy asked.

"I've got to get to a phone."

It took them the better part of twenty minutes to make long-distance connections with the United States. The better part of Cain's sanity was lost in that time. He'd abandoned his wife and in doing so had set her in a death trap.

When he finally was able to reach the house, there was no answer.

"It may not be as bad as it looks," Murphy said, looking anxious himself. "According to my calculations, it's three in the afternoon. She might be outside. Try again in a couple of minutes."

"Mallory," Cain said next.

"But he's in Washington State," Murphy said, apparently not understanding.

Cain was well aware of exactly where Mallory lived. "If Enrique was looking for a brother to kill, Mallory's as close to me as any relative."

No one answered at Mallory's place, either.

In desperation Cain contacted John Stamp. "Where's Linette?" he asked when Patty answered the phone.

"Cain, is that you? Good grief, you sound like you're phoning from the moon."

"Where's Linette?" Cain pleaded a second time. "Patty, listen, it's very important that I speak to her immediately."

"I'm sorry, but I haven't seen her all day."

"Where is she?"

"Honestly, I don't know why you're so upset, but I don't have a clue where she might be. Funny, now that you mention it, but the truck's here, and I didn't see her leave. Are you sure there's no answer at the house?"

17

Mallory didn't venture far from the house these days. Francine was due to deliver their baby any time now, and frankly he didn't know how much more of this suspense he could take. When he'd first learned Francine was pregnant, Tim had been justifiably proud. It hadn't taken long for his seed to take root, and there was a certain amount of male pride associated with the speed with which he'd impregnated his wife.

Now that the baby was due, Mallory's thoughts were consumed with Francine's well-being. He'd wanted temporarily to move off Vashon Island, where only minimal health care was available. It seemed perfectly logical to him that they rent a hotel room close to the hospital to await the blessed event. But his stubborn wife would hear none of it.

Francine, who hadn't been delicate and small before the pregnancy, was as big as a house now, yet Mallory was convinced he'd never seen her look more beautiful. Her stomach protruded halfway into the next room, yet every move she made was marked with grace and poise.

He marveled at her and not for the first time recognized that he was damn lucky to have married this remarkable woman.

The other day he'd found her in the nursery, preparing the room for their child. He'd seen her fold a minute T-shirt and found it impossible to believe that any child of his would ever be so small.

His son or daughter. The significance of his as-yet-unborn child hadn't fully impacted Mallory. At first the baby was a something rather than a someone. They'd talked about the baby, but the reality of him or her hadn't struck home until Mallory had watched his child blossom and grow inside Francine's womb. This new life had stretched and explored its world, and Mallory had been amazed to have his child kick against his own hand.

Mallory was worried. He was a man who'd spent the better part of his adult life on a battlefield. Yet nothing had concerned him more than this young life he'd created with Francine.

His gaze followed his wife as she set their dinner on the table. He didn't want her to know how anxious and fretful he'd become. Yet it had become harder and harder to hide his distress.

"It really isn't necessary to watch my every move," Francine said, one hand braced against the small of her back. "Trust me, Tim, we'll have plenty of warning before Junior makes an appearance."

"I don't know why you won't listen to reason."

Francine smiled and her eyes brightened, and Mallory swore he would love this woman on his dying day. "We'll have plenty of time to get to the hospital, I promise you."

"The ferries—"

"Run every half hour. Now stop worrying and come to the table. Dinner's ready."

Mallory set aside the evening newspaper and joined his wife at the dining room table. He discovered as her time drew near that he didn't have nearly as hearty an appetite as usual. If this waiting went on much longer, he'd be skin and bone.

"Would you stop," she snapped. "You'd think I was the only woman in the world to be nine months pregnant."

Mallory reached across the table and squeezed her hand. "As far as I'm concerned, you are." It was in his mind to kiss her, but he decided against it. They hadn't made love in three weeks, two days, and ten hours, not that he was counting. The problem was, Mallory had never desired his wife more. Kissing her just then was more temptation than he could handle.

"Take heart. I talked to my mother this morning, and she'll be here for two weeks following my release from the hospital. You can relax and let Grandma take over."

Mallory didn't know how other husbands felt about their mothers-in-law, but frankly, he was overjoyed that Martha would be with them.

"Good," he said, and reached for the bread and butter. "But I still think we should be hiring a nurse or a nanny or whatever it is other families do."

"We aren't going to need a nanny. We're going to care for this baby ourselves. We'll take turns changing diapers."

"Hey, just a minute," Mallory said, holding up his right hand. "No one said anything to me about messy diapers."

"I'm saying it now. You wanted to be a father, re-member?"

Mallory grinned. "As I recall, I was far more inter-ested in the creative process."

The phone rang just then. Francine looked to him. "Let the answering machine get it," she pleaded. "You know how much I dislike having our dinner inter-rupted."

It was a small request, and Mallory agreed. "I doubt it's important."

They finished their meal, and as Mallory carried the dishes to the sink, he noticed Francine staring out the window above the kitchen sink.

"Something wrong?"

"The light's off inside the barn."

Mallory glanced out the window himself. A still, ee-rie darkness permeated the night.

"It'd be just like Bubba to use this as an excuse to raise all kinds of hell," Francine murmured.

The male llama had been a thorn in Mallory's side from the first. After months of working together, man and beast had a grudging respect for each other.

"You'd better see about getting the bulbs changed. Do you want me to come with you?"

"Every light's off," Mallory said, wondering what had blown the breaker. It wasn't likely that every light bulb had malfunctioned at the same time.

"I'll finish up here," Francine told him, and opened the dishwasher.

Mallory kissed her on the cheek on his way out the door. Humming to himself, he made his way across the yard. His steps slowed. Tension filled the night air. It was almost as if he were on a mission again, and Cain

McClellan were at his side. The hair on the back of his neck rose, and it wasn't from static electricity.

He was only a few steps away from the barn door when he heard Francine.

"Tim. Tim," she called, her voice filled with controlled fear.

Mallory whirled around to discover his wife standing on the porch steps, her arms cradling her grossly extended stomach. The light above the door illuminated her face. Her eyes were round and imploring.

Mallory swore his blood ran cold. "Is it the baby?"

"JOHN," Cain said hurriedly into the telephone receiver. His plane was scheduled to depart in twenty minutes, but he was frantic to learn what he could of his wife's whereabouts. "Have you talked to Linette yet?"

"I can't say that I have. But don't you worry, I'm sure everything's fine. I've sent Patty over to the house to check up on her."

"No," Cain cried. "Don't send Patty there alone."

"I'm sorry, Cain, but I'm having trouble hearing you. There's a bunch of static on the line. Can you hear me?"

The irony of the situation was that his end of the telephone was as clear as Austrian church bells. Rarely had Cain felt more helpless. He'd spent the better part of two fruitless hours attempting to warn those closest to him that he suspected they were in grave danger.

Unable to talk to Mallory personally, Cain had been forced to leave a cryptic message on his answering machine. This was his second, or was it his third call to the Stamps? He didn't remember any longer. The local sheriff had promised to send someone out to check on Linette, but that could be hours yet.

"John, listen to me, and listen carefully. Linette may be in danger. There's a man seeking revenge against me. He knows about Linette."

"Cain, listen, I apologize, but I still can't hear you. Your voice keeps fading in and out. From what I understand, you're worried about Linette."

"Yes!" Cain screamed. Worried was the understatement of the year.

"I'm sure everything's fine. By the way, I understand congratulations are in order."

"Congratulations?" He didn't know if his wife was alive or dead, and his foreman was issuing congratulations. It didn't seem possible that in this nightmare there might be news that was good.

"Patty went to the doctor with Linette. So you're going to be a father."

Cain felt the sudden need to sit down. Linette hadn't said a word. Hadn't so much as hinted at her condition, not even when she might have used the information to keep him from leaving with Murphy. He closed his eyes and braced his forehead against the wall.

"Patty gave her one of those home test kits, but Linette wanted a GYN to confirm her condition. You'll like Dr. Adams. He delivered both our boys."

"Find Linette," Cain shouted into the receiver. "Keep her safe. I'll be there as soon as I can."

"You haven't got a thing to worry about," John assured him. "Just relax and you'll be home before you know it."

"I'm sorry, I didn't mean to alarm everyone," Linette said, looking to John and Patty Stamp. The couple stood at the end of her bed, looking slightly embarrassed for having walked uninvited into the house.

"It's just that Cain phoned and said he was worried about you," John explained.

"Worried. Whatever for?"

"John couldn't make it out. Apparently the line was bad," Patty said. "Men . . . I doubt we'll ever understand them."

"I haven't felt good all day. I think I might be coming down with a case of the flu." Linette felt mildly guilty. The phone had been ringing off the hook all morning. She'd finally unplugged it in order to sleep without constant interruptions.

"You say Cain's been trying to reach me?"

"That's what he said. He's on his way home. I don't understand it myself, but he wants you to stay with us until he's back."

"That's ridiculous."

"He's probably concerned about your being pregnant," Patty offered.

"He doesn't know," Linette admitted sheepishly. "I didn't tell him."

John Stamp buried his hands in his jean pockets and shifted his weight from one leg to the other. "He knows now. I didn't realize you were keeping it a secret. I congratulated him when he phoned."

"He knows?" This left Linette to wonder if this was the reason Cain was rushing back to Montana.

"He didn't act surprised."

"He wouldn't," Patty muttered.

Linette understood why. No man would willingly admit to his hired help that he'd been left in the dark about his own wife's condition.

"Did he say when to expect him?"

John rotated the brim of his hat in his large hands. "I

can't rightly say. He seemed far more concerned about you staying with the missus and me for the next couple of days."

"But that's ridiculous."

"It's what Cain wants."

"I'm not leaving this house, John Stamp, no matter what instructions my husband gave you. Not when I can barely lift my head off this pillow. I don't know what's gotten into Cain, but I assure you, I can take care of myself."

Still John hesitated. "You're sure about that?"

"Positive."

"Then so be it. Just be sure you let Cain know that the decision was yours. I've seen that man when he's upset, and I don't want to be on the receiving end of his temper."

"You won't be," Linette promised.

"How are you feeling now?" Patty asked.

"My stomach's queasy." Her head throbbed with a killer headache, and she alternated between sweats and chills.

"When was the last time you had anything to eat?" Patty asked.

Linette shook her head. She didn't remember. "Morning, I guess." Tea and dry toast. Neither had stayed down for long, but she wasn't sure if that could be attributed to the flu or to morning sickness.

"It might be a good idea if I stayed the night with her," Linette heard Patty suggest to her husband. "You and the boys can manage one night without me, can't you?"

"No problem," John assured her.

"Patty, that isn't necessary. All I do is sleep. You can

check on me every four or five hours if you want, but there's no need for you to spend the night here."

"Nonsense. Don't deprive me of this night of peace and quiet. It'd be like a minivacation for me." Patty kissed her husband and shooed him out of the room ahead of her. "I'll be back before you know it," her friend told her.

Linette tried to smile, but her head hurt and she discovered she was sleepy again. She'd rest her eyes a few moments, she told herself, and be awake by the time Patty returned.

"WHAT is it?" Mallory asked as he raced toward the house.

"I think it's time," Francine said. "I felt this sharp pain, and the next thing I knew my water broke."

"Okay," Mallory said, sounding calm and collected when he was anything but. "We'll phone the doctor, get your suitcase, and head for the hospital."

"You phone the doctor," Francine said. "There are a couple of items I still need to stick inside my suitcase."

Mallory froze on the top step. "You mean to tell me that after nine months you still aren't ready for this baby?"

Francine smiled calmly and kissed the corner of his mouth. "Don't panic. Everything's going to work out just fine."

Panic was an adequate word to describe Mallory's brewing emotions. They'd been waiting for this moment for weeks, and now that their child's birth was imminent, Mallory wasn't sure he was mentally prepared for the ordeal. Already it felt as if his bad leg were about to go out on him. He tried to disguise his fear from Francine and doubted his playacting worked.

As calmly as possible, he walked over to the phone and picked up the receiver. He looked up and punched out the Seattle number, then realized there was no dial tone. To make sure he wasn't imagining things, he tapped the plunger several times. Nothing.

The flashing red light of the answering machine blinked on and off, reminding him the phone had been working only moments earlier. He hit the switch on the machine and was surprised to hear Cain's voice.

"Mallory . . . Cain here. Listen, I hate . . . alarmist, but . . . danger . . . lurking about. Don't . . . chances. Enrique . . . revenge. I'll explain everything . . . worried . . . take care."

Mallory rewound the tape and listened to it a second time. The connection was bad. One thing was certain, Cain wouldn't have left the message if he didn't believe Mallory and Francine were in danger.

That explained what had happened to the lights and the phone.

"Tim?" Francine stood just inside the doorway to his small office. "What's wrong?"

"The line's dead." He couldn't very well tell his wife, who was in the first stages of labor, that they didn't dare leave the house for fear of what they'd encounter outside their back door.

"Someone's out there," Francine said without emotion. "Someone who wants you dead."

Mallory frowned. This woman never ceased to amaze him. "How'd you know that?"

"I heard part of Cain's message. Who's Enrique?"

"The hell if I know." Mallory ran a hand down his face. "He wouldn't be the first man who wanted to see me six feet under. He probably won't be the last."

"What are we going to do?" Francine asked, and bit into her lower lip. He admired her for staying calm and wasn't sure there were many women with her coolness.

"Don't worry about a thing," Mallory said, hoping to reassure her.

All at once Francine sucked in her breath and widened her eyes.

"What is it?" he asked, hurrying toward her. He gripped her hands in his own, surprised at the strength with which she held on to him.

After a moment she relaxed and smiled up at him. "That, my darling husband, was a labor pain."

"How strong was it? Is this your first one? How far apart are they?" His heart was pounding so loud, it was sounding out taps in his ear.

"Slow down," Francine advised, her hands squeezing his. "I'm fine, and so is the baby. I got a bit frightened there when my water broke, but everything's going to be all right. What's our situation like?"

Mallory closed his eyes in an effort to calm his heart and his head. "I don't know. My guess is that we're being watched."

"Can we leave the house?"

"I don't know that yet."

"I'm going to lie down," Francine said without emotion. "More water leaks out every time I have a pain, and I don't think it's a good idea for me to be walking around so much."

Mallory nodded and, taking her by the elbow, escorted her into the master bedroom. He left the lights out and helped Francine onto the mattress.

After adjusting the pillow and bringing her a fresh supply of towels, he asked, "Can I get you anything more?"

"I'm fine."

Unfortunately Mallory couldn't say the same thing. He was a wreck. He didn't know who or what lurked outside his front door. His wife was in labor, and for all his medical experience in the field, he didn't know a thing about delivering a baby.

His phone was out of order. As far as he could see, only one option was left open to him. He had to discover for himself exactly what danger awaited them before he brought Francine out of their house.

His camouflage gear was tucked away in a trunk in the attic. Using a flashlight, Mallory climbed the stairs to where his equipment was stored. He changed clothes quickly and smeared a mixture of black and green paint over his face.

"Tim?"

He heard Francine's timid voice almost immediately. "I'm coming, sweetheart."

Francine gasped and levered herself on one elbow when she saw him. A smile softened her features. "Just what do you think you're doing?"

"I don't know," he said sarcastically. "It seemed like a good time to dress up for Halloween. What the hell do you think I'm doing?"

"Just where are you going?"

"Outside."

All at once she bit into her lower lip, closed her eyes, and breathed in deeply. She seemed to be counting silently, her head moving almost imperceptibly. "How long will you be gone?"

Mallory knelt down on the floor beside the mattress. "I don't know. Will you be all right alone for a few moments?"

"Of course." How confident she sounded, as if she gave birth once a week the way some women did the washing. "Just promise me one thing."

"You got it."

"Please be careful, Tim," she whispered, her hands resting over her rounded tummy. "I don't want to have to deliver this baby on my own."

"You haven't got a thing to worry about, sweetheart," he said with supreme confidence. When it came to fighting for money, Mallory had been one of the best, but this time it was his family. He was protecting his wife and their child; he'd be more than good.

He'd be lethal.

"Are you feeling any better?" Patty asked Linette. She sat on the edge of the mattress and held a tray in her hand. Linette noted that her neighbor had been thoughtful enough to bring her soup. Chicken noodle, from the looks of it, along with several soda crackers.

Somehow Linette managed a weak smile. She felt worse now than earlier. "I don't know that I can eat anything."

"Give it a try. A couple of spoonfuls of soup and we'll see how your stomach handles that. Have you been drinking plenty of liquids?"

Linette closed her eyes. She'd barely gotten out of bed in two days.

"Don't answer that, I can tell that you haven't. Here," Patty said, setting a glass of water next to the bedstand. She stayed with Linette until she managed two pitiful mouthfuls of the soup, and then shook her head, unable to take more.

"Is there anything else I can get you?"

"No. I'm fine. Really. I'll rest and feel better by morning."

"I'm sure you will," Patty said, brushing the hair away from Linette's brow. "At least your fever's broken. That's a good sign."

"See, I'm already on the road to recovery."

Cain was on his way home. Linette wasn't sure how she felt about that. He'd broken his word. He'd walked out on her. Now he seemed to think that all he needed to do was come rushing back and everything would return to the way it had been before.

Wrong.

What Cain failed to realize was that if he had the option to pick and choose which promises he opted to keep, then she did as well.

Although she'd sold Wild and Wooly to Bonnie, she still felt very much a part of the business. Bonnie was a wonderful manager, but for all her business finesse, the older woman didn't have the strong personal relationship with the customers that Linette had worked so hard to build. From what Bonnie wrote, several of her former clients had asked about Linette. Even more had inquired about the evening classes she'd once taught.

As much as she tried to tell herself otherwise, Linette missed San Francisco and her life there. She could understand the desire Cain felt to go back to Deliverance Company. Murphy had offered him the perfect reason.

She could understand, but she couldn't accept that he'd broken his word. He'd left her sitting at home, twiddling her thumbs, waiting like a dutiful wife for her husband's return.

Patty came back a few minutes later and removed the dinner tray. She carried a thick novel with her. "I can't tell you how long I've been waiting to read this book. I'm going to soak in a bubble bath until my skin shrivels up into tiny wrinkles. You'll call me if you need me, won't you?"

"I'm feeling much better already," Linette assured her friend. "Take your time and enjoy yourself."

"I will. I can't remember the last time I took a bath without little green army men camped along the edge of the tub. This is going to be pure heaven."

It might have been the soup or the fact she had company, Linette didn't know which, but she did feel better. Sitting up in bed, she reached down and plugged in the phone. To her amazement it rang almost immediately.

"Hello," she said into the mouthpiece.

"Linette? It's Cain."

"Hello. Cain?" She wished she didn't sound so pleased to hear from him, but she was, despite everything.

"Are you all right? Is someone there with you?"

Her hand tightened around the receiver. "I'm perfectly fine. I don't need a keeper, you know."

"Who's with you?"

"Patty Stamp."

Cain's response sounded very much like a string of swear words.

"Where are you?" she asked.

"I just landed in Florida. Listen, babe, I don't know if John fully understands the situation."

"What about Jack?"

"He hasn't been found yet," he answered impatiently.

"Then what are you doing back in the States?" She closed her eyes, already knowing the answer to her questions. "Is it because I'm pregnant?"

"Where's John?" he asked, ignoring her words.

"His house, I suppose."

Again his response was followed by a list of words she'd never heard her husband use in her presence before. Linette frowned, not knowing what to think.

"Cain, what's wrong? Patty said the sheriff stopped by to check up on me."

"Nothing you need to worry about," he said in a tight, strained voice that said otherwise. "I was thinking maybe it would be a good idea if you visited Nancy for a few days."

"My sister-in-law, Nancy Lewis? Whatever for? Cain, there's something you're not telling me." She could hear the alarm in his voice, and if she read him right, it had little or nothing to do with her pregnancy.

"Linette, listen, I made a mistake in leaving you. Jack's capture was a setup to get me out of the country."

"A setup?"

"There's a man by the name of Enrique who wants me to suffer, and the way to hurt me is through the people I love. He's knows I'm married, and I'm afraid it won't take him long to discover you're alone at the ranch."

Linette sucked in her breath. "Oh, dear God."

"I've already hired a couple of men to watch the house for any unusual activity, but for the love of heaven, Linette, don't trust anyone. I made a mistake in not making John understand the seriousness of the situation, but I didn't want to alarm him. I don't have the luxury of that any longer."

"What do you want me to do?" Linette's hand was trembling so badly that it was difficult to keep hold of the telephone.

"You'll be safer with Nancy. Get there as soon as you can make the arrangements."

"What about you?"

"I can take care of myself," he assured her. "But damn it all to hell, Linette, I can do a better job of it if I'm not worried sick about you."

She stiffened at his words. "I apologize for being such a burden to you."

He swore again, this time with regret. "I couldn't live with myself if anything were ever to happen to you or the baby. You're my life. I was a fool to have ever left you. Trust me, this isn't a mistake I'll soon forget."

"I sincerely hope not," she told him.

"I don't want you to worry, you're safe for now."

A thought suddenly occurred to her. "But how will I know the bad guys from the good guys?"

"You won't, but then it's unlikely that you'll ever see either. Just get to San Francisco as soon as you can."

"But what if I'm followed?"

"You will be," he assured her.

"I mean by the wrong people," she insisted. "I don't want to put Nancy or her family in jeopardy."

"You won't, babe, I assure you. Just promise me you'll take care of yourself."

"I will. You too."

"I will. I will."

"And Cain?"

"Yes."

"Get that son of a bitch."

Her husband chuckled. "My thoughts exactly."

18

There were two men, Mallory decided. The first had positioned himself outside the barn, and the second was stationed behind a tree and was studying the house. Mallory didn't know how much time he had before they made their move. He wasn't sure how much time Francine had, either.

Cold fury tightened his muscles until he had to force himself to relax. He didn't have the luxury of venting his anger. Just yet. Soon, though. Soon enough these men would pay.

Try as he might, Mallory couldn't get Francine out of his mind. It was vital on any mission to clear his head of distractions. His wife, her body twisted with labor pains, was more than a minor distraction, however.

She'd attempted to disguise her fears, but Mallory had seen through her brave front. She was frightened. Hell, so was he.

Mallory worked his way around the outside of the barn, circling the first man, taking care to remain as silent as possible. Only he wasn't quiet enough.

Mallory stopped breathing when a shadowy figure emerged from the barn no more than ten feet from where he was standing. For one horrible moment he assumed there was another man he hadn't known about and he'd blithely walked into their trap. His heart beat in slow, irregular thuds for several seconds until he realized the figure wasn't that of a man.

It was Bubba, his cantankerous male llama, the bane of his existence.

Bubba had heard Mallory. Apparently the llama assumed that if Mallory was in the vicinity, it must be feeding time, whether the sun was out or not.

Mallory's attention went to the gunman positioned alongside the barn. The man, dressed in army fatigues, lifted his head and peered into the thick darkness like a wild beast testing the wind. After a moment he signaled to the second man, who zigzagged across the yard before joining him.

Mallory was a safe distance from the pair but close enough to pick up the majority of their conversation. Luckily he was fluent in Spanish and understood every word.

"What the hell's that? It looks like a horse," the gunman stated.

"It's a llama."

"A what?"

"A llama."

"What's it doing out here?"

"Hell if I know."

The second man checked his weapon. "Are they still inside the house?"

"The woman is."

"What about Mallory?"

The second man was silent for a moment, then, "He knows we're here. He's out here somewhere, watching, waiting."

"Let's get the woman. That'll flush him out."

The other man's soft laugh lacked humor. "Trust me, neither one of us would make it two steps inside that house."

After a bit more, the two separated. The first man returned to his post near the front of the barn.

Thinking all these visitors should pay him heed, Bubba followed the gunman at a leisurely pace. He stopped and craned his long, sleek neck over the fence, seeking a handout. At first the man ignored the beast, but Bubba, bless his miserable, black heart, didn't take kindly to being ignored.

He spat at him.

The gunman swore and wiped the slime from his face.

If circumstances had been any different, Mallory would have laughed outright. The hired killer whirled around and cursed the llama vehemently. This was the moment Mallory had been waiting for. Bubba had provided the distraction he needed.

Mallory slithered forward from his hiding place. For an instant all he could think about was Francine and his need to get back to her. All he could see was his wife, waiting inside the house, frightened and worried. His wife, giving birth to his child alone, not knowing if he'd return.

Deliberately he wiped her image from his mind. No longer was he a husband. No longer was he a soon-to-be father. For that moment he was a trained killer.

The first man went down without knowing what had

hit him. Mallory ducked behind the side of the barn and waited for the second hired gun to realize something was amiss.

All around him was silence. The kind that broke through sound barriers and rocked men's souls. The kind that throbbed like a breathing, living beast. The waiting game was about to end.

Inside, Francine's nails dug into her thick comforter and she struggled not to cry out as a contraction twisted her body. Tim had been gone for hours. Time lost meaning. Between pains she prayed for his safety, knowing that if anything happened to him, the killers would come for her and the baby.

Francine tried not to think about what was happening outside the house. Every ounce of energy she possessed was tunneled into the birthing process.

The pains became stronger. She didn't know how much longer she could withstand the agony without crying out. Yet she dared not.

"It wasn't supposed to happen like this," she whispered to her unborn child. Her hand rested on her tightening abdomen, which she rubbed, wanting to reassure both her and her infant.

The labor pain came on slowly, working its way from the small of her back around her abdomen, growing in intensity.

"Tim," she pleaded into the dark silence between deep, even breaths. "Please, oh, please hurry."

Knowing she'd have two, possibly three minutes to rest between contractions, Francine closed her eyes and tried to relax. She tried desperately not to think about what was happening outside her home. Tried not to think if her husband was alive or dead.

She wasn't one to give in to panic, but she felt the emotion bubbling up inside her like fizz ready to explode from a pop bottle.

Another contraction arrived, this one more acute than the others. Francine bore it as best she could. By the time the pain receded, she tasted blood and knew her teeth had cut into her lip.

A door slammed, followed by the sound of running footsteps. Before she drew another breath, Tim was kneeling on the floor next to her. He gathered her in his arms and hugged her as if he wanted never to let her go.

"Are you all right?" she asked, brushing the hair from his face, looking for signs that he might have been hurt.

"Yes. Yes. Let's get you to the hospital."

"No," she said softly, gripping his large hand with both of hers. "It's too late for that now."

"Too late? What do you mean, it's too late?"

She loved the way his voice rose and cracked with a loving kind of hysteria.

"In case you didn't know, we're about to have a baby," she told him softly, her strength fading.

"I've known that for close to nine months. I was there in the beginning, remember?" He spoke fast, running the words together.

"I mean we're about to have a baby *soon*."

"How soon?" He was on his feet and backing away from her as if he suspected what she had was contagious.

"Within the hour, I'd guess. The pains are less than two minutes apart. I'm about to enter the second stage of labor." Briefly she closed her eyes, sensing his fear, facing her own. "I'm going to need your help."

Tim looked down on her as though he were tempted

to turn and run. Again he knelt on the floor beside her and gripped her hands.

"Tell me what you want me to do."

She smiled up at him through her tears. "I love you, Tim Mallory."

"You must," he agreed, rolling up the sleeves of his camouflage shirt. "Otherwise you wouldn't be willing to go through this."

JOHN Stamp carried Linette's suitcase out to the car and glanced about him suspiciously. "You're sure about driving out of here alone?" he asked as if he were looking for her to change her mind. He stood back, waiting for her reply.

"I'll be fine," Linette assured him. She didn't say it, but it was probably safer as well for John and the Stamp family that she left.

John looked to his wife as if seeking confirmation. Patty didn't seem any more confident than her husband. "This doesn't seem right to me," she said to her husband. "I don't see anyone out here who's going to protect you."

"Cain said I should go. Now stop worrying."

"I wish Cain had said something to *me*," John muttered.

"Is there a phone number where I can reach you?" Patty asked Linette.

Linette hesitated, uncertain she should give out Nancy's phone number. "I'm feeling much better now, don't fret. I'll give you a call once I'm settled." She opened the car door and slipped inside the driver's side. John held the door open, and it seemed to Linette that he was looking for an excuse to keep her.

"You promise to keep in touch?" Patty asked a second time, her voice slightly higher than normal.

Linette nodded. She reached for the door, and John released it reluctantly. He wrapped his arm around his wife's shoulder, and the pair stepped back as Linette started the engine. The driveway had never seemed so long as when she pulled out of the yard.

Once on the main road, Linette reached for the radio and turned on the local station. Anything to fill the silence. Anything to take her mind off who might be watching her every move.

She'd phoned early that morning and booked the first available flight to San Francisco. A call to Nancy and Rob had assured her of a warm welcome. Cain had promised to contact her in San Francisco to be sure she'd arrived safely.

A glance in her rearview mirror revealed a black luxury car coming behind her at a fast rate of speed. Her heart started to pound, but she forced herself to repeat Cain's reassurances. He'd promised her that she would never see either the good or the bad guys.

The car gained speed. Linette certainly hoped these folks were patient because it might be several miles before there was a chance to pass her on these twisty, curvy roads.

The sedan was practically on her bumper. Suspicious, Linette sped up. The other car increased its speed. Her nervousness mounted with every moment. At long last the car chose to go around her. Linette wondered at their wisdom. The edge of the road led to a steep embankment, and it made her nervous to look over the side. It had always bothered her to drive this stretch of road without guardrails.

The vehicle pulled alongside her, and Linette knew then that something was very wrong. The two men in the car were looking at her. The two cars were so close, their side panels touched.

Linette refused to give ground. There was none to give. Another two or three feet and she'd be forced over the embankment.

Her heart raced like an oil drill pumping out raw crude. Her fingers felt as if they were fused to the steering column.

So much for Cain's reassurances. This wasn't a silly game played by two overgrown teenagers. These men were attempting to kill her.

Adrenaline shot through Linette like liquid fire. The sedan slammed hard against the side of her vehicle, the hit jolting her. Linette screamed in terror at the sound of metal scraping against metal. Her hands gripped the steering wheel as firmly as she'd hold on to a life preserver in a sea storm.

The wheels on the right side of the car were off the road now, spitting up gravel and dirt. She'd lost ground, precious inches.

She realized she wasn't going to be able to save herself. She'd barely talked to Cain about their baby. She hadn't had the chance to tell her husband that she'd never been more pleased about anything. Her baby. She refused to allow these men to destroy her child.

From some reserve of strength and determination she hadn't known she possessed, Linette turned the car directly into the other vehicle. Sparks flew from the clash of steel. Again she was jarred; she felt her head whip to the side and slam against the window. Struggling to remain conscious, she decided she wasn't going to let them kill her without putting up a fight.

Her concentration was absorbed in staying on the road. In staying alive. All at once, without warning, she noticed a third vehicle headed straight toward her. A head-on collision was inevitable.

Everything happened in slow motion. Linette slammed on her brakes and instinctively raised her arms to protect her face. The instant her hands were off the steering wheel, the car veered to the right. Two wheels teetered on the ledge of the embankment before catapulting over.

Linette screamed as the car rolled again and again and again. Her cries reverberated inside the car, playing back to her as if from a Swiss mountainside.

Then she knew nothing.

$\mathcal{I}$T hurt to breathe. Jack Keller suspected he had four broken ribs and an equal number of broken, nailless fingers. This was what he got for being so stupid. He'd walked right into that trap. After all his years of training, he should've known better.

His one good finger on his right hand tentatively investigated the extent of his injuries, and he felt one rib bone jutting out against his skin. He moaned softly. He tried to open his eyes, but both were swollen shut. What he did manage to see between the narrow sliver of light wasn't encouraging. It looked as if he were behind bars. How long he'd been there, he could only speculate. Too long.

He heard a pair of voices from the other side of the wall. One sounded vaguely familiar. Enrique's? No, he decided. He hadn't seen the drug lord in several days and had no wish to make the other man's acquaintance again.

Enrique had been full of questions about Cain. Jack had pretended not to know anything. His silence had cost him dearly. He'd talked plenty, but he hadn't told them anything they could use against Cain.

The faintly familiar voice drifted toward Jack a second time. If he didn't know better, he'd think it was Murphy. But even Murphy's accent was better than that.

It wasn't Murphy. It couldn't be. No one knew where Jack was. This stinkhole was too deep for him to ever be found. The way he figured, with his internal injuries, he wouldn't last much longer anyway.

He had regrets. Didn't everyone? He thought about his life. The turns in the road he'd taken, the choices he'd made. Good and bad. He would have preferred to live to a ripe old age and pass on with a loving family gathered around his bedside. Instead he was likely to die without anyone ever learning what had happened to him. He'd decided, early in his army career, to live by the sword. He expected to die by it. And he would.

Consciousness started to fade. Jack welcomed the oblivion.

A war seemed to be going on outside his door. Fitting, really, that he should go out surrounded by gunfire. The door burst open, and Jack feared Enrique's gorillas had come to torture him again.

"Jack."

It was Murphy.

"It's about time," he mumbled.

"Sweet Jesus, what have they done to you?"

Jack tried to smile. He knew he must look like crap. Well, that adequately described the way he felt.

"Never mind what you look like," Murphy said, chuckling. "You never were that good-looking anyway."

𝒯IM wiped a cool cloth over Francine's face. "How are we doing?" he asked, and his voice shook slightly, as if he'd paid a heavy penalty for each of her contractions.

Her eyes remained closed, but she managed a weak smile. "So far so good." Her breathing was hard and labored. Giving birth was by far the most draining ordeal of her life.

A pain gripped her at the small of her back, and she whimpered, unable to disguise her agony as the contraction knotted her uterus, attempting to force the baby from her body. By the time the last of the pain had ebbed away, she was panting and weak.

"Can you see the baby's head?" she asked when she had her breath back.

Tim moved to the foot of the mattress. "Yes," he cried excitedly, sounding shocked and more than a little frightened. "The baby's almost here."

"I know," Francine whispered.

The time between contractions seemed like none at all. The next one gripped her body like a vise, and she had the strong urge to push. Her hands found and locked around the rails of the headboard as she bore down with all her might. The effort half lifted her from the bed.

"Good, sweetheart, good," Tim praised her.

After the next contraction, she felt the baby's head spill between her legs. Tim's gentle hands cradled their infant's tiny head. A mewling cry filled the room as their child drew its first breath.

"We have a son," Tim announced in a strangled voice that sounded nothing like his own.

Rising up on her elbows, Francine watched as her husband severed the umbilical cord and gently wrapped their freshly washed child in a soft, warm blanket. Tears fell unrestrained down her husband's cheeks as he gazed upon his son.

"A boy," he repeated, as if he didn't quite believe it even now. Taking exquisite care, he placed their child in Francine's waiting arms.

"He's beautiful," she whispered, weeping silently.

"It's little wonder when you're his mother."

Francine stared down at her son, completely enraptured by the pink, crinkly face topped with a crown of dark hair. Then she unwrapped the blanket to inspect his hands and feet, count his fingers and toes.

"I told you he was a boy," Tim said, as if she'd doubted his word.

"I love you, Tim Mallory," she whispered through her tears. She felt shaken by the enormity of the love that swept through her for her husband and for her baby. Never had she experienced anything so powerful.

Tim sat on the mattress and wrapped his arm around her shoulders. "If you aren't partial to any name, I'd like to suggest one."

"Sure," she said, eager to hear his suggestion.

Tim smiled and gently kissed the crown of her head. "How about Bubba?"

19 ✖

*K*nowing Linette was safely on her way to San Francisco left Cain free to hunt down Enrique. He tracked the man deep into the heart of Central America.

He ended up in a known hangout of Enrique's, a cantina. Wearing a disguise, Cain pretended he was there to quench his thirst. Knowing it was best not to ask questions, he made himself comfortable and listened in on the conversations around him. Within a few hours Cain learned everything he needed to know. As he'd guessed, Enrique was in town. He left his killing to others—not that he didn't have the taste for it himself, but there were problems waiting for him in the States and he dared not take the chance of crossing the borders.

By nightfall Pretty Boy stopped by the cantina himself, his mood jubilant. Before long he had his arm around the waist of a lusty señorita, and it soon became apparent the two had matters other than conversation on their minds.

Cain watched Enrique closely from the shadowy

corner in the back of the room. Pretty Boy was both careless and overconfident as he stood and followed the woman out of the bar.

One of his men looked up and called out in Spanish, "Hey, man. When you're through, I'll have a turn with her myself."

Enrique laughed, and his hand stroked the woman's slim buttocks. "Be patient, my friend," he said. "I have the feeling this may take a very long time."

His men booed, and in an effort to appease them, Enrique ordered a fresh round of drinks.

Cain left by means of the side door and made certain he wasn't being followed. By now Jack would have been rescued and Linette was safely tucked away with family. He followed the couple for several blocks.

"I understand you've been looking for me," Cain said, stepping close behind the other man.

Pretty Boy froze, then viciously pushed the woman away from him before he turned to face Cain. He swore violently, then smiled, revealing even white teeth in a humorless display.

Cain smiled in return, enjoying the advantage of surprise. "You're stupid," he told the other man, "to let yourself get caught like this. I would have thought better of you."

"I'm celebrating," Enrique told him, gesturing with his hand. "The news of your wife's death reached me this afternoon." He laughed sadistically. "Perhaps you should join her, McClellan." He pulled a gun from his pocket and fired the weapon in rapid succession.

Cain flung himself to the ground, shooting as he went down. It was over within seconds. Enrique lay dead on the dusty street, his eyes staring blankly into the night sky.

Cain studied the man and felt no thrill in the death. No thrill in eliminating one who brought only suffering and heartache into the world.

A shout could be heard in the distance, and Cain made haste leaving town. He rendezvoused with Murphy an hour later.

"He's dead," Cain said without expression.

"Good." Murphy's eyes refused to meet Cain's. "Listen, I have some bad news. It's about Linette. You'd best get back to Montana fast."

The hours it took him to reach Montana were the longest of his life. Cain paced the hospital waiting room like a beast until an older couple glared at him, silently requesting that he stop.

The woman left the room, and minutes later a chaplain came into the area.

"Are you all right, son?" asked the minister, claiming the vacant chair next to Cain.

Cain looked over at the compassionate man, and his throat constricted. He wasn't anywhere close to being all right. Fear and anger festered inside him like a raging infection. Rarely had he tasted hate in such a bitter form.

"I'm fine," Cain said tightly, and clenched his fists so hard that the blood drained from his fingers. He stood then, because sitting for any length of time was impossible.

"Is there someone I can phone for you?"

"No one." Cain had sent both John and Patty Stamp home for fear his frustrations would spill over onto them. Neither deserved to receive the brunt of his anger.

The minister gently pressed his hand on Cain's shoulder. "The chapel's on the bottom floor if you change your mind. I'll be there until six this evening."

Cain nodded, eager for the man to leave him alone. The minister left, and Cain returned to the chair and buried his face in his hands. He hadn't slept in two nights. Hadn't been able to close his eyes without picturing Linette being pulled from the wreckage that had once been their car.

He could hear her screams of terror, feel her pain. The torment of those last moments hounded him like an evil spirit.

All this had happened to his wife because of him. Because of what he was and what he did.

A shuffle of footsteps attracted his attention, and Cain looked up to find Murphy standing just inside the doorway. He walked across the room and sat down next to Cain.

"Enrique's henchmen have been rounded up," he announced.

Cain regretted that he hadn't had the pleasure of killing the sons of bitches himself. "What about Jack?"

"He's been better."

"Is he going to make it all right?"

"Sure. Give him a month or two and he'll be good as new."

"I'm glad to hear it."

Murphy leaned forward and braced his elbows against his knees. "What about Linette?"

Pain tightened his chest, and Cain found he couldn't answer. He shrugged. She'd been badly hurt, but it could have been much worse. He felt helpless to reach her, helpless to comfort her. The guilt of knowing he was the one responsible for what had happened ate at him like sharks in a feeding frenzy.

The two men sat side by side without speaking for the next hour. No sooner had Murphy left than Linette's physician stepped into the room.

Cain stood, his eyes connecting with the other man's. He instinctively squared his shoulders, dreading the worst.

"I'm sorry, but we couldn't save the baby. We did everything possible."

"My wife?"

"She's resting comfortably for now."

Cain's legs felt as if they'd gone out from under him, and he slumped onto the chair. The physician sat next to him, going over the extent of injuries. The prognosis for a complete recovery was excellent.

"When can I see her?"

"Soon. Let her sleep for now, that's what she needs most. Her body's been badly battered. The seat belt and air bag saved her, but the shock of losing the baby has taken its toll. I suggest you let her sleep."

Cain would have agreed to anything just then. "Fine. I'll be here."

A few more hours later Linette squinted against the bright light and rolled her head to one side. She discovered Cain sprawled on the red vinyl chair next to her hospital bed, asleep. His head drooped to one side and his arm dangled over the cushioned armrest, his knuckles brushing the polished floor.

She stared at her husband for several moments. The memory of everything that had happened flooded her mind. She'd lost the child. Nothing mattered but her baby. Not the men who'd attempted to murder her, not the fate of the occupants of the other vehicle. Nothing. Only the death of her child.

It was easier to close her eyes and sink back into a drug-induced sleep than deal with reality.

The next time Linette woke up, Cain was standing at her bedside, her hand cradled between both of his.

"Hello, honey," he whispered.

She blinked up at him, finding the lights inordinately bright. "The baby," she said. There was no question in her voice, only certainty.

His response seemed to require a long time. "There'll be other children," he said gently.

"I wanted this baby," she said, choking on a sob.

"I wanted this baby, too."

His words were meant to reassure her, but she felt no comfort, only pain, only grief, her old friends. After Michael's death, Linette had given up the hope of re-marrying and having children. Then she'd met and married Cain, and it seemed that she'd been given a second chance at love and life. Now she realized it was only a second chance at grieving. A second chance of dealing with loss and pain.

Cain raised her hand to his face and pressed it against his cheek. "The sooner we get you home the better."

"Enrique?"

"Dead."

She bit into her lower lip, amazed at the amount of hate she felt for the dead man. "I hope he rots in hell."

"I don't think there's any question of that."

"The other people in the accident?"

"They weren't hurt. As for the men who ran you off the road, they're sitting in a jail cell, and I sincerely doubt that they'll see anything on this side of the bars for a good long while. It seems they're wanted for a long list of offenses."

"Good," she said without much enthusiasm. "What about the men you hired to protect me?"

"It doesn't matter, honey, nothing does but you getting well."

"Tell me," she said, louder this time, draining her strength.

Cain's eyes became dark and fierce. "Their bodies were found yesterday."

Linette closed her eyes. "Dear God."

"You don't need to worry. It's over now. Neither Enrique nor anyone else is ever going to hurt us again."

All this was more than Linette could take in at one time. She felt as though the world were caving in on her.

Physically Linette healed, but the emotional scars cut deep grooves into her heart. She grieved for the loss of her child the way she'd grieved for the husband who'd been taken in his prime. She had no energy, no will.

Cain was at her bedside every day. The room was crammed full of flowers, stuffed animals, gifts galore. Linette thanked him, but none of the trinkets he brought her meant a thing.

"Linette, please," he said the night before he was scheduled to take her home from the hospital. "What is it?"

She shook her head. The world felt gray and cold, and even the warmth of Cain's love couldn't chase away the chill.

"Tell me." He squatted in front of her and gripped her hands in his. "I can make it right, whatever it is."

"You can't fix this," she said through her misery.

"I can't bear to see you so unhappy. Are you in pain?"

She shook her head. She was in pain yes, but not the kind that a kiss and a Band-Aid would cure. This agony was familiar, one she'd lived with those first weeks and months after losing Michael.

"What can I do to help you?"

Linette closed her eyes. "I want my baby."

Defeated, Cain buried his head in her lap.

Home offered little solace. Linette sat and stared into the distance. She ate only because it was easier to give in to Cain's urging than to argue. Each day she gained a little more strength, but she hadn't the will or the conviction to pull herself out of the lethargy that trapped her emotions.

At night Cain held her in his arms. He hadn't attempted to make love to her since the accident, in the beginning for practical reasons, later because she had no desire. It had died with their unborn child.

Their once active sex life came to a grinding halt. She shied away from his kisses, and soon he stopped offering them. Linette suspected Cain was losing patience with her, but she couldn't help herself.

Then one afternoon, about three months after the accident, when spring seemed to burst overnight onto the countryside, Cain came into the house for dinner.

"You'll never guess what I found this afternoon," he said conversationally, sitting down at the table and reaching for the bread. "A stray calf. It looks like her mother's dead. I brought her into the barn for the night."

"Her mother's dead?"

"John says this sort of thing is common. I'll bottle-feed her for a few days and then sell her at the auction."

After dinner dishes, Linette wandered out to the barn, thinking she'd find an adorable calf to pet. It might be fun to watch Cain feed it a bottle, she mused.

Instead of a cute, cuddly calf, Linette found a scroungy-looking thing leaning against the rail, its head drooping to the ground. It was ugly and filthy with cuts and mud caked all across its back side.

"You poor baby," Linette murmured.

Cain came out of the shed with a milk bottle, looking none too pleased to have to deal with a stray after a long day on the trail. "John said this should work."

"I'll do it," Linette found herself offering.

Cain looked at her as if he weren't sure he'd heard her correctly. "You're sure?"

Linette offered him a small smile and reached for the makeshift bottle. Although Cain made an excuse and left her, Linette knew he wasn't far away. More than likely he was waiting to come running when she called.

"Hello there, Funny Face," she said gently, moving into the pen where the calf waited. She patted her hand against the top of its head. Not having been around live-stock much, she wasn't sure what to expect.

She certainly didn't anticipate feeding a calf from an old milk bottle to be as easy as it turned out. Funny Face took to the improvised method as if born to it. She drank the last drop and then raised her ugly face to look at Linette with big brown eyes.

The following day, just before Cain had left with John Stamp, Linette asked, "What about the stray?"

Cain muttered something under his breath. "I forgot to feed her. Could you give her another bottle for me?"

She nodded, when that was what she'd wanted him to ask her all along. Why she should be so shy about it, she didn't know.

After the men were gone Linette wandered out to the barn. Funny Face rushed to the gate to greet her. For the next few days the calf mewled and came running the instant she caught sight of Linette.

Despite her depression, Linette found herself smiling at the ugly heifer. The calf wasn't so much interested in her as she was in the milk bottle.

After a week, when Funny Face had finished her morning feeding, Linette decided to give the heifer a long overdue bath. The entire back side of the stray was caked in thick, dark mud.

By the time she finished, Linette was convinced all she'd done was transfer the mud from Funny Face to herself. Cain found her like that, on her knees on the barn floor, brushing the snarls out of the calf's tangled hair, talking to the disgruntled stray in soothing tones.

"Don't you dare laugh at me, Cain McClellan," Linette warned. After wrestling with a stray calf for the last two hours, she was in no mood to be teased over her appearance.

"I have no intention of laughing at you," Cain said, letting himself into the gate. "If anything, I was thinking of kissing you."

"Kissing me . . . when I look like this?" Linette gazed down upon her mud-speckled shirt and water-soaked jeans. "Either you're desperate for a kiss or blind to my many faults."

"Both," he assured her.

Deliberately he removed the brush from her hand and set it aside. Then he gathered her in his arms and slowly, in painstaking inches, lowered his mouth to hers.

It had been weeks since he'd touched her this way. Weeks since she'd wanted him. But she desired him now with a strength that left her shaking.

Cain took her mouth fully, slanting his lips across hers, giving her his tongue. The hot rush of sensation took the starch out of Linette's knees, and she clung to him.

"You left me," she whispered, trembling. "You broke your word and left."

"I was wrong," he whispered huskily. "I'll never do it again."

"How can I believe you?"

Cain gently relaxed his hold on her. "I can't give you a single reason why you should. I've been so afraid I've ruined everything with my selfishness. It's because of me that we lost the baby. It's because of me that you were in the car accident. I don't know that I'll ever be able to forget that."

"It's over now."

"But it isn't," Cain said bitterly. "Each night I hold you in my arms and wonder if our lives will ever be the same again. If I were any kind of man, I'd release you, but I haven't got the courage to let you go. I need you too damn much."

"I need you, too."

"I'm asking for a second chance. God knows I don't deserve it, but I've learned my lesson, honey. I discovered what Mallory did when he realized he was in love with Francine. I didn't have the heart for fighting anymore. I left it with you."

"You're sure this time?"

"Positive. There's nothing more I want in this life than to settle down on this ranch with you at my side. I like it. Even John's surprised by how well I've taken to managing a herd." He laced his hands together at the small of her back. "But it means nothing without you. Are you willing to give me a second chance?" He brushed his lips close to her ear. "I promise to make it worth your while."

Linette snuggled close into her husband. "I'm willing to put the past behind us." All at once the future looked clear and bright.

"Let's go inside," Cain said, breathing hard and fast.

"I'm a mess."

"You're the most beautiful woman in the world." He captured her lower lip between his teeth and sucked gently.

"Do you mean to have your way with me, Cain Mc-Clellan?"

"Without a doubt."

"It isn't even noon." She didn't know why she was putting up arguments when she was as eager for her husband as he was for her.

"I don't care what time it is."

"Eleven-fifteen."

Cain chuckled. "You know what they say about striking when the iron is hot." He kissed her again and it was wet and wild and Linette swore the two of them sizzled together.

Their mouths were fused together when Cain hoisted her into his arms and carried her across the barnyard and directly into the house.

"Take off your spurs," Linette cried as he started across her kitchen floor.

Muttering under his breath, Cain set her back on her feet and removed his spurs. Then, for no reason she could think of, he sat down and with some difficulty removed his cowboy boots as well.

"Anything else?" he asked.

Linette laughed. "Oh, yes, lots more."

Cain grinned and lifted her into his arms once again. He couldn't seem to make it more than two or three stair steps before he'd stop and kiss her. Their lips mated, and he used the time to unfasten another button of her western-style blouse. By the time they reached the top of the stairway, she was half naked, embarrassed some- one might see her in her skimpy underwear.

"I need a bath," she protested.

"Later," he promised, and carried her into their bed- room. He laid her on the bed and stared down on her. His eyes were bright with need, bright with love.

"I've missed you so much," he whispered.

Linette helped him undress, her hands aggressively removing his clothes. His hips were taut and lean, and the evidence of exactly how much he'd missed her was all too evident.

She needed him now as never before, as she might possibly never need him again.

Her release came like an explosion. She cried out and whimpered and clung to him, crying and laughing both at once. Cain followed her shortly and seemed to share the same cataclysmic experience.

Cain's breathing was hard and fast as he lay sprawled across her. He was heavy, but she needed the feel of him. Needed him. It felt good to say that, if only to herself.

Linette smiled up at her husband.

He smiled down on her, then kissed her long and sweetly with an uncharacteristic lack of haste. Tunnel- ing his fingers through her hair, he raised his mouth a mere inch from hers.

"What changed?"

She knew what he was asking but wasn't sure she had the answer. "Funny Face needed me," was the only explanation she had to offer.

"Hell, woman, I've been walking around like a wounded calf for three months, and it didn't so much as faze you."

"We're going to be all right now," she said, brushing the hair from his temples. "Everything's going to be fine."

"I'll never leave you again," Cain promised, and he said the words as if speaking a solemn vow.

"I know." She became thoughtful, thinking of the men of Deliverance Company. "Murphy's not so bad, you know. He's just a poor misguided soul. What he really needs is a wife to straighten him out."

"Is that what you've done to me? Straightened me out?"

Linette had to think about that. Smiling, she shook her head. "No. All I had to do was love you."

Cain buried his face in her neck and linked their bodies. "Let me love you again."

"Yes," she whispered, placing her arms around his neck. Soon her body sang and her breathing stopped, only to start again in startled gasps of ecstasy. All that was necessary was love. She had the feeling it would be all they needed the rest of their lives.

What She Wants by Lynsay Sands

Earl Hugh Dulonget of Hillcrest was a formidable
knight, used to getting what he wanted. This time,
he got himself into a bind. His uncle's will had a
codicil: He must marry. And Hugh had just insulted
his would-be bride by calling her a peasant! How
could he win back her esteem—and her hand?

The Wrong Marquess by Vivienne Lorret

Elodie Parrish can feel spinsterhood breathing down
her neck. That's the trouble with waiting for the
marquess next door her entire life. But Ellie knows
if she gives him one last Season, he'll finally propose.
The only problem is, her path keeps crossing with
Brandon, the arrogant Marquess of Hullworth, who
is convinced she has designs on him.

A Scot to the Heart by Caroline Linden

Captain Andrew St. James always knew he came
from a noble family, but his branch grew far from
the wealth and status. He is shocked to learn that
he now stands as heir presumptive to his distant
cousin, the Duke of Carlyle. There is much for
Drew to learn and adjust to—including the spirited
Ilsa Ramsay, his sister's irresistible friend.